Z

SIFP

W9-BKV-328

STEP
1 C

SPLIT SECOND

A Selection of Recent Titles by Fern Michaels from Severn House

CAPTIVE EMBRACES
CAPTIVE INNOCENCE
CAPTIVE SECRETS
DEAR EMILY
SARA'S SONG
SINS OF THE FLESH
SINS OF OMISSION
TENDER WARRIOR
TEXAS FURY
VALENTINA
TO TASTE THE WINE

SPLIT SECOND

Fern Michaels

This first world edition published in Great Britain 1999 by
SEVERN HOUSE PUBLISHERS LTD of
9–15 High Street, Sutton, Surrey SM1 1DF.
This first world edition published in the USA 1999 by
SEVERN HOUSE PUBLISHERS INC., of
595 Madison Avenue, New York, NY 10022.

Copyright © 1999 by Fern Michaels.

All rights reserved.
The moral right of the author has been asserted.

British Library Cataloguing in Publication Data

Michaels,   Fern
   Split second
   1.   Suspense fiction
   I.   Title
   813.5'4 [F]

   ISBN 0 7278 5431 3

All situations in this publication are fictitious and
any resemblance to living persons is purely coincidental.

Typeset by Palimpsest Book Production Ltd
Polmont, Stirlingshire, Scotland.
Printed and bound in Great Britain by
MPG Books Ltd, Bodmin, Cornwall.

Prologue

She covered her face with her arm, shielding her eyes. The light was so bright. It came suddenly, without warning. Unlike a sudden flash it didn't fade. It stayed, blooming brightly towards the center and radiating outward in streaks of red brilliance. The sound rocked her brain, low, booming, lethal. There was fear. A chest-crushing panic stealing her breath, denying her air.

She knew where she was, yet she was lost. She had been here before and never before. She wanted to run but her feet were heavy, stuck in something thick and gluey, something that would not let her escape.

There was fire. Angry yellow fire bursting through doors and eating through the roof. The fire was inside and she was outside in the cold. Something wet fell on her cheeks. Snow. She saw everything; she saw nothing. People, a huddle of humanity. Mothers with open mouths screaming for their children. Men, taken unawares, stricken with confusion, frozen, helpless. Children, staggering beneath the impact of explosion, their little arms reaching, seeking safety. And over it all a pall of red, denying her a clear view, permitting only impressions. And yet she knew she had walked this place before.

There was more, much more, presented to her in rapid-fire succession. Fire. Explosion. Screams. Cries. Red. Always red. Pain. Loneliness. Anger.

Confused, lost, she concentrated on locating herself. Slowly, creeping through her consciousness, realization penetrated her senses. Crazily, a cheery Christmas carol piped through her ears. Glittery holiday decorations swung in erratic rhythms before crashing down, plummeting from great heights into the maelstrom below.

Squeezing her eyes shut and willing herself to concentrate, she panned the scene. Recognition came with disbelief. Timberwoods Shopping Mall!

Curling herself into a fetal position, she huddled under the bed covers. She was trapped, and nothing could save her if she stayed here in this dream world.

Sobs tore through her chest and tears erupted behind her tightly closed lids. She must wake up, she must, otherwise she would be imprisoned forever in her own nightmare.

Her body sat upright in the narrow bed. The haze of red clouded her vision, seeming to steal into the corners of her room, seeping beneath the window sill and dissolving into the light of day. Shuddering with fright and shackled with a sense of doom, she opened her eyes and screamed.

One

A credit to Versace and Chanel, she slid her still shapely arms into her silk suit jacket as she watched her teenage daughter out of the corner of her eye. A frown pulled her finely shaped brows together as she turned to face the girl. "Angela, why are you fidgeting?" Her voice held the barely disguised note of harshness which was always present when she addressed her only child; so different from her usual languorous speech.

"Mother! I have to talk to you. It's important," Angela pleaded, her too-closely-set brown eyes watching her mother intently. "You have to listen to me. I had another vision."

Sylvia Steinhart evaded Angela's plea. "For heavens sake. Can't you see I'm in a hurry? You always do this to me. Today is the stockholders' meeting and I don't have a spare minute."

"But I need to talk to you," Angela persisted, reaching out to touch her mother's arm. "It's about those things I see . . ."

"You mean those things you say you see!" Sylvia Steinhart backed off a step, a look of impatience on her face. Then, to change the subject, to talk about anything besides Angela's delusions, she asked, "When was the

3

last time you had a bath? You positively reek of cigarette smoke."

"Please, Mother. It's a matter of life and death! You have to take the time to listen to me."

"Oh, really, Angela," Sylvia snickered, turning her back on her daughter. "Not now. I've got to look and be my best and you're upsetting me."

"It's always 'not now.' Every time I need you, you're either going to the office or the theater. If it isn't the theater, then it's the hairdresser. When will you have time to talk to me? Give me some idea!" Angela's exasperation dissolved into sullen petulance and she lit a cigarette, inhaling deeply. Her small sharp features were defiant, but her eyes were filled with unshed tears as she blew a puff of smoke in Sylvia's direction.

Sylvia glanced up from fastening the clasp on her watch and saw that Angela hadn't budged. "Money. Is that it? You need money? Here." Sylvia reached into her purse, opened her wallet and pulled out three crisp twenty-dollar bills. She tossed the money on the shiny surface of the cherrywood table, hoping to distract her daughter.

"I don't want your money, Mother." Angela's voice shook with emotion. "I want to talk to you. I said it was important. I saw something. It was terrible. I have . . ."

"I knew it was a mistake to listen to your father. I refuse to hear anything more about these so-called visions of yours. Even the psychiatrists say it's only another of your bids for attention. Psychiatrists at seventeen," Sylvia scoffed. "If the Rabbi could only see you and hear you, I'd never be able to show my face in public again."

"The Rabbi? What's he have to do with anything?" Angela rolled her eyes and shook her head. "Good God,

4

isn't there someone in this family who'll listen to me?" Sylvia remained unmoved. "Oh, forget it. Just forget it," Angela spat viciously, grinding out the cigarette into the powder-blue carpeting. "Admit it, Mother, you're afraid to hear what I have to tell you because you know that once you hear you'll have to do something, and that will take precious time out of your precious day!"

Sylvia looked at the charred black hole appearing beneath Angela's booted foot. Anger and frustration fanned her features. "For that little stunt, sweetie, you'll get no allowance for a month."

Angela spun around. "And they say my generation is all messed up. God, they should throw you under the lights and see what makes you tick!" She groped across the table for the three twenties, but as they came beneath her badly bitten fingertips, she suddenly became distracted. Her gaze was fixed on a bottle of bourbon that was resting too near the edge of a low shelf near Sylvia's elbow. "Look out!" she shouted, reaching a hand out towards her mother.

Sylvia reflexively jumped back from Angela's outstretched hand, bumping the shelf and sending the bottle crashing onto the bar directly below. The neck of the bottle splintered, spraying a shower of glass and amber liquid over the skirt of her designer power suit.

"Oh, no! I'm ruined!" she shrieked. Suspicion narrowed her eyes and stretched back her lips. "Did you . . . ? Oh, my God. You made that happen, didn't you?"

Angela shook her head. "No . . . no, I just knew it was going to fall. I tried to push you away."

Sylvia stared at her daughter, her expression wavering between belief and disbelief. Then she looked down and

5

surveyed the damage. "You knew that bottle was going to fall over . . . you made it happen."

"You can't have it both ways, Mother. Either I knew it was going to fall or I made it fall. Which do you think?"

"You did it. You deliberately did it to keep me from being on time for my meeting." She waved her hand. "Now, I have to change. Get out of my way." She pushed past Angela, heading for the stairs to her bedroom.

"Are you going to listen to me or not?" Angela demanded, trailing her mother. When she reached the master bedroom she found that Sylvia had closed and locked the door. "You're going to listen to me! You're going to hear me out. It's about the Timberwoods Shopping Center. It's going to blow up! I saw it all! A lot of people are going to die in there, Mother, and if you're not careful you may just be one of them."

Behind the door of her luxurious green-and-white bedroom, Sylvia was hastily changing into another of her designer suits. In spite of herself she couldn't shut out the sound of Angela's voice or the girl's description of the explosion she predicted for the Timberwoods Shopping Mall. A series of shudders traveled the length of her spine. Angela's voice penetrated the two-inch wood door and Sylvia imagined she could see her crouched outside the door, gloating, reveling in the horrible pictures she was creating for her mother. Fire, death, panic . . . a holocaust.

Angela called them visions, but the psychiatrists had assured Sylvia they were nothing but bad dreams, some like scenes out of horror movies, but dreams nonetheless. It had long been decided that Angela created them as a ploy for getting attention.

Sylvia's hand trembled and an expression of anguish spread across her features. Why couldn't she have a nice normal daughter? One who was interested in the nicer things life had to offer. Clothes, travel, boyfriends . . .

She massaged her temples with long manicured fingers. Regardless of what the psychiatrists said, it wasn't normal for anyone to have dreams like those Angela called her 'visions'. Somewhere, deep in her soul, she wondered if Angela didn't actually cause things to happen. Like the bourbon bottle falling . . .

The heartrending sound of a sob filtered through to Sylvia. The long suppressed urgings of motherhood stirred deep within her. There had been a time when the two of them were the model mother and daughter, going places and doing things together. Sylvia recalled taking Angela shopping for that special party dress. And then, another time, for Angela's tenth birthday she'd invited eleven little girls, bought a cake and party decorations. She'd even hired a clown to perform magic tricks. She smiled at the memory of all those little girls in their frilly dresses, their hair in ribbons and bows. Those had been the good times, Sylvia thought, when her daughter acted like everybody else's daughter, like little girls should act. Sugar and spice and everything nice.

When had Angela changed? When had she become so . . . belligerent, so . . . strange? Sylvia tried to think of a specific incident, something she could point to and say 'that was what did it' but nothing came to mind.

And so now here they were, mother and daughter, still living in the same house but worlds apart. Poor Angela, she really needed someone who understood her, someone who had all the time in the world to talk to her and listen to her. Sylvia toyed with the idea of going to her daughter, but she had no idea what to say to her or how to calm her fears. Instead she reached for her purse, swung open the door and rushed past a crouching Angela, fleeing the house.

Hearing the purr of the Mercedes in the driveway, Angela knew she had been deserted again. She tore through the rooms of the house. Looking for someone, needing someone. Anyone! Gleaming cherrywood tables winked back at her, mocking her confusion and loneliness. Her narrow face was streaked with tears and flushed with frustration. Her dull brown hair adhered to her perspiring brow in frizzy ringlets. She caught her lower lip between her even white teeth. Seven thousand dollars to straighten them and Sylvia had complained to the orthodontist: "But they still look so . . . so big!"

Having as little thought for Angela's presence as Sylvia, the doctor had retorted: "Her teeth are beautiful, Mrs Steinhart. I've done a creditable job if I say so myself. If only her face weren't so narrow. Perhaps cosmetic surgery . . ."

Angela had raced out of his office, ignoring the baffled expressions on the faces of her mother and the orthodontist. Even now, almost two years later, the incident still stung. She didn't care what that idiot of a doctor thought; it was the sudden look of interest on Sylvia's face that had terrified her, as if she were considering the possibilities.

Angela's panic and feelings of loneliness were too urgent for tears. She contemplated her next move. Daddy. Maybe Daddy would listen. Somebody had to!

In her bedroom she fished for the white cordless phone

buried beneath a mound of soiled clothing. She dialed her father's office from memory and waited. "Daddy. This is Angela. Could you come home for lunch today? I have to talk to you; it's important. I wouldn't bother you otherwise."

"Honey, if it was any other day but today I could swing it. What is it? Boyfriend trouble? You are taking the pill, aren't you?"

"No . . .I mean yes. No, it's not boyfriend trouble. Daddy, please, could I meet you somewhere for lunch? Can I come to your office . . . ?"

"Money? Is that all?" he interrupted. "There's five hundred dollars in my top dresser drawer. Take what you need."

"Daddy, it's not money. I have to talk to you, I really do. It's about those things I see. Daddy, this is the worst and I'm scared. Please, I have to see you!" She struggled to control her voice, to stifle the sobs rising in her throat.

"Look, honey, today is bad. It's probably something you ate. Why don't you take a nap? I'll see you over the weekend. I'm leaving for London this afternoon. Be a good girl till I get back and I'll bring you a present." The connection was broken and Angela found herself staring at the phone in her hand.

Well, what had she expected? He was just as messed up as her mother. They had cut her off again, just as always, but it still hurt. It always hurt. More angry now than wounded she rubbed away the tears with the backs of her hands.

She needed someone, but who? Someone. Fleetingly she thought of her psychiatrist then dismissed the idea. Never. Between that shrink and Sylvia they'd have her committed to an asylum. It was a recurring thought that terrified her. Somewhere there had to be someone who would listen to her, listen and believe. Someone who would try to understand. Someone who would take the weight off her shoulders and absolve her of all responsibility. Then it would be in their hands. Angela knew there was no way she could handle this one alone. No way at all.

Angela revved the motor of her black and orange Porsche and careened down the street. "I may be all screwed up, but I have to do something!" she thought.

Easing up on the gas pedal she turned into Timberwoods Drive and stopped at the changing amber light. Her eyes were murky as she gazed down the incline at the crowded parking lot. Cars, as far as the eye could see. The Christmas season. Happy people hurrying to get their shopping done. The light turned green and Angela swung into the lot. She rode up one lane and down the other, mentally counting the cars. Thousands of people. All those little kids looking at the Christmas displays. She parked the Porsche directly under a 'No Parking' sign and climbed from behind the wheel. She was halfway to the long green awning which led to the entrance when a guard called for her to stop. She looked over her shoulder and tossed her head.

"You have five minutes to move that car or it'll be towed away!" the guard shouted.

Angela waved her hand and continued her long-legged stride. "So tow it away. I'll just get another one."

The burly guard swore beneath his breath as he watched Angela progress through the throngs of shoppers, the frayed hems of her baggy jeans scuffing the pavement.

Why would a kid whose folks could afford to let her drive around in a Porsche dress like that? Bums! All of them! He saw them every day, looking like filthy beggars. Yet when you frisked them you came up with a wad of cash big enough to choke a horse.

He looked back at the Porsche and knew he wasn't going to do anything. He'd worked for Timberwoods Shopping Mall for six years and he only had a few more weeks until his retirement in January. He'd bucked the big boys in the front office before and the kids always got off while he got chewed out. "You must be more delicate in your handling of the youth," that asshole Richards, the manager of Timberwoods Mall, had said. He knew the big man's concern was for the parents who spent their money at the center. Delicate – shit! A few more weeks, the guard reminded himself; then the whole damn place could blow up and he wouldn't care.

Inside the mammoth mall Angela headed down the long hallway leading to its center. She was jostled by the crowds of good-natured shoppers and little children holding their mothers' hands. She headed straight for the administrative offices. She wasn't sure who she was going to talk to or what she would say but she'd worry about that when she got there. She glanced down at herself. Maybe she should have taken a bath and changed her clothes. Looking the way she did they might not take her seriously. They might take her for a gang member or a crackhead, or both. Oh, well. Either they'd listen or they wouldn't. It was as simple as that.

Angela decided she would ask to speak to the young woman in security – well, not really so young. Twenty-five or six would be her guess. Heather something. Angela remembered her from the day she'd been mistaken for a shoplifter and brought into the offices and searched.

The reception area was small. Three comfortable chairs and pots of brilliant Christmas poinsettias lined the walls. An undersized desk with a girl slightly older than herself completed the small cubicle. "I want to talk to Heather," Angela said boldly as she stared down at the young, fresh-faced receptionist.

The girl set her face in a smile and pressed a button on the phone. She spoke quietly then nodded at Angela. "She'll be right out. Take a seat, please."

Angela slumped down in one of the chairs and idly picked up a booklet from the round glass table. She blinked as she looked at an architect's drawing of the Timberwoods Shopping Complex. She was so engrossed in the bold type at the bottom – Steinhart Assoc. Architects – that the receptionist had to speak twice before Angela heard her. "Miss Andrews will see you now."

Pushing open the door to Heather Andrews's office, Angela was greeted by a young attractive brunette wearing a dove-gray suit. "I'm Angela Steinhart. We met a few months back when . . ."

Heather Andrews looked at Angela with recognition and gestured for her to sit down in the chair opposite her desk. "I remember. That was a most unfortunate incident."

Angela had thought so too. "I have to talk to you," she said now, letting the past go.

Heather closed the office door and sat down at her desk. "What can I do for you, Miss Steinhart?"

Angela looked at Heather's wide blue eyes fringed with thick dark lashes, her smooth pink cheeks and her bright pretty smile beneath the short crop of dark glossy hair. She wondered vaguely if her own life would be different if she were as pretty as Heather Andrews.

"Miss Steinhart – Angela," Heather repeated softly, "what can I do for you?"

Angela had crossed her right leg over her left and was fiddling with the frayed hem over her jeans. "I . . . I came to you because I didn't know where else to go, or who else I could . . . I could tell." She took a deep breath then let it out in a rush. "I know you think I'm a spoiled rich kid. It's true, but I'm not here to explain or defend my lifestyle. I'm here to . . ."

Heather watched the young girl with a mixture of emotions. Here goes another lunch hour, she moaned silently. With a patience she found remarkable under the circumstances, she said, "I can see that you're upset. Why don't you start at the beginning?" She took a covert glance at her watch. The girl was obviously agitated, and there was fright in her desperate glance. Calm her down and get her out, Heather told herself.

Angela fished in her bulky shoulder bag. Heather noticed how severely bitten her fingernails were, the cuticles were ragged and scabbed. Angela withdrew a cigarette. "I hope you don't mind if I smoke," she said, her tone slightly shaky and unsure as she held the slim white cylinder aloft. "I'll try to start at the beginning. Before I came here, I tried to talk to my mother, but she didn't have time to listen, and she didn't really want to. Then I tried my father. He was worried that I might be pregnant. I'm not, so he offered me money. Believe me when I tell you that there wasn't anywhere else for me to go."

Heather nodded, her mind churning. What was wrong with this haunted-looking teenager?

"I'm seventeen – I'll be eighteen the day after Christmas. My problem – if that's what it is – started when I was twelve. I see things," Angela blurted. "I used to tell my parents when I saw them – when they would listen, that is. They always explained it away as a bad dream or an upset stomach. These . . . these. . . things I see, they happen. . . they happen to other people. At first it only happened once in a while but then it became more often. By that time I was so scared I didn't know what to do. I guess I scared my parents too," Angela fretted. "Their answer was to take me to a shrink. This hot-shot psychiatrist said I was making a bid for attention. That was all my mother had to hear! She started following doctor's orders by ignoring me, which is what she's been doing for as long as I can remember."

Heather licked her dry lips and stared at the girl. "Tell me, what are these things you see?" There was an intensity about Angela that gave Heather gooseflesh. This job certainly had its drawbacks, and sitting here listening to this crazy kid was one of them. Everything the girl said seemed rehearsed, like the dialogue of a bad actor or the story of a liar. "The first time it happened it was our neighbor's dog. I saw it get killed by a truck. I even saw the kind of truck it was – one of those telephone trucks, you know, with the basket that hoists men up to the top of the poles."

Heather nodded.

"Well anyway, it happened. A couple of hours later right there on my own street! The second time it happened it was a baby falling into a redwood swimming pool. I didn't know who the baby was and I didn't know anyone who owned a redwood swimming pool." Angela's voice became strident, her face flushed and the words came out in a rush. "Two days later there was a picture on the front page of the evening paper! It was just the way I saw it! The list is endless. What I'm trying to tell you is, what I see happens. It comes so fast, I'm never prepared. It comes without warning!"

Angela's voice had risen to a shriek. The cigarette from which she had taken only one or two puffs had burned down, scorching her fingers. She was shaking and her face, which had been flushed a moment ago, was now drained of color.

Heather was frightened . She considered calling for the emergency staff stationed at the clinic. Taking Angela's hand and shaking it over the ashtray to dislodge the smoldering stub, she could see the reddened skin between the girl's fingers.

For the first time Angela seemed to be aware that Heather had moved from behind the desk to her side. Her expression registered surprise but she continued rubbing her fingertips as she spoke. "I saw a busload of little children going down a hill. There was something wrong with the brakes on the bus. I saw the number painted on the side of the bus. Seventy-three. It was after a storm and trees were down all over the roads. And I saw the street sign – Melrose and Archer. I was scared. It still scares me. I had to do something. I rode my bike to the top of the hill and stopped the bus. I told the driver to please check his brakes. I told him he was going to crash at the bottom of the hill. He . . . he laughed at me, but he was mad. Really mad! He wouldn't listen. Thirty-seven little kids died."

Angela's eyes were wide and staring. The flesh on Heather's back crawled.

"About a month later I saw the driver shopping in town. I went over to him, but before I could say anything to him, he recognized me and acted as though I was some kind of disease. He said, 'Get away from me, kid. You're walking death.' I got so sick they put me in the hospital for a week. The doctors said I was hyper. God!" Angela exclaimed pitifully. "Wouldn't you be hyper if these things happened to you?"

Heather could only nod. She remembered that fatal crash and the long procession of mourners at the mass funeral. "Angela, why did you come to me? Even if I believe what you're telling me, what can I do? Perhaps a competent psychiatrist . . ."

"I told you, I've had the pleasure. Several times. Different psychiatrists," Angela sneered. "All they wanted was my father's money. I'm here now because I've had another one of my 'fits,' as my mother calls them. I want to ask you a question. When's the height of the Christmas season?"

"The week before Christmas usually."

Angela paled as she mentally counted the days. "Today's Monday the fifteenth. It's now! It's now!"

"Yes, Angela, Christmas Day is next Thursday. The stores are open until six on Christmas Eve," Heather said, alarmed. "Why?"

Angela rubbed her temples. "Ten days to Christmas." Her voice was a choked whisper, frightening Heather. Strangling on the words, Angela blurted, "I saw this mall burst into flames. I saw it collapse. I saw people trapped and buildings falling on them. I saw people die, babies, children, their parents searching for them. Worst of all, I saw the blind panic, the stampede . . ." She couldn't go on. She covered her face with her hands and sobbed.

Heather was at a loss. "I . . . I don't think . . . If this . . . is a joke . . ."

"Miss Andrews, I may not be the town's most adored person, but I wouldn't lie to you about something like this! Go speak to the bus driver. His name and address are engraved on my brain – I'll be glad to give it to you, or you can get it from the old files in the newspaper office. Make up your own mind after you've talked to him. I can't help you with this! Somebody will have to do something!" She was almost screeching by now but the look of impatience on Heather's face forced her to control herself. "Wait! You have to let me finish. The day following the first vision, yesterday, I had another . . . another . . . you know. This one was clearer. I saw a man – he was doing something bad, and I knew he felt so sad inside but he was doing it anyway. Everything was in a red mist and it was hard to tell exactly what was happening. All through the vision I could hear Christmas carols. I saw you get hurt!"

"Angela, calm down," Heather insisted. She stood up behind her desk, ready to physically restrain the girl if necessary. It was obvious she wasn't dealing with a stable personality and that the girl needed help.

"Calm down? How can you ask me to calm down? I've just told you about some diabolical plot to destroy the shopping center and kill all the people in it. How can I be calm?"

Heather spluttered, "There must be some explanation for this . . . these things you – "

"Believe me, if there is an explanation, I haven't found

17

it." Angela's voice had lowered to a hiss. Disgusted, she sneered, "Look, I've lived with this since I was twelve. I know what's going to happen, and now I've told you. You've got the ball now – you run with it."

"Angela, your parents – what if I went with you to tell them?" Heather's manner was slightly cajoling as though humoring a sick child, which was exactly what she thought of Angela.

"What for? They'll tell you it's a nervous condition or another of my bids for attention." Angela laughed uneasily. "My mother wants me locked up. If she finds out I've come to you, it'll give her all the ammunition she needs to have it done. Regardless of what my father wants. And do you know something? At this point I almost don't care. Sometimes I think my mother's right. Maybe I am crazy."

Heather was speechless as she watched the slim girl leave the office. She breathed a sigh of annoyance. Why did she have to come and dump on me? she thought. Now, I'll probably have to fill out a report. And the report will have to be filed with the chief of security. It did come under the heading of strange and unusual circumstances. Heather groaned. Security would blow everything out of proportion. Instead of seeing that Angela Steinhart was in need of psychiatric help, they would create chaos. The bomb squads would arrive with their sniffer dogs, all the employees would have to work overtime, the Steinharts would be alerted and Angela herself would be hauled in for questioning. And all because she couldn't get her parents' attention and had looked for someone else to dump her grief on. Well, that worked two ways. Heather would do what everyone else did around here – she would dump on Felex Lassiter, head of public relations.

Breezing through the outer office, past the receptionist's desk and down the wood-paneled corridor, she opened the door to the office which bore Felex Lassiter's name and title. Nodding to his secretary she said, "I'd like to talk to Felex."

She opened the door marked 'Private'. "Something's come up. But first, pour me a drink, will you? A stiff one," she directed firmly.

Felex Lassiter pushed his chair back from his desk and frowned at the beautiful woman opposite him. His eyes narrowed. She was upset. She didn't belong here at the center. Her guts weren't encased in steel like the others in security. She should never have been hired in the first place, but Dolph Richards, the center manager, had insisted, saying she had the best-looking legs he had ever seen.

Lex had to agree. His pulse took on a faster rhythm as he watched her. He'd been attracted to her from the moment he'd laid eyes on her and instinct told him she had felt the same. So why hadn't he ever asked her out? A simple movie, a dinner, something? Shrugging away his thoughts he walked over to a compact glass and chrome bar and poured a hearty jolt of Jack Daniels. "Easy does it," he said as he handed her the glass. "That stuff grabs your guts and does strange things."

"Lex, I want to talk to you about something. I'm not quite certain I know how to handle this – I don't even know where to begin."

"Start by finishing your drink and we'll take it from there."

Gratefully Heather sipped at the liquid. She sipped again and felt herself relax. Leaning back in the chair, she crossed her legs and asked for a cigarette. Dragging deeply, calming herself, she played for some time and reviewed what she knew about Felex Lassiter. He was cool in a crisis, level-headed and always considerate. A man whose strength could be depended upon. In his early thirties, his good nature and quiet authority won him the respect of his associates, while his handsome blond looks and athletic build won winsome smiles from the secretaries. Heather agreed with the consensus that Lex was long on charisma and short on razzle-dazzle – unusual for a public relations man. It seemed people just naturally responded to his sincerity. Wasn't this the reason she had sought him out now to help her gain some perspective on the Angela Steinhart problem? In truth, Heather was strongly attracted to him, but he had never made a move to kindle a relationship outside the office.

"Lex, do you remember me talking to you about Angela Steinhart?" she finally began.

Lex nodded.

"One of the guards mistook her for a shoplifter and brought her up here to security. Angela is a very disturbed young girl and it doesn't seem as though there's any help coming from her parents."

Lex nodded again, patiently waiting for Heather to make her point.

"Today the Steinhart girl came to see me and told me something incredible." Heather gulped at her drink and plunged into telling. "She claims to be a seer, says she has prophetic experiences. Visions, she calls them."

Heather recounted Angela's story, pointing out the bus

incident. Lex sat upright, listening intently. Concluding her story, Heather lowered her voice. "Angela told me that during the height of the Christmas season Timberwoods is going to explode and thousands of people are going to die. She told me I was going to be one of the people hurt." Heather had left her chair by now and was nervously pacing the office.

"And do you believe this?" Lex asked, his tone measured and calm.

"I don't want to believe it. I'd rather think that this is what she says her parents think it is – another bid for attention, pitiful though it may be. However, I do have to file a report and when security reads it we both know what's going to happen."

"Right," Lex agreed, considering her last statement. "They'll go off the deep end."

"Exactly. I'd hate to bring all that grief down on Angela's head, but what else can I do? I can't even make an intelligent judgment since I don't know anything about prophetic occurrences and ESP."

"I do, in a limited way. Do you believe her, Heather?"

Heather hesitated, remembering the expression in Angela's eyes. An expression that revealed the girl's futile acceptance of the inevitable. "No!" she stated resolutely. Somehow her answer rang false in her ears.

Arriving back at Timberwoods Mall from his supper hour, Charlie Roman lifted his large frame from behind the wheel of his dilapidated '89 Chevy. The wind caught his sandy hair and whipped it into strings resembling shredded wheat. Squinting against the whirling snowflakes, he surveyed the ominous dark sky and wished for a heavy snowfall. Perhaps the weather would keep the shoppers and their greedy little brats at home. He could use an easy night – playing Santa Claus in an enormous complex like Timberwoods was no cushy job.

Charlie slammed the door of his Chevy twice before the catch held. He pulled the collar of his gray wool jacket closer about his thick neck. People hurried between the mall and the parking lot but Charlie plodded toward the entrance doors with a slow careful gait. He wasn't taking a chance on slipping on the thin film of ice and falling.

Passing through Parking Lot Five he noticed Heather Andrews heading for her car. She seemed lost in thought, oblivious to the snow. Miss Andrews was always friendly to him. Several times, at employee meetings, she had smiled at him and said hello. He liked Heather and had toyed with the idea of asking her out. She was one person who seemed to see beyond his shyness to the sincere sensitive man inside. Charlie had even fantasized that she would accept his invitation with a sweet smile lighting her pretty face. The thought of a date with her had exhilarated him for weeks.

Charlie's eye caught a familiar figure coming toward him. Felex Lassiter. Nice guy, Mr Lassiter. Preparing himself for Lex's greeting, Charles was thinking of something non-committal to say about the weather when Lex veered off to the left, towards Miss Andrews. Charlie took a few more steps and turned around. They were both getting into the car – together! Charlie's anger rose. He hadn't known they were a couple. So much for his fantasy. It was a silly fantasy anyway – Heather never would have looked twice at him. He wasn't one of the 'beautiful people'. He was a nerd and an awkward nerd at that. What a fool he'd been.

He laughed out loud, a great roaring laugh. Forgetting to watch his footing, his leather soles slipped on the ice and down he went. Red-faced he quickly glanced around, expecting to see hordes of people standing around, pointing and jeering. Instead there was only a too-thin girl watching him with worried brown eyes.

"Hey, I'm sorry. I wasn't watching where I was going! Give me your hand." Angela extended her arm, bracing her feet against Charlie's weight.

Charlie denied her assistance, hefting himself up with agility. Immediately the girl began to brush him down. "Hey, I'm sorry, really I am."

Peering intently into her eyes, he tried to judge whether or not she was putting him on. Nobody cared about him. Ever.

"Are you all right? I didn't mean to . . . I've got something on my mind. I didn't even see you." Angela herself was surprised at her reaction. The mood she was in she could have knocked down the President of the United States and she wouldn't have given him a backward glance.

"Yeah, yeah, I'm okay. I've got to get back to work." His tone was harsh, annoyed.

He saw the girl's eyes focus on his face. He answered the question in her glance "I'm the Santa Claus here. The kids are waiting."

"I thought Santa Claus was supposed to be kind, but . . . Oh, well, never mind." Angela snapped back at him and turned to leave.

"Hey, wait a minute," he called after her as she nimbly

ran across the ice, dodging cars as she went. "I didn't mean . . ."

"Forget it," she retorted. "I never did believe in Santa Claus anyway."

Charlie watched her go, a knot of strange emotions choking him. For one instant there he had thought he'd seen some real concern in the girl's face. Then "Nah! She's just an airhead like all the rest," he grumbled. He ran a hand through his damp hair, pushing it back from his face.

Heather Andrews peered through the windshield as Lex piloted the car through the parking lot. "Did you see that?" she asked. "That was Charlie Roman and Angela Steinhart."

At the mention of Angela's name Lex showed interest. "Where?"

"Oh, she's gone now. But that's a likely pair, don't you think? Poor Charlie."

"It's that 'poor Charlie' attitude of yours that keeps him pining after you like a sick puppy," Lex stated.

"Oh, Charlie's okay, I guess. He seems so lonely sometimes. And I suppose he does have a crush on me, but he's harmless."

"Christ," Lex laughed, "if there's one thing a man never wants to hear anyone say about him, it's that he's harmless."

Heather glanced at the tall blond man beside her. "Don't worry, Lex, I can't imagine a woman saying that about you. Now, where's this place we're going for dinner?"

Two

Charlie Roman woke up and lay for a moment contemplating his day. He might get overtime if he decided to work. On the other hand, he had no real need of the extra money since the check wouldn't arrive till after the start of the new year. Still . . . "Ho! Ho! Ho!" he muttered to himself as he crawled from his warm bed. Everything was almost finished. All he had to do was decide on the day and carry it through.

Charlie padded into the bathroom. He peered at his reflection in the cloudy mirror and wondered why his eyes were so bloodshot and his skin so blotchy. And it was getting harder and harder to swallow. He would have to gargle and hope for the best. This was no time to get sick. He brushed his teeth and then gargled three times, slowly and methodically. The medication had better work. These days everything was such a rip-off. Well, he was about to even the score a little. And when he bailed out, he was going to take along a lot of company. He smiled at the thought of all the mourners that would fill the cemeteries. Christmas should be outlawed. Everything was too commercialized. And those vicious little brats who tried to poke his pillow-stuffed stomach and make him say, "HO! HO! HO!" Dirty, snot-nosed little kids. Gimme this, gimme that, and never a please or thank you.

He emerged from the shower a few moments later and toweled himself dry. HO! HO! HO! He dressed quickly, aware of the chill in the room then, satisfied with his appearance, he trotted downstairs to make coffee. Perhaps he should go to work. He had never turned down overtime before. This was no time to do anything that might give people cause for taking a closer look at him. A niggling ache seemed to be settling between his shoulders. He reached into the kitchen cabinet and withdrew the aspirin bottle. He gulped down four of them and sat down to wait for the coffee to perk. What day to choose? Christmas was on a Thursday this year so he had ten days if he counted today. Not Christmas Eve.

It was too big a decision for so early in the morning. He would decide later that evening. The coffee pot uttered a loud 'plop' then was silent. Charlie poured himself a cup of the fragrant brew and settled back on the wrought-iron chair. It was a pleasant kitchen, he thought, as he gazed around. He would miss it. The hanging baskets with the early American decor made him want to live in a different time, a time when things were done slowly and thoroughly. The shiny copper utensils hanging next to the stove gleamed in the light. His eyes focused on the long trailing bridal veil plant that he had given his mother for her birthday. Plants didn't have emotions like people, even if his mother used to say that talking to them helped them grow. Plants were nothing but a bunch of leaves that bugs lived in.

He drained his coffee and rinsed the cup in the gleaming sink. Turning on the radio for the weather report he heard the soft strains of 'Oh, Come All Ye Faithful'. Charlie shuddered as the song ended. Where were the faithful? Where was the joy? Who was triumphant? His head began to ache as he listened to the jovial announcer: clear skies this morning, clouding up by late afternoon, snow beginning in the early evening. Would the threatened snow deter shoppers from coming to the mall? Not likely, as long as they had their pockets full of money and charge cards. Reassured by his thoughts, Charlie slipped into his jacket and pulled on a warm woolen cap.

While he waited for the old Chevy to warm up, his thoughts wandered to the mall. He had noticed something strange yesterday. There seemed to be more security guards patrolling the mall. They looked more alert than usual and kept checking and rechecking the same areas. One of them had even had the gall to tell him to move on and keep Ho! Ho! Ho!-ing.

A small knot of fear crawled around Charlie's stomach as he shifted the car into gear. There was no way anyone could know what he was planning. No way at all. Stopping for a red light, he let his mind wander again. Everyone would be gone. All the men in the maintenance department, all those superegos – all gone forever. In a way it was a shame that no one would ever know that he was the one responsible for the destruction. But as long as he knew, that was all that counted. He wouldn't have to set foot on the loading docks ever again. Did they care that he had a bad back? Six years of honest loyal work had counted for nothing. When he had protested, he had been told he could take a transfer or a lay-off. There had been no choice. His stint as Santa didn't count for anything either. He didn't need it. He didn't need anyone.

27

He'd had enough. All those wisecracking idiots in the maintenance department constantly ribbing him about this and that. They loved to tease him about his shyness around women. That's all they cared about – women and sex. Nothing else mattered. Not friends, not family, not their jobs – nothing. But he was smarter than all of them put together. Hadn't he proved that by graduating from refrigeration school? And not from some dumb correspondence course either, but from an accredited evening course at Woodridge High School. They'd told him he was one of the most promising students.

But then there had been that incident halfway through the course when the instructor had taken him aside and asked whether he intended to pursue a career in refrigeration and air conditioning. If he did, the instructor said, Charlie had better do something about the extra weight he was toting about. The job market was tough on overweight men and job bosses wanted guys slim enough to crawl around the air ducts. Well, he'd done it, hadn't he? He'd lost almost fifty pounds before the end of the course, and it hadn't been easy. It was wonderful how a pizza or two could ease loneliness. That had been eight years ago, just about the time they were beginning construction on the Timberwoods shopping complex. With a glowing recommendation from his instructor, Charlie had landed a job with the refrigeration crew. Night after night he had studied blueprints, munching down the facts and figures along with home-baked cookies and milk. By the time the duct was being installed on the roof he had regained twenty pounds.

Charlie's face flamed red with the remembered humiliation of being stuck in a shaft where they were stringing the main air-vent duct. It had taken a crew of six men forty-five minutes to extricate him. Ten minutes later he had left the site with the foreman's cruel words and his co-workers' laughter ringing in his ears. Dumb shits, what did they know? He had vowed to show them all, to make them sorry.

After that he'd nearly starved himself to death to get the weight back off. He'd lost most of it but it was a constant fight to keep it off – a fight he would be glad not to have to worry about any longer.

His flesh tingled with excitement; he'd show them all, and the very air duct which had caused him so much humiliation would become his means of retribution. Charlie Roman laughed, a light, thin sound. All this planning was making him hungry – he longed for a thick slab of homemade apple pie.

The great glass-walled conference room at Timberwoods Mall looked down on the parking lot. It was only eleven in the morning when Harold Baumgarten, chief of security, called the unscheduled meeting. Now, fifteen minutes later, the conference room was filled with the forty-three men and women who comprised the mall's security force.

Harold squared his shoulders and shed his ominous frown. It wouldn't be seemly for the security chief to look anxious. His men could handle any crisis, and this was a crisis; he could taste it. His hands were perspiring freely as he shifted the crumpled letter from one hand to the other. He wiped his palms on his trousers, sucked in his breath and opened the door to the conference room. A sea of faces greeted him as he walked on his short legs to the platform from which he would address his crew.

He held up his hand and waved the letter in the air. The buzzing group began to quiet. Baumgarten's eyes raked the room, searching for Heather Andrew's face before he remembered it was her morning off.

"You all know that I run a clean shopping center and I intend to keep it that way. I have here, in my hand," he said briskly, "a bomb threat." He paused importantly, waiting for the gasps of shock and wide-eyed displays of interest. His audience, being inured to their chief's dramatics, gave him no satisfaction. They merely waited politely for him to continue. Clearing his throat, Harold obliged. "According to the police the first two bomb threats were sent by the same person. I don't have to remind you that this is the third such letter I have received in the last three months. The police and the bomb squad are on the way. The men will be in civilian dress and I want all of you to assist them in any way that you can. As of right now the security in this mall is doubled. In no way are you to alert the shoppers of this bomb threat. If there's one thing we don't need now, it's a panic."

"Do you think this is just another scare like the last two?" asked Eric Summers, a detective on loan from the local police department who was acting as special assistant to Baumgarten over the holiday period.

Harold stared into Summer's serious face. If there were a bomb and it did go off, he almost wished Summers could be standing next to it. He schooled his face to be objective and answered: "It's the same type of letter. The words were clipped from newspapers and pasted onto plain white tablet paper. The only difference is that this time they are saying the bomb will go off in seventy-two hours. That difference is what's causing us the worry. I want all of you out there sniffing out this bomb."

Summers stood up. "You do realize that we could comb this center from one end to the other and find nothing. We have to consider the fact that the bomb might not be planted until the eleventh hour. The police department will want to concentrate on finding the person who sent that letter – which is evidence and might have helped in finding the sender had it not been so carelessly handled." Any time he could give Harold the needle, he did.

Baumgarten flushed deep red. Covering his embarrassment with bravado he shouted, "It's up to the police to find that person! Your job is to cover each area then cover it again. Do I have to tell you how to do your job?"

"No, sir, you don't. I'm the best in the business and I have nine citations to prove it."

Harold pointedly ignored him. "Mr Richards will be here shortly so we'll have to wait. Meanwhile, I'd like for each of you to come up and take a look at this letter – without touching it, of course," he added sarcastically. His mind was racing. Goddamn it, where the hell was Richards? Probably sacked out with some chippie from hosiery. Here they were, faced with a bomb threat, and he was screwing around with some girl, he thought viciously.

Summers smirked. He'd be willing to bet five bucks that Dolph Richards would keep them waiting till he'd finished laying some broad. He wondered what the prick's screwing average was.

Richards appeared as if on cue, his fly unzipped. Summers guffawed. He knew Richards would deliberately wait until he got up on stage to zip it so Harold could see. The two of them had a running feud that went way back.

Dolph Richards walked up to the platform and waved a greeting. He was slim and tall with a youthful lift to his step which belied his fifty years. He plucked at the lapel of his Italian suit and passed a hand over his glossy black hair. He silently mouthed a greeting to someone in the room, displaying perfect teeth. Squaring his shoulders he slowly and deliberately checked the zipper on his fly. Satisfied with the look he received from Harold, he started to speak.

"Ladies and gentlemen, happy holidays to all of you. I understand we seem to have some sort of problem. Another one of those nuisance letters that Baumgarten keeps getting." He sighed wearily, as if the weight of the entire mall rested on his shoulders. "I've come to the conclusion that these pesky letters are aimed at the chief himself. I think, Harold, that some place in this complex you have an enemy. No one in his right mind would dare to blow up my center! I won't allow it! You men and women were hired to see that things like this don't happen, so go out there and find whoever this is who has it in for our security chief. When you find him, bring him to my office."

Richards glared at Summers from beneath quirked brows. His wide smile froze into a stiff line. "Understand this, Summers, I don't want the police crawling all over the place."

Baumgarten reddened and mumbled, "The authorities have already been notified."

Richards bristled then visibly brought himself under control. He threw his hands in the air, breathing a sigh of resignation. "All right, all right. If you think there's someone out there, go and find him. This is the Christmas season, a time for goodwill and euphoric sentiment. People don't plant bombs at Christmas time." He offered his audience his 'Mr Congeniality' smile. "Thank you, ladies and gentlemen, for giving me your time. Go out there and do your job – and don't be surprised if you don't find anything." With a jaunty wave of his hand, he was off the platform and striding through the doorway.

The chief of security's face looked pained as he too waved a hand in dismissal. "Quarter-hour reports," he shouted after the retreating staff.

"Amen," snarled Summers.

Angela awoke to the gray light penetrating the filmy drapes at her window. She yawned and blinked her eyes, grateful for the night's undisturbed sleep. She glanced at the clock. Eight o'clock. She had slept nearly fifteen hours!

Yesterday evening, after her unpleasant encounter with the mall's Santa, she had come home, smoked a few cigarettes and crashed. Now, in the half-fog of too much sleep, her fears returned. Pulling her football jersey down over her underpants, she padded across the soft carpeting and out the door. Her first stop was her mother's bedroom. Empty. She traced a path through the house and discovered she was alone. Again.

Enraged, she fled the emptiness and ran back to her bedroom. The same dirty jeans she had worn the day before were in a heap near the bed. Hastily she pulled them on then reached for her combat boots. Ignoring the tears streaming down her cheeks, she dug in her purse and

33

withdrew a wad of crumpled bills. Forty, sixty, eighty, one hundred and forty dollars. How far would that take her? Wait a minute – Daddy had said there was money in his dresser. Five hundred dollars. He'd told her to take what she wanted. That gave her six hundred and forty dollars. She could sell the Porsche, take off for Hawaii. Then she'd be the one doing the leaving. They could think what they wanted. When the damn place blows up, she'd be halfway around the world. I did what I could and no one would listen, she thought, no one will believe me. Her hands were trembling so badly that she could barely light her cigarette. All those people . . . all that blood.

Angrily she reached for the phone and placed a call to TWA. A pleasant voice wished her a happy holiday and asked if she could be of assistance.

"I'd like a reservation for Hawaii as soon as possible."

"I'm sorry," the voice returned after a moment's silence. "There are no seats available until December twenty-eighth. I can put you on standby if that will help."

"You don't understand! This is an emergency! I have to leave as soon as possible," Angela shouted, tears choking her voice.

"I am sorry but TWA is booked. Shall I try the other airlines for you?"

"Yes."

The voice returned. "There's one cancellation on the morning of the twenty-sixth. If you care to leave your number I'll call you back . . ."

Angela slammed down the receiver. Flinging herself on the bed she let the tears flow. Damn everybody and everything, she raged. Just this once, why couldn't you help me, Mother? I tried so hard to be what you wanted.

Why can't you accept me the way I am? I know I'm not pretty like you, and I'm all arms and legs, but I'm your child and that should count for something. If you'd only look at me, really look at me. Touch me, tell me that you love me. Just once. Is that too much to want?

It hadn't always been this way, she reminded herself. There had been a time – a long time ago – when she had led a normal life. She and her mother had been comparatively close and she'd felt loved. As a family they had all shared meals, gone on trips together and talked to each other. When had it all changed?

When she was twelve, Angela realized. Right after she'd had her first vision. Her mother had shrugged it off as a bad dream. But as the visions had become more frequent she and her mother had become more distanced from one another. Angela's bad dreams had become her mother's nightmares and the only cure for that was to visit a psychiatrist. But it was Sylvia who needed a psychiatrist. She couldn't accept that the incidents Angela saw really happened, even when they made front-page news.

Suddenly Angela jerked upright. "When was the last time you had a bath?" her mother had asked. "All right, Mummy darling, a bath it is," Angela shouted to the empty hallway as she darted into her mother's dressing room. She scooped up three two-ounce bottles of Givaudan 50 and raced into the bathroom. Pouring the costly fragrance into the tub she turned on the hot tap. Two hundred bucks an ounce ought to set her dear mother back on her heels a trifle and make her take notice.

She watched with clinical interest as the water gushed into the bathtub. The aroma of Givaudan was suffocating, it wafted into the bedroom in a cloud of steam. Angela swiftly calculated how long it would take to flood the upstairs and ruin the downstairs ceiling, then stuffed a washcloth into the overflow drain and turned the water on full force. She repeated her actions with the sink and then with the sinks and showers in the other two upstairs bathrooms. Before she could regret her actions she turned back to her room and collected her purse and jacket.

Shortly after noon Heather Andrews tapped on Felex Lassiter's office door before storming in. "Lex, I guess you know I'm going to hang for this."

Lex lifted his blond head from the file folders on his desk. "What?"

"For this," Heather said in exasperation. "This was my morning off. When I came in I learned about this new bomb scare. Lex, I never wrote out that report on the Steinhart kid for Harold. How am I going to tell him about it now? I'm gonna swing for this one. Did you know the whole mall is crawling with security? Eric Summers had to bring in the local police . . ."

"Sit down, Heather, take it easy. It isn't as bad as you think." Lex's protective instincts kicked in; he put his arm around her and led her to a comfortable chair.

"The hell it isn't! Oh, why should I care anyway?" She sat down and buried her face in her hands. "I hate the job anyway. I've got enough time in to collect unemployment . . . Oh, hell, Felex, I should have written out that report. Not just for Harold, but for Eric and the rest of those poor people who are wasting their energy trying to track down a bomb and find the person who wrote the threat. I've known who it is all along."

"You don't know that. You only know what the girl told you yesterday. It's perfectly understandable . . ."

Heather reached for his cigarettes and lit one with shaking hands. "The hell it is! I've been through this before, remember? I know what goes into checking out these threats. From what I hear this one is different."

"Right," Lex encouraged. "I didn't come forward with what I knew about Angela because I thought it was your place. Secondly, things just don't fit. The note says seventy-two hours, but Angela said the peak of holiday shopping. If it was Angela who sent the threat, wouldn't she have been more specific in trying to back up her story to you about her visions?"

"I . . . I guess so. Still, it's my neck for not telling Harold."

"Look, we'll square it with Eric. Okay? I'll have him come up here and we can both talk to him."

Heather managed a grateful smile and touched his hand. "Yes, Lex. Please."

Eric Summers brought the walkie-talkie to his lips and spoke softly. "Summers here. Give me the head count."

"Are you ready?" a voice asked. "We're up to 276,543. Alderman's has a two-day sale going on. This mall is so jammed you can't move and the pickpockets are out in droves. Four of them are on the way back to the chief's office right now."

"Are you sure of the count?" Eric asked sharply.

"Positive. I double-checked it and Manners verified it. Wait till Monday. I just saw the flysheet for Walden's. They're having the same sort of sale, and you know what happens when Walden's says 'half-price.'"

Eric quickly calculated the timing of the sale with the seventy-two hour deadline of the bomb threat. He shivered. Christ! These pre-Christmas sales were for lunatics. And only a lunatic would conceive of destroying a complex like Timberwoods Mall, he acknowledged. It was a monument to human construction skills. Millions of square feet of shops, food stands, indoor waterfalls, living trees and exotic plants. There was a Japanese lotus garden with a fishpond, a German beer garden, a Parisian bonbon shop, an Italian villa – all of it sheltered beneath a single roof. Movie houses, restaurants and auditoriums, all housed within a climatically controlled atmosphere. It was spring all year round in here. People came from all over the state and beyond to shop at the famous Timberwoods Mall, so imagine the lives that would be lost if there was a bomb.

The beep of the walkie-talkie interrupted Summers's horrified thoughts; he brought the box to his lips. "Summers."

"Conrad on the promenade. A-okay. Listen, Baumgarten just squawked my box and said he was pulling me off the upper level and assigning me to the Christmas parade on Friday. Thought you should know."

"No problem. Out."

Jesus, another problem. He'd totally forgotten about the parade. He counted on his fingers. Friday. Seventy-two hours away. He pressed a button on the phone and asked for last year's attendance figures on the parade. "And give me the estimated headcount during Walden's half-price sale as well."

Seventy-two hours. The best that could be hoped for

was that it would pass without incident. In the meantime, everything had to be checked out. All those innocent people. Would Dolph Richards close the mall? Would Walden's go along with the shutdown? They were the biggest and loudest of all the stores. Summers knew in his gut that it would be business as usual.

The black box squawked again. Grateful for a reprieve from his thoughts, he answered quickly, "Summers." Felex Lassiter wanted him in his office right away. Some new information.

Eric paced Lassiter's office, his coffee-brown eyes coming to rest again and again on Heather. "Do you or don't you think that this Steinhart kid is the one who sent this bomb threat? Could she be responsible for the first two letters as well? They're all similar – words and letters cut from newspapers and magazines."

"I don't know. I don't know what to think. Yes, I think she's connected somehow . . . but I don't know how. Look, if you could have seen her you would have felt sorry for her. She's so frightened of being put away. She says her mother thinks she should be put in an asylum. I'm sorry to say I almost agree with her."

"All right, so you do think she's involved?" Summers fired off his words with machine-gun rapidity. His pleasant face was set in serious lines, his brows drawn together in concentration. He turned to Lex who was standing near the window, his back turned to them. "What about you, Lassiter? What do you think? Did you see the Steinhart girl?"

"No. Heather came to me almost immediately afterwards though. And ease up – badgering Heather isn't going to solve your problem. She's already explained why she didn't immediately file a report with Baumgarten."

Balancing on the corner of Lassiter's desk, Summers looked at Heather again. Making no apology, he said, "You have a home address on this kid, I assume."

Heather nodded. Her pretty face revealed her inner anguish. If only she had reported to Baumgarten, or at least to Eric himself. She alone was responsible for the havoc being created out there in the mall. Why, oh why had she taken the morning off? Then again, would she have had the courage to stand up at Baumgarten's meeting and say what she knew? Could she have let everyone know how she'd failed in the job?

"I want the two of you to go out there to talk to the kid. And to her parents. She must trust you, Heather, if she came to you first. If she didn't send the letters maybe she knows who did and she's feeling guilty about it. And Lassiter, that Joe-college smile of yours would charm the stars out of the sky. Besides, Heather will need a back-up."

"I can't," Heather protested. "I don't want anything to do with it."

"It's too late for that now." Eric overrode her objections. "You're in it, like it or not! I'll get things moving on this side. It's not going to be easy to tell Baumgarten. Take your choice – Baumgarten or the kid."

Defeated, Heather slumped in her chair. Talk about being between a rock and a hard place.

"Did you bring the kid's address? Good." Lex unlocked the car door and watched her slide into the passenger seat. He wished to hell he could do something to ease her worry but his hands were tied. At least for now. Maybe later, after the interview, he'd take her out, buy her a few drinks and a nice supper. She deserved that. She deserved a lot, and from now on he was going to do his damnedest to see to it that she got it.

"I don't like this one bit," Heather complained as he turned the key in the ignition of his Ford Bronco.

"Don't worry, it'll be all right." He smiled at her. "Where does this Angela live?"

"Clove Hills. Do you know where that is?"

"Doesn't everyone? As my mother used to say, 'That's where the elite meet to eat.' Did you know that Dolph Richards lives in Clove Hills?"

"Who cares? Lex, what are we going to do after we've talked to Angela?"

"That's up to Eric Summers." His eyes on the road, he was silent for a moment. Then, "I don't know, Heather," he said honestly. "I really don't know."

Three

Angela parked her Porsche at the curb and walked into the house, glancing over her shoulder at the various trucks lining the driveway. A plumber, an electrician and a van with 'Sumpy Pumpy' painted on its side.

Her watch told her that six and a half hours has passed since she had jammed the overflows and left the water running. She closed the door behind her and waded through the several inches of water flooding the kitchen floor. Ignoring the workmen, who stared at her, she climbed the back stairway. I really did a number on you this time, old Mummy, she thought. This should set you back a bundle and keep you home for a while redecorating. She felt a moment of remorse then laughed at herself. Maybe she shouldn't have jammed all the upstairs overflows.

She ran to her room, sat down at her computer desk, flipped on the CPU and waited for it to boot up. A triumphant expression on her face she typed furiously for several minutes, checked her spelling then printed it out. Ripping the paper out of the printer, she read what she had written:

As a concerned citizen of Woodridge, I'm warning you that an explosion will happen at Timberwoods Mall during the height of the Christmas season.

Thousands of people will be killed. You've got to do something to stop it.

One who knows.

"That should give them some food for thought," Angela muttered. She was going to send it directly to the mayor. Would he send out a bomb squad? He couldn't afford to ignore the letter but would he close the mall? The management at Timberwoods would have to believe the mayor if they didn't believe her. She knew she had frightened Miss Andrews but she also knew that Miss Andrews didn't really believe Angela could see into the future.

A thought struck Angela. She had to be careful. If they discovered who had sent the mayor the letter, they would descend on her immediately. They'd say she was mentally unstable. Just what her mother would need to put her away.

Another thought struck her like a blow. They could accuse her of planning the explosion. They'd say she belonged to a subversive group or something. Her head buzzed, her thinking apparatus seemed to have short-circuited. "Why me?" she moaned. "What did I ever do to deserve this?"

Angry tears streamed down her thin cheeks as she lit a cigarette. Eventually she crumpled the letter into a ball and dropped it into the trash can. There was no way she could send that letter to the mayor – or to anyone else for that matter. She was too close to the edge as it was. It would be just the ammunition her mother needed. "A nice long rest," they would say when the men in white coats came to get her. Striking a match, she touched her cigarette to the edge of the paper and watched it burn.

It was no use. No one could escape the inevitable, and that meant the people at the shopping mall too. Somewhere in her gut, Angela knew that what she had envisioned was not a freak act of nature. Somebody was making plans to blow up the mall. Maybe, just maybe, if she hung around the center and kept her eyes open, she could find out who it was.

Crushing out the cigarette in an onyx ashtray, she hopped up from her chair and pulled a Gucci suitcase from the huge walk-in closet. Without thought to color or coordination, she pulled a mass of clothes from the scented hangers and tossed them into the depths of the soft-sided suitcase. Scooping up a handful of little plastic cases and jars she dumped them into a plastic pouch and buckled the suitcase. She would check into the nearest hotel and decide what to do next.

A timid knock sounded at the door and Irma, the old housekeeper, poked her head around the corner. "Miss Angela, we have to go to a motel for a while. I talked to the plumber and the electrician and they said we can't stay here. Your mother asked me to pack a bag and she'll pick it up. She wants to know where you're going to stay. She's upset over this . . . this . . ."

"Is she now? Tell her I'll let her know where I'm staying when I decide."

"Miss Angela, I told her one of the pipes in the bathroom broke. I didn't tell her . . ."

"You didn't tell her it was me who flooded the house? I appreciate you covering for me but it wasn't necessary. I'm sure my mother knows what happened. I'll own up to it. Don't worry about it. Thanks anyway, Irma."

"And, Miss Angela," the elderly housekeeper continued, "there's a man and a lady downstairs to see you."

"Me? Who are they?" She snapped to attention.

"I don't really know, Miss Angela. With all the confusion and your mother not here . . . ."

"All right, Irma, I'll be right down."

Angela's hands were shaking. She needed something to calm her. In her mother's bathroom there were tranquilizers. That would do it.

Biting her lower lip, Angela walked down the stairs, her boots squishing on the water-sodden carpet. In the foyer she saw a tall good-looking blond man with his back to her. Not an insurance man. He was with pretty dark-haired Miss Andrews from Timberwoods Mall.

"Angela, this is Felex Lassiter," Heather intoned gently when she saw Angela. She pasted a friendly smile on her lips but had a haunted look in her eyes. "We'd like to talk to you for a few minutes. Okay? Is there somewhere we could go that would be out of the way?" She glanced at the crew of electricians parading through the foyer.

Angela nodded, heading for the den. She wondered briefly if the water had reached her father's private sanctuary at the far side of the house. She smiled as she sloshed into the room and plopped down on the nearest chair. The tranquilizers hadn't really had a chance to work yet but just knowing she had taken them seemed to calm her.

Lex addressed the girl. His voice was pleasant and contradicted his frown. "It appears there was some sort of accident with the plumbing."

"Yes. I accidentally left the water running upstairs," Angela said shortly.

"You accidentally left the water running?"

45

"Uh huh," Angela answered with a smile.

Heather looked down at her new forty-dollar shoes and grimaced. It would cost a double fortune just to replace the carpeting, to say nothing of the damage to the wiring. She considered the cost of her shoes and sighed.

"Angela, we want to talk to you about your visit to my office yesterday," she said quietly. "I want you to tell Mr Lassiter what you told me, word for word."

"Why?"

"Why? You came to me and told me an incredible story. I want Mr Lassiter to hear it. If you're telling the truth, then perhaps we can help."

"It's too late. What do I have to do to make you understand? Nothing is going to change what I saw. No matter what you do, no matter what you say, you can't do anything. There's no stopping it. It's going to happen. Period."

The effect of the pills in her empty stomach was dulling her senses.

"Maybe it isn't too late," Lex said quietly. "I want to help if I can."

Angela felt herself responding to the man's soft concern. Then, discounting it as another effect of the tranquilizers, she sighed. "You won't listen. I already saw it. When I see it, that's the end. You can't change what I see. I don't know why I went to the center yesterday. I just had this need to tell someone, to get somebody to listen to me. I felt I had to try. Well, I'm not trying anymore. I'm never going to try again. I can't change anything."

Lex sat quietly, listening to the tone of Angela's voice. The slight sing-song quality alerted him. "Are you on something, Angela?"

"Just a couple of tranquilizers. I was jittery, I needed something. What business is it of yours anyway?"

"Angela," Lex said softly, ignoring the girl's defiance. "Miss Andrews has given me a rough sketch of what you told her. I want to hear it from you."

"Well, forget it. I don't want to go over it again. It was bad enough seeing it."

"I can understand that," he sympathized.

Heather's eyes flew to Lex. He wasn't going to let her off this easily, was he?

Lex continued to speak, his voice soft and soothing. "How did you know it was Timberwoods Mall in this vision of yours?"

"Because I was there. I was standing outside and all of a sudden there was an explosion and then another. Buildings collapsed. First one and then another!" Her voice rose in hysteria and even the tranquilizers couldn't calm her down. "And fire," she continued. "Thick black smoke. Flying glass. People were trapped in the stores. The exits were blocked. Children were lying dead, their parents searching for them. Everybody was screaming for help. Rivers of blood. I tried closing my eyes but all I could see was red and red, fire and fire . . ." Her voice rose to a wail.

"Easy does it." Lex reached out and took Angela by the shoulders. He held her against his body, could feel her quaking and trembling.

But now that Angela had started she couldn't stop. "People were trapped under mountains of stone and rubble. Everyone was screaming. I couldn't see to get to the trapped ones because of the fire, but I knew they were there. I could hear their screams . . ."

"Angela, Angela, hush, it's all right." Lex looked over Angela's head to Heather, who was sitting quietly with a stricken expression on her face. The girl's words were vivid, her panic was genuine. Heather believed her.

Angela calmed, wavering for a brief moment, indecision written on her face, a plea in her eyes. Then it was gone. "Come on, I did my good deed by telling you and now that's it. Get out of here. I'm out of it. I don't care if you believe me. Why should you be different from the rest of them? Close the damn mall or let it blow up." She broke out of Lassiter's grip. "I have to get out of here before my mother gets here. All this water and the ruined carpet is going to cause her to blow. I don't want to be around, if you know what I mean."

"No, wait a minute. We've received a letter – a bomb threat. We have to know – did you send it? Did you?" Lex shook her violently now, trying to break through the effects of the tranquilizers.

"Let go of me! I didn't send anybody anything!" Suddenly Angela was grateful she had burned her letter to the mayor. There was no way they were going to pin this on her. No way! She had already said too much. She could almost see the men in white coats coming for her.

"Let me go!" She pulled away and ran out of the room.

Heather looked at Lex, her face worried. "I can't help it, I believe her! God, I believe her!"

"I do, too. Stoned on tranquilizers and she told it like she was there, had actually seen it happen. She's so damn scared she doesn't know what to do. All that hardness – it's all part of her cover. She couldn't handle it without the front."

"She was right. I told you I believed her . . ."

"Easy, take it easy." Lex saw that Heather was begging him to reassure her, to tell her it was all a drug-induced hallucination, but he couldn't. "Angela didn't send that bomb threat. I'll go one step further and say she doesn't know who did."

Heather rubbed her temples as she watched Lex's face.

"Angela seemed to think her mother would be here soon," he continued. "I say we wait for her. I'll call Eric Summers and tell him what happened. Okay?"

"Okay. Where do you think Angela went? Shouldn't we have kept her here?"

"She'll run for a while, but she'll come back to us eventually. No matter what she says, she can't walk away from this and forget it. She's got to try to do something. She hurts too much not to try. Tranquilizers aren't her answer and she knows it."

Sylvia Steinhart turned the Lincoln Continental onto the New Jersey Turnpike in a state of controlled fury. "Wait till I get my hands on Murray," she muttered. "Angela doesn't get this . . . strange behavior from my side of the family. When I get my hands on her I'm literally going to choke the life from her!"

Irma had tried to tell her that the pipes had broken, but Sylvia knew better. It wasn't cold enough for pipes to break, and even if it were the pipes were heavily insulated. It was just another of Angela's attention-getting ploys. God knows, she had done everything she could to give Angela a proper upbringing, certainly more than her mother had given her and more than most of her friends gave their children. She'd done all the required things, hired all the right people but it hadn't been enough. Nothing was ever enough for Angela. She needed more – much more.

The first psychiatrist Sylvia had sought out had suggested family counseling; three sessions a week to start. Sylvia had snipped that idea in the bud right away. Who had time to just sit around and talk? Murray certainly didn't. He had a business to run. And she certainly didn't. Stupid man. He must have got his license to practice from a mail-order magazine.

Sylvia had been more careful in selecting the second psychiatrist, making sure he was more on her wavelength before taking Angela in to see him. He had suggested that Angela was simply seeking attention and had reassured Sylvia that Angela's problems were nothing to do with a poor upbringing.

There had been other psychiatrists after that, all of them carefully briefed by Sylvia prior to meeting Angela, and all of them coming to the same conclusion. They recommended a variety of ways to deal with her daughter, everything from giving her the attention she needed to ignoring her completely. But nothing had worked. Angela had got worse instead of better. No telling what she would do next!

"Damn," Sylvia said through tight lips as she narrowly missed a tractor-trailer. "This has gone on long enough." Her anger was building. "I won't stand for anymore. Not another thing. If Murray had let me get her help when I wanted to this wouldn't be happening now. It was for her own good, but oh no, he couldn't see it. If I'd done what I intended I wouldn't be getting these migraine headaches." She continued her tirade against her absentee husband and daughter until she came to her exit.

She would never make it back to the city now for her dinner engagement with the Mosses. She had waited so long for the invitation and now – all spoilt by Angela, as she managed to spoil everything. The girl needed a strong hand, someone to put a stop to her mischief. And while they were at it they might take a hand in her appearance too. She would pay extra if she had to.

The sleek Lincoln purred to a stop outside the house and Sylvia noted the line of cars and trucks. She moaned as she slid from the car.

She threw open the door and stood outlined in the doorway. She bit into her full lower lip as her eyes swept around the brightly lit foyer, taking in the sodden powder-blue carpet. The water was already seeping into her doeskin shoes. Another claim for the insurance man. All this beautiful carpet – it would be impossible to replace. And the wooden floors underneath the thick carpeting – were they ruined too? Probably. All it needed now was for the ceilings to collapse. When Angela did something she made a thorough job of it.

Sylvia's face brightened momentarily. She couldn't be expected to stay here. She would take a cruise and let the insurance company take care of the repairs. If she complained long enough and loud enough they would handle everything. Or Murray could handle it. It was all his fault anyway. She would place a call to London, tell him the situation and make him come home and take charge. He'd damn well better listen!

"Mrs Steinhart, there's a lady and gentleman waiting to see you in the study. They came to see Miss Angela but she went out and left them sitting here." Irma sounded agitated. She gestured towards the carpet: "I was out shopping when the pipes broke and when I got back everything was flooded. I didn't know what to do

"You did the right thing in calling me, Irma," Sylvia said, trying to comfort her frazzled housekeeper, even though she felt she was the one who needed comforting. After all, it was her house that was ruined and her daughter who had ruined it.

"The insurance man you called is upstairs, along with a man from some cleaning crew. He's drawing up an estimate of how much it will cost to clean the house. The plumber was here too, but just left. The electrician is checking the wiring. He says we can't stay here. Mrs Steinhart, I hate to do this but I have to give my notice."

Sylvia nodded wearily. Another problem to deal with, thanks to Angela. "I understand. But if you would consider changing your mind, I'll give you a raise and put you up at a motel until things are straightened out. I'll pay your wages for as long as it takes. Please reconsider, Irma. You know how hopeless I am in the housekeeping department."

"I just don't know, Mrs Steinhart. Let me think about it. Shall I tell the lady and gentleman that you'll see them?"

"Tell them I don't have time. If there's one thing I don't need right now it's a conversation with perfect strangers about Angela. Oh, and by the way, Irma, you don't need to cover for her. I know she's the one responsible for this mess."

The housekeeper twisted her apron between her hands. "Please, Mrs Steinhart, that's one of the reasons I want to leave. Now, don't get me wrong, Angela has always been respectful to me and even offered to help at times. I just feel that she needs . . ."

"You won't have to worry about Angela much longer. I'm placing a call to her father in a few minutes and he'll be home tomorrow. I've made the decision to have her institutionalized. It's for her own good."

The old housekeeper nodded dourly. Angela wasn't the one who should be in an institution, she thought uncharitably. "I'll tell these people you were detained and don't know when you'll be back."

Sylvia nodded absently as she rehearsed her speech to her husband. Her doeskin shoes made squishing sounds as she waded across the waterlogged carpeting to the front room. Fixing herself a double Scotch on the rocks, she downed it neatly in two rapid gulps before placing her call to London.

With a long arm she reached back, grasped the Scotch bottle and poured herself another drink. She hated people who drank to excess, and a woman who couldn't hold her liquor was worse. However, there was an exception to every rule.

Her call was connected. "Yes, I'm still here. Then interrupt him! This is an emergency! What do you mean he can't be disturbed? If you don't interrupt then I'll place a call to the nearest police station and have them interrupt him. Now, hurry, this is an emergency! Very well, call me back. Yes, yes, I understand. Fifteen minutes."

Irma opened the door of the study. She was surprised to see the gentleman listening on the phone. She hated lying and it seemed that was all she'd done since coming to work for the Steinharts. First for Angela and now for Mrs Steinhart. In Angela's defense, the girl had never asked her to lie for her; Irma had taken it upon herself to shield her whenever she could.

"Sir," she said coolly, "Mrs Steinhart has been unavoidably detained and won't be home for some time. Perhaps if you call tomorrow . . ."

Lex swiveled to face the housekeeper. "Detained? I just heard her identify herself to the overseas operator. Tell her we have to speak with her. It concerns Angela and it's extremely important. I can't tell you how important. Where is she?" he asked briskly.

No more lies, Irma thought. She'd told her last lie for the Steinharts. Mr Lassiter had said it was about Angela, maybe he was here to help the girl. God knows, somebody needed to help her because her parents never would.

"The front room, two doors down the hall," she said, pointing the way. "I don't care if you tell her I told you or not. It's time someone did something for that poor girl."

"There's no need for me to mention it at all," said Lex. "I heard her myself. After all, we want to help Angela. Surely she'll take the time to talk with us. She is her mother."

"I wouldn't count on anything," the ageing housekeeper muttered as she turned on her heel and marched from the room. "If there's one thing that lady isn't interested in it's her daughter."

"Come on, Heather." Lex was already halfway out of the room. "We'll have to talk fast to cover a lot of territory in the fifteen minutes until her husband calls back."

Lex rapped smartly on the door, opening it at the same time. The tall willowy woman in the room downed her drink and thumped the glass on the shiny surface of the desk.

"Felex Lassiter," he introduced himself, "and this is Heather Andrews. We're from the Timberwoods Mall and we want to talk to you about Angela. I was placing a call to the center and overheard you on the line. I apologize." He grinned at her.

"Mr Lassiter, is it? I really haven't the time to speak with you right now. I'm expecting an overseas call any second." Sylvia's tone was frigid.

"That's why we need to speak with you immediately. After we've finished you can relay the matter to your husband."

"What has my daughter done now?" Sylvia asked in a bored voice. "Whatever it is, can't you just send me the bill? I'll have my husband take care of it immediately, I assure you. Now if you'll excuse me . . . ."

"Mrs Steinhart, your daughter hasn't done anything to require you to be billed. She came to the center yesterday, very distraught, and spoke with Miss Andrews here. She told her a most fantastic story. She said she'd had a vision that the Timberwoods Shopping Mall was going to explode and collapse during the height of the Christmas season and thousands of people were going to die. Now do you see why we need to talk with you?"

Sylvia Steinhart paled and grasped the edge of the desk. Heather noted her white clenched knuckles and the dark spots of rouge standing out sharply on her high cheekbones. She's afraid, she thought. No, she's petrified. She knows it's true.

Controlling herself with an effort, Sylvia wet her lips before speaking. "And . . .you . . .you believe her? My dear man, Angela has been doing this for years. She'll go to any lengths to get some attention. We had a slight arg . . . discussion yesterday and this is Angela's way of getting back at me. It doesn't mean a thing. Really, it doesn't. You know how these teenagers are." Her eyes were bright and staring.

Heather Andrews spoke up. "Your daughter and I talked at length, Mrs Steinhart. She told me she's been having these visions since she was twelve. She mentioned an incident that I vividly remember."

"I believe her, Mrs Steinhart," Felex added. "And Miss Andrews believes her too. Look, it was obvious that Angela was upset and wanted help. Someone to listen to her. Even if it is a bid for attention, as she says you seem to think it is, we have to check it out. You must understand our position. Do you have any idea how many people shop in the center during Christmas week? Angela said it would be a series of explosions. She described things no one could possibly know."

"Angela . . . has . . . this gift of a fertile imagination," Sylvia said waving a hand in dismissal. "She can make people believe what she says she saw by describing it so vividly. She has these . . . these nervous fits. I assure you they don't mean anything. You must not take her seriously. That's what she wants, to make people jump to her command."

"Mrs Steinhart, I don't buy what you're saying. I listened, really listened to Angela in this room not more than half an hour ago. What she told me was not a product of her imagination, nor was it a 'nervous fit', as you called it."

"Don't you see that you're playing right into her hands?" Sylvia retorted. "This is what she wants. She always wants to be the center of attention!"

"Mrs Steinhart, please . . ."

56

"I don't want to discuss it any further. If you don't leave I'll be forced to call the police."

"Mrs Steinhart, Angela told Heather about a psychiatrist she had been seeing."

Heather didn't think it was possible for the woman to pale still further, but she did, her face turning chalky as she moistened her lips. She swayed and Lex rushed to put an arm around her.

"Sit down, Mrs Steinhart, you don't look well. Heather, could you get her a drink."

Heather poured some more Scotch into Sylvia's glass and held it to the trembling woman's lips. "Drink this."

Sylvia, her face a mask of rage, knocked the snifter from Heather's hand. "Get out of my house! Get out this minute! What right do you have to come here and upset me? Get out!"

"Not until you tell us what you're so afraid of, Mrs Steinhart." Heather's voice was insistent.

"Afraid? I'm not afraid. I'm mad! Mad as hell as a matter of fact. Mad because I have a daughter who doesn't just see things in the future but makes them happen. Now you take that any way you want to and do with it anything you want to do. I don't care. It's your mall, your responsibility. Not mine!" Sylvia was shaking, her teeth chattering violently.

"Mrs Steinhart, are you saying that what Angela fears for Timberwoods will come true? Or are you saying that she's the one who will blow up the mall?"

"I've said all I'm going to say. Look around you – does this look like the work of a sane person? Get out, get out!"

Heather and Lex quickly exited the room, heading

57

for the front door. Behind them they could hear Sylvia Steinhart's wails.

Sylvia collapsed against the soft padded chair and allowed the trembling to consume her. The implication of what the man had said finally penetrated her numb mind. Thousands of people. Explosives.

The phone rang and it was all she could do to make her legs obey her. Clutching the receiver, she gasped, "Murray, is that you? Listen to me, you have to come home. Take the next plane. It's about Angela. I know you just got there but you have to take the next plane home."

"For God's sake, what is it this time?" Murray asked impatiently. "I told you before I left that this was an important deal. Why can't you handle whatever it is? If you'd stay home once in a while and talk to Angela maybe she wouldn't get into so much trouble. Take a drink and calm down."

"Don't tell me to take a drink. I've already had three double Scotches and the problem isn't going away."

"Then sleep it off, you're probably drunk," Murray answered shortly.

"Damn it, Murray, I'm not drunk. Listen to me. First of all, Angela's flooded the whole damn house. Everything is ruined. And when I say ruined, I mean ruined, Murray. Floors, ceilings, carpets, wiring, the whole bit. We're going to have to move out. And that's just the first thing. When I came home to inspect the damage there were two people from Timberwoods Mall here. They wanted to talk about Angela. This Mr Lassiter said Angela went to the mall yesterday and told them she'd had a vision of the center being blown up. She also told them about Doctor

58

Tyler," she continued slowly and distinctly. "They said they believed her!"

"Where's Angela now?"

"How in the hell do I know where she is? She's like some phantom – she comes and she goes. After she'd ruined the house, she left. What do you want from me, Murray? She's your daughter. My family is normal, she gets this . . . this craziness from your side. I think she's actually planning on blowing up the mall! Now, are you going to get on a plane and come home or not? I told you she should have been put away. It would have been for her own good. But oh no, you said she needed a little freedom and time to try her wings. Well, your fledgling has turned into a hawk and it's all your fault!"

"If we're going to start laying blame, let's put it right where it belongs – on your doorstep. If you had listened to me years ago this wouldn't be happening now. All you were concerned about was the social stigma and Angela's appearance. Now you can see where all your conniving has got you. The whole world is going to know about your daughter now, not just a few psychiatrists. I'll be home some time tomorrow – tonight, if I can get a plane. And for God's sake keep your mouth shut till I get there!"

The line clicked off in her ear and Sylvia stared at the silent receiver. She slowly replaced it and quickly poured herself another full tumbler of Scotch. The whole world would know . . .

Four

The customized Porsche sliced down the highway, weaving boldly between the other vehicles. Angela shifted from fourth to third then down to second with a speed that strained the transmission, finally careening around the bend that led into the Timberwoods Mall car park.

The question was, why did she feel compelled to come back here? She hated the place, feared it. Who did that spit-and-polish Lassiter think he was fooling?

She shifted again to third and pressed her foot down on the accelerator. If there was one thing she didn't do it was lie to herself. Lassiter believed her vision that the center was going to blow. Beyond that, there was no way he would commit himself, especially to her. And what good would it do to have Lassiter believe her anyway? Pretty soon, if not right this minute, somebody was going to come right out and say that she was responsible for the bomb-threat letter Lassiter had told her about.

She raced the car up one aisle and down the other, looking for a parking space. A sleek Miata backed out of a narrow slot. Angela maneuvered into the space and cut the engine. Her shoulders slumped as she pocketed the keys. The gray cloud of despair that had been hovering around her was rapidly growing in size and deepening to black. She shivered.

"I should be out looking for someplace to stay and instead I come to this place," she muttered.

The tinny sound of 'Jingle Bells' wafted through the parking lot as she made her way along the slippery frosting of snow to the mall entrance. She pulled open the door and walked aimlessly down a section of the center called The Alley. Ignoring the brilliant Christmas displays and the bustling crowds, she made her way to a railing that over-looked a tropical garden setting. A flash of red registered on her mind as she let her gaze travel beyond the crowds to the squared-off section that was Santa's workshop. The Santa from the parking lot was there.

Jamming her hands into her pockets Angela continued her trek around the mall, always returning to the tropical garden. The Santa was still there. She could tell he was pretending to enjoy the children who insisted on sitting on his lap. A flashbulb went off. Angela sighed. Everything was wrong. Wasn't Santa supposed to take a kid up on his lap and ask, 'Were you a good little boy? What do you want for Christmas?' Now all Santa did was pick the kid up, face him towards the camera and say, "Smile and look at the birdie."

The little boy sitting on Santa's lap became difficult and yanked at Santa's white beard. Angela watched with interest as Santa extricated his beard with forceful fingers and dumped the child on the floor. The boy howled angrily, demanding a candy cane as his mother whisked him out of sight.

Angela frowned and walked into a bath shop. She stared at a bright array of bath towels trimmed in frosty lace then grinned as she spotted a saleswoman watching her suspiciously. Did the woman really think she was going to stuff one of the towels into her hip pocket? Evidently, for she was approaching, an uneasy look in her eyes. "Just looking," Angela muttered as she moved over to the shower curtains. What was she doing here anyway? Why was she torturing herself this way? There was nothing she could do.

She made her way again to the center of the mall and the tropical garden. All the benches were filled with squealing kids sucking on candy canes or dribbling ice cream down the front of their snowsuits. Her eyes went again to the red-suited figure on the gilt throne. Curiously she began to clock the kids who went to climb on Santa's lap. One minute flat was as long as Santa permitted them. Just enough time to snap a picture.

What was there about this Santa figure that kept drawing her back here? Maybe she'd secretly wanted to be a Gentile when she was a little kid. She snorted. Had she ever been a little kid? She couldn't remember. It seemed as though she'd been a teenager all her life. Suddenly it was important for her to know if she had ever acted like all the squealing rambunctious kids racing around the center. A feeling of panic washed over her as she struggled to revive a memory, any memory, good or bad. It didn't matter. She squeezed her eyes shut and forced herself to think back. With relief she recalled a shopping trip with her mother. They had been looking for a special dress – a Christmas dress, she remembered. Her mother had wanted something in velvet with a white lace collar and bows. They were in a store, a big store with several floors and lots of departments. Not a mall. Timberwoods hadn't been built yet. They'd had lunch in the store dining room and watched a fashion show. Afterwards her mother had taken her to visit Santa. When Santa had asked her what she wanted for Christmas, she couldn't think of anything she didn't already have so she'd shrugged and said nothing at all.

Her mother had snatched her off Santa's lap and chastised her for not telling Santa what she wanted. Instead of looking for the dress they'd gone home, and on Christmas Day she'd worn an old dress. Now she wondered why her parents had celebrated Christmas at all when they were Jewish. Was it the in thing to do back then? There hadn't been any more Christmas celebrations after that one. And from then on, whenever she needed new clothes, the nanny had taken her shopping.

The queue to see Santa had diminished and the photographer had placed a sign in front of the roped-off area which said, 'Elves off-duty for fifteen minutes.' Which probably meant the young girl in the elf outfit was going outside to smoke a cigarette and Santa was going to sit there and wait until she got back. Angela ran to the escalator and down the moving steps, too impatient to wait. At the bottom she slowed, then walked towards the North Pole display. She waited impatiently for the man in the red suit to acknowledge her. He said nothing, just stared at her.

"Hi," Angela said finally in a cracked voice. Why had she even come down here? she wondered. But here she was, as if drawn by an invisible thread.

"You know, you look exactly the way a Santa should look," Angela said, hoping to draw the man into conversation. He just shrugged in response.

"Listen, would you like to have a cup of coffee or a soda with me after you finish up here?" Angela said, hearing the hint of desperation in her voice. Even though the fake moustache and beard masked his face she should be able to feel some interest from the silent man. A person's eyes were supposed to hold hidden messages and reveal untold stories. But from the way he was behaving this man was dead from the neck up.

"All right. Where?"

Angela blinked in surprise. She shrugged, "Wherever. Burger King is just over there, or there's an ice-cream parlor down at the end of The Alley. You name it."

With or without the Santa suit he was a big man, not fat, not muscular, just big and sort of awkward. Did that have something to do with why she was here – because she felt some sort of common bond?

"Burger King is okay with me," came the flat reply.

Why was she so drawn to this man? It had to be the Santa suit, or what Santa represented. Maybe she should try another approach, just to see if there was any kind of life behind those flat eyes.

"Look, working here in the mall like you do, you must know a lot of people, right?" All she got by way of response was a shrug. "I need a place to stay for a while. Two, three days, maybe even a week. I have money – a hundred dollars for a week. Do you know anyone who has a spare room?"

She waited patiently, knowing the man was mulling over her words. There was still no change of expression, nothing alive in the flat eyes. When he finally decided to speak, his answer stunned her. "You can stay with me."

Angela felt as though a heavy weight had toppled from

her thin shoulders. She stared at him feeling relieved, not because of his offer but because it meant she would be near him. She could continue to feed this strange obsession.

"Would you like your picture taken with Santa?" the young elf with the camera demanded. "Only $6.50 a shot. No? Then you have to move on. The kids are lining up again."

Angela stared at Charlie Roman. He met her gaze blankly. "I'll wait in Burger King for you."

Charlie said nothing but Angela knew his small flat dun-colored eyes would follow her until she was out of sight. She let out a long sigh and searched for a bench to sit down. She felt different now, almost calm. She hadn't felt that way in days. If she were honest with herself it had nothing to do with finding a place to stay. There was always somewhere to crash; she'd even slept in her car before now. No, what was making her feel different was the Santa with the flat eyes.

Harold Baumgarten led the small parade into Dolph Richards's office. He'd just listened to Eric Summers's story and he wasn't impressed.

"I hope your migraine is better, Miss Andrews," he said testily, turning to Heather.

"You wouldn't believe the pain I've been in, Mr Baumgarten. You simply wouldn't believe it."

The chief of security shot her a suspicious look as he opened the door to Richards's inner sanctum.

As always when entering his boss's office, Harold blinked at the lavish decor. Heavy wheat-colored curtains complemented the ankle-deep chocolate carpeting and oversized display pieces of every description cluttered the large space. The huge kidney-shaped desk was bare of anything resembling work. Someday, Harold thought, he would work out what all the buttons on the phone were for. Possibly some sort of warning system to tell Richards when someone was hot on his tail. Harold's eyes went to the large tufted sofa upholstered in lemon yellow. How in the hell did Richards keep it clean?

Dolph Richards beamed an expensive movie star smile at the small group. "Sit down, everyone. Can I get anyone a drink? I've got some good imported brandy. Why don't we try it out? You all look so serious."

"I don't drink and you know it, Richards," Harold said peevishly.

"That's right, Baumgarten. You don't drink and you don't smoke and you don't womanize. And you frown on those who do. Loosen up, Harold, the world is going to pass you by. Live," Richards exclaimed expansively, "for tomorrow you may die."

Harold developed a coughing fit while Heather tried to swallow past the lump in her throat. Lex winced slightly but kept smiling.

Richards was generous with his imported brandy as he poured it into elegant snifters and handed them around. Harold eyed the glasses with distaste, picturing in his mind the long-haired beauty who worked in the crystal shop. The whole goddamned office was a shrine to Richards's sexual conquests. He felt nauseated as he watched the grinning Richards playing benevolent host. Still, in a few days he wouldn't have to worry about him any more. He was quitting this thankless job and taking off for Florida. The hell with everything.

"How long is this going to take?" Richards asked.

Heather grimaced. Harold smiled at his private thoughts and waited for Eric to take up the reins.

"I only ask so I can call my wife. The decision to hold dinner is up to you folks." Richards flashed his too-white teeth.

"Tell her not to hold dinner, this may take a while," Summers advised, sipping his brandy.

Richards played with the buttons on the phone. "Darling, don't wait dinner for me. I'm in a meeting and I don't know how long I'll be. I'll catch a bite here."

"Is she blond or brunette?" The strident voice carried into the room.

"Neither," Richards said, pressing the receiver closer to his ear in an attempt to muffle the sound.

"Oh, a redhead. One of these days, Dolph, I'm going to catch you red-handed and then I'm going to cut off your dick just like that woman on TV did."

Richards blanched slightly but answered pleasantly, "See you in a little while. Love you, darling."

"You bastard, you don't know the meaning of the word. Sit on it, Dolph!"

"Wives! Sometimes they don't understand," he said, laughing, hoping her voice hadn't been overheard.

Harold felt his stomach heave; he wanted to smash that handsome, lying face. If there was any justice in the world someone would make a eunuch out of Richards and present him to his wife for Christmas. He forced his mind back to the matter at hand as Eric Summers spoke.

"Heather Andrews came to me with a rather interesting story. I think she should tell you herself and then I'll pick up from where she leaves off."

Heather moistened her lips and spoke quietly. "Angela

67

Steinhart came to see me yesterday. She just wanted to talk to me. You do know who she is, don't you?"

Richards sighed. "Yes, I know her. Know the family rather well. We get together once in a while for a game of bridge. Strange girl. Willful. Spoiled. You know how some of those poor little rich kids are."

Heather nodded. "She told me a horrible story that made my blood run cold. She said that for years she's had these visions, premonitions of things that are going to happen. She's a sort of seer, I think that's the word for it. She told me she saw Timberwoods Mall collapsing at the height of the Christmas season and thousands of people losing their lives. She said there would be a series of explosions which would demolish the whole center. I believed her then and I believe her now."

"Miss Andrews, surely you're joking," Richards said indulgently. He could forgive this idiocy. After all, she did have the best legs in the center. "Angela was playing a joke on you. I admit it was in poor taste, but it must have been a joke."

"It's no joke," Lex said curtly. "Heather and I went over to her house and talked to her. She described the vision and what happened. The kid isn't lying. Lives are at stake here. Timberwoods is at stake. We have to do something. Angela says that what she sees happens. It's as simple as that. You'll have to close the mall."

"You're out of your mind!" Richards was horrified. "Why, if one word of this ever gets out this center is doomed. The loss of revenue and failure to renew leases – it would be catastrophic! Harold, what do you have to say?"

The chief of security had developed a grayish pallor.

"Christ, first the bomb threat this morning and now this," he said hoarsely. "I knew there was something different about it."

"It's all a joke. For whatever reason, Angela is playing a trick on you, that's all. Teenagers do that sort of thing. Especially spoilt little rich kids." Richards sounded relieved now he was on surer ground. "They've got nothing better to do."

"At first we thought Angela might have sent the bomb threat but she didn't. We know that now," Eric stated. "The police say the MO is the same as the others. I checked with them before I came in here."

"The girl is probably on drugs! All teenagers are on drugs these days," Richards cried. "You're believing the word of a druggie?"

"Drugs or no – I believe her and so does Heather. If you could have seen her, heard her . . . Something has to be done," Lex said.

"Nothing is going to be done. This whole thing is ridiculous. I don't believe in all this shit you're spouting. I believe in the here and now. No one can foresee the future. If either of you utter a word of this . . . if this gets out . . . you'll be fired on the spot. Do you hear me, Harold? I'm holding you personally responsible. I'll sue you . . . all of you. And that's not a damn threat, that's a promise!"

Harold was having difficulty speaking so he just nodded and wiped damp hands on his trousers.

"Listen to me, Richards," Lex insisted. "We went to see Mrs Steinhart at her house. It was a disaster. The whole downstairs was flooded, thousands of dollars in damage. Mrs Steinhart intimated that Angela did it, that she wasn't sane. On the other hand, she also intimated that she knows

69

about Angela's visions and that they come true. She didn't come right out and admit it but she might as well have. She probably thinks that if the word gets out it will ruin her social standing in the community. When we mentioned that Angela told us she'd seen a psychiatrist, she almost fainted."

"What was his prognosis?" Richards asked craftily.

"Who knows. But her mother calls Angela's condition nervous fits."

"There, you see!" Richards laughed heartily. "The girl is some sort of mental case and the psychiatrist recognized it. I can almost understand your being taken in by her. It sounds like she really worked you over." He shook his head. "Forget it. Why don't you both go out to dinner and forget the whole thing? Everything will look differently in the morning. And remember, not a word of this to anyone."

"Mr Richards," Harold said hesitantly, "what if it is true? What if the girl can predict these things? When you stop and think about it, it doesn't sound too far-fetched. I read about things like this in the papers every week. Not necessarily something as catastrophic as this, but things of this nature. Do you know how many people will be in this mall next week? My God!" he exclaimed, horror spreading across his face.

"You always were a mealy-mouthed son of a bitch, Harold. I just told you it was a trick, and you know damn well that no one in his right mind would blow up my shopping center. Remember, all of you . . . if one word of this gets out, you're fired!"

"You can sit here and pretend till hell freezes over that we never talked to you," Lex said, his temper rising, "but

I'm going to talk to anyone who will listen to me, and that includes the police. I want to be able to live with myself. I have to try to do something. You can't play with human lives. You're going to be forced to close this center!"

"I won't close the center. You're crazy, Lassiter. Isn't he, Baumgarten?"

Harold frowned as something stirred in his gut. He squared his plump shoulders and said quietly, "I don't know if he's crazy or not. But if I were in your position I'd close this center. If this ever comes to pass and word gets out that it was your decision to keep the mall open . . . you're a dead man. These bomb threats could be some sort of warning. The seventy-two hours takes us right into the Christmas parade."

"But she's a mental case! You'd believe some kid who's so screwed up she doesn't know what day of the week it is? Fools! This center stays open and I don't want to hear another word about it."

"Over my dead body," Eric shouted. "Don't be stupid! Get your brains out of your jockey shorts and do something now before it's too late!"

"You're going too far, Summers. I don't have to sit here and listen to this," Richards shouted angrily.

"You don't have to but you'd better. All this is too much of a coincidence. The bomb threat, the Steinhart girl coming to talk to Heather . . ." Lex faced Richards's fury.

"You're a jackass, Lassiter. I'm warning you, stay out of this. No one is closing this center. No one is going to tell me what to do. I'll have the lot of you thrown in jail."

"Try it," Summers said coldly.

Harold stood up, his short legs trembling. "I'm on your

side, Summers, for whatever it's worth. I vote to close this center and I'll tell the police so. I am the chief of security."

"Not any longer. You're fired!" Richards shouted.

"My contract says you have to give me two weeks' notice," Harold laughed, enjoying his own private joke. "I really don't care if you fire me or not. I'll stay for my two weeks and you can't do anything about it."

"You're too stupid to get a job anywhere else. I'll kill you, Baumgarten, if this garbage gets spread around the mall."

Harold continued to laugh. He walked around to the portable bar and poured himself a glass of brandy. He held the glass aloft and said, "To all the stupid fools the world over." He took one gulp of the fiery liquid and poured the remainder over Richards's desk.

Stunned, Richards watched the brandy seeping into his trousers before jumping to his feet "You're out of your minds, the lot of you! Get out of here before I throw you out."

Outside Richards's office, Lex turned to Heather and put his hands on her shoulders, gently squeezing them. "You need to get some rest. Go on home. I'll be in touch."

Heather leaned towards him, needing his strength. "But what are you going to do?" she asked, knowing there were purple shadows of fatigue under her eyes and not caring. Something was developing between Lex and herself, something that went deeper than smudged make-up and disheveled hair. This was something that came from the inside out.

"Lex is going to come home with me," Summers explained. "I've got a connection through the police force with a man by the name of Noel Dayton. I've already called him and he's going to meet me at home. I don't want to make this official by talking to him in the office or downtown at the station."

"Who's Noel Dayton?" Heather asked.

"He's a police psychiatrist from New York City. I'd like him to talk to Angela."

Lex wrapped an arm around Heather's waist and started walking. "You've had a long day. I'll walk you down to your car." Lex smiled down at her, his concern evident. "We'll get a fresh start in the morning. And another thing – I don't want you losing sleep over this," he added sternly. "We're going to do our best and that's all any of us can do."

Heather nodded gratefully. "Will I see you later?" she asked, hoping he would catch her silent invitation.

"I'll give you a call," he said, smiling.

"Harold, you should be in on this too." Summers turned to address the chief. "You will come home with me, won't you?"

"Of course. I'm chief of security, I'll do everything I can."

"Thanks for the back-up in Richards's office. If we stand together maybe we can get to the bottom of this." Summers's voice was weary. "I don't know what to believe at this point. All I know is that the bomb threat was real and tangible. I could hold it in my hand and look at it. This Steinhart thing, well, I just don't know. But I do know that we've got to follow every lead, look into every corner. If Angela knows something, we've got to make her tell us. That's where my concerns lie. I had an old sergeant in police academy who used to say, 'No threat is an empty threat.' I tend to agree."

Harold worked his mouth into a smile and patted Summers's back. "Exactly. And don't worry about Richards. He's an ass. I'll get my coat and meet you by lot number five."

Lex hurried Heather through the cold windy parking lot to her car.

"It's over there," she said, pointing a gloved hand. "You don't have to do this, you know."

"I know, I know, all that women's lib stuff. Let's just say I like to do it; it doesn't mean I don't think you're not capable of getting out to your car yourself."

Heather laughed. Being with Lex was so nice, so easy. In the past two days their relationship had deepened and it was as though she had known him a lifetime. "Here it is. Now you hurry over to number five. Eric and Harold are probably waiting for you."

Lex grabbed her arm and pulled her towards him. "Let them wait. I've got something important on my mind." He rested his hand on the car roof and leaned close to her. His breath was soft and warm on her cheek and his eyes held hers softly.

Heather lifted her face, offering her lips to his kiss. He gathered her in his arms and held her close, tight against him. "Mmmm," he sighed into her ear. "I wish I was going home with you rather than Summers."

Heather laughed lightly, "I do too, but you can't stand up Eric and Harold. No way am I going to be responsible for breaking up the three musketeers. On your way, mister."

She gave him a gentle push. "If it's not too late when you're through, give me a call."

"I'll keep my fingers crossed," he told her, touching her lips with his once again.

Angela scanned the interior of the Burger King restaurant for an empty booth. It was dim and she had to peer intently between the tinsel and artificial greenery that hung from the beams overhead. God, she was tired of the sound of 'Jingle Bells.' Didn't they have any other Christmas recordings? Even 'Rudolph' would have been an improvement.

Fighting her way between strollers pushed by harried mothers, Angela made her way to what looked like one of the waiting lines. She tapped her foot impatiently, to the undisguised annoyance of the woman behind her. As if she cared. If the woman could put up with the snotty-nosed little kid pulling on her trouser leg, she could certainly put up with Angela's nervousness. She switched from floor-tapping to nail-nibbling as she moved slowly to the front of the line. "Two coffees," she muttered finally.

She should have taken plastic lids for the scalding coffee. It was slopping all over her hands and wrists. She waited patiently for an elderly couple to vacate the booth next to her and immediately sat down. The woman with the little boy fixed her with an angry look and spoke in an offended tone, "You could have taken a small table. Why do you have to hog a whole booth?"

"Not that it's any of your business but I'm waiting for someone," Angela said, indicating the second cup of coffee.

"I just bet you are. You damn kids are all alike, you take over and hog everything."

Angela frowned at the woman. What had she done to upset her so? Adults! Go figure. She looked pointedly at the child with the dripping nose who was demanding an ice-cream cone, a seat and some French fries. Maybe if she had a child like that she would be rude too.

Several minutes later Angela was startled as a shadow fell across her table. She glanced up and sighed with relief.

"I wasn't sure if it was you. It's so dim in here," Charlie Roman said as he wedged himself between the orange table and the brown plastic seat.

"You're right. It looks like they took out all the over-head lights and put in those tiny colored ones. More Christmassy, I guess. Here," she said, sliding the coffee towards Charlie, "I thought you might want coffee. I hope it isn't cold. I drank mine while I waited."

Charlie reached for the coffee, his eyes on the girl across from him. He wondered what she was all about. "How much do I owe you?"

"You don't owe me anything. What's a cup of coffee between friends? You can buy it next time."

Friends? Charlie frowned. They didn't even know each other and she was calling them friends. He'd never had a girl for a 'friend' before. "Yeah, sure, I'll buy the next time."

"Well, now that that's settled, why don't you relax and enjoy it – the coffee, I mean. I got it black because I didn't know what you took in it."

"Black is fine," Charlie mumbled. He hated black coffee. He liked it with lots of cream and at least three sugars. And he hated lukewarm coffee with a passion. But he would keep his complaints to himself.

"My name's Angela Steinhart." Angela held out her hand.

Charlie looked down and saw her ragged nails. "Charlie Roman," he said, holding out his own hand hesitantly.

Angela noticed that he wiped his palm on his trousers before he offered it and she wondered vaguely why he should have sweating palms. Playing Santa Claus must be tougher than she thought. All those whining kids.

"Do you shop here often?" Charlie asked, wondering why he hadn't seen her around before.

"Not really. Lately, though, I've been killing time here a lot," Angela volunteered. She would have liked to tell him the real reason she was there but she didn't want him to think she was crazy.

Charlie was uncomfortable. He squirmed on the hard plastic seat. He didn't know how to talk to girls and she looked uncomfortable too. The knowledge that she might be nervous pleased him and he relaxed for the first time in days. He'd had reservations about meeting her but now he was glad. She was anything but pretty but she wasn't homely either. He frowned, trying to decide if it was her nose or her teeth that made her face look irregular. Somehow one didn't seem to go with the other. Aside from that she was as skinny as a rail, but what the hell? He could put up with her. It wasn't like they were going to jump into the sack together. They were just having coffee and talking.

"Do you pick up guys all the time?" he blurted. She was staring at him and God only knew what she was thinking.

"Nah. You never know what you're getting. You're different, though. You work here and you're a Santa Claus and all. That makes you a responsible adult." She giggled, waiting to see Charlie's reaction. There was none. Then she asked, "Do you pick up girls often?"

Charlie's eyes widened and he almost burst out laughing. Did she really think he picked up girls? A guy like him who was big and awkward and nerdish? She was obviously putting him on. Still, she didn't look like she was poking fun at him. All the guys he knew lied to girls; why couldn't he?

"Sometimes," he said quietly. Let her make whatever she wanted out of that.

Angela pursed her mouth. "Well, I'm not a pick-up so get that idea right out of your mind. I don't go in for one-night stands and I don't sleep around."

Charlie's face drained. Wow! She was no Heather Andrews but she had something Heather didn't. Honesty! He liked the feeling that was starting to stir in his nether regions. "So who said you did? I don't remember inviting you anywhere. You invited me, remember?" he said testily.

"I just don't want you to think I'm some kind of cheap pick-up. I sort of like you and I don't want us to have any misunderstandings later on. Sex does that to people," Angela replied knowledgeably.

Charlie stared at the girl a full minute before he replied. "You've made your point."

"Have you worked here long?" Angela questioned, hoping to change the subject. Sex seemed to be a taboo subject with the Santa.

"Close to six years. Why?" he asked bluntly.

"Why not?" Angela replied just as bluntly. "Is it a secret?"

Secret! Jesus, just the word sent a chill up his spine. She was out of her mind. "You certainly ask a lot of questions," he said coldly, not liking the stiffness that was building up in his pants. Here he was getting a hard-on for a string bean who would probably jab him to death with her hip-bones if they ever got together. How was he going to tell her he had never had a woman before? She looked experienced. Hell, he would just have to bluff it. A bright flush stained his cheeks and he was thankful that his Santa trousers had yards of play in them. "I never had a secret in my life," Charlie lied.

"That's hard to believe. Everyone has secrets. Everyone has a skeleton in his or her closet. I bet you have one and just don't want to tell me," Angela pressed, enjoying the crimson stain of Charlie's cheeks. It matched his Santa suit.

He had to be careful, she was clever. She almost acted like she knew something. What could she know? "Well, you're wrong. My life's an open book."

"Actually," Angela said, searching her memory for some kind of compliment to pay him, "you have a nice open kind of face, very readable, if you know what I mean."

Holy Christ, did that mean he was giving away that fact that he had a hard-on? Oh Jesus, he had to get out of here and he had to do it now. "Look, I have to get back to the mall. I still have part of my shift to finish and then I have to clean up the area."

"Do you want me to help?" Angela offered, hating to see him leave. "Say, where do you live?"

Charlie debated a second. Then, what the hell, he thought. "I live on West End Avenue, second house from the end." Without another word he trotted out of the restaurant, his stiff member rubbing against the rough velvet of the Santa suit.

Angela stared after him, still trying to figure out why she was drawn to this man in the midst of the terrifying threat to Timberwoods Shopping Mall.

Five

Eric Summers opened his front door and invited in Harold and Lex. He took their coats and introduced them to his very pregnant wife, Amy.

Lex looked into her soft doe-like eyes and grinned, "The big day is soon, right?"

Amy ran her long tapered fingers through her short-clipped natural hair. Her tea-colored skin glowed with vitality as she laughed happily, "Christmas Day, what do you think of that? What better Christmas present could I give Eric?"

Eric's gaze was clear and direct as he explained to Harold Baumgarten, "This is the closest we've come in six years. Amy has had two miscarriages and the doctors told us we couldn't have children. Someone up there must like us," he said, smiling.

Harold blinked. "I didn't know . . . what I mean is . . . I'm sorry." Suddenly he reached out and grasped Amy's dark slender hand in his. "Congratulations. I wish you both the very best," he said sincerely.

Eric looked across at Lex. "How about a drink?" he asked, massaging his square jaw, his fingers making a rasping sound against his five-o'clock stubble.

"I'll have a double Scotch. What about you, Harold?"

"I'll have the same. I've never had Scotch before. Is it any good, Lassiter?"

"In answer to your question, Baumgarten, it grows on you."

"Oh, I'm sorry, I forgot you don't drink," Eric apologized.

"Don't be sorry. I just took up the habit. A double Scotch," Harold said firmly.

"Honey, why don't you . . ." Eric turned towards his wife.

Amy laughed, a bright tinkling sound that fell softly on Harold's ears. How long since he'd heard a woman's warm laugh? "I'm going, I'm going. I think I'll make some brownies. Do you like brownies, Mr Baumgarten?"

"I love 'em." Harold beamed. "With lots of nuts."

"One pan of brownies with lots of nuts coming up."

"Amy," Eric said anxiously, "don't overdo it, okay?"

"Honestly, did you ever! If I need you to slide the pan into the oven, I'll call you," she complained as she waddled toward the kitchen.

Eric sighed. "I just don't want anything to go wrong at this stage of the game," he said defensively.

He filled the glasses and settled down to await the arrival of Dr Noel Dayton. A few minutes later the doorbell sounded. "I'll get it, honey," Summers called through to the kitchen.

He opened the door and admitted a slightly built man whose overcoat was pulled up over his chin. He wore a knitted hat low over his ears.

"Christ, it's gonna blow out there."

When Dayton lifted his face, his ingenuous smile and electric blue eyes met Lex's and Harold's. "How do. Pleased to meet you both."

"Gentlemen, this is Dr Noel Dayton. Noel – Felex Lassiter and Harold Baumgarten. Here, give me your coat."

"Where's Amy?" the doctor asked, a slight New-England twang in his voice.

"The kitchen. How about a little something to take the nip out? Still drinking bourbon?"

Dayton headed for the sofa. "Yep, thanks. Well, gentlemen, Eric here tells me we have a problem."

Lex wondered if Dayton used the collective 'we' as a leftover from medical school and hospital training. But as Harold took the initiative and broke the ice, telling Dayton about the bomb threat and Angela Steinhart, Lex became convinced that Noel Dayton had used the collective term because he was the kind of man who involved himself.

Once Harold had finished, Lex reported on his visit to the Steinhart house.

"Is the kid on drugs? Is that it?" Noel asked.

"She'd taken a couple of tranquilizers to calm her down, she said. But I don't think she's an addict," Lex explained.

"Did she send the bomb threat?"

"She says she didn't," Lex replied. "And frankly I believe her."

"Where's Angela now?" Dayton's questions were fired off efficiently. Harold sat back, relaxing for the first time that day since Summers had come to report Angela's visit to Heather the day before. It was evident that Dayton had a very good grasp of the situation and he wasn't panicking.

"I have no idea where she is," Lex answered. "Heather and I were the last to see her at her home. She wanted to avoid her mother so she ran out on us. But she can't get away from this. It's with her all the time, I could tell. She's scared. She'll turn up – I know it in my gut."

"And if she doesn't?" Summers demanded.

"Jesus, I don't know. You were top at the police academy. You tell me, Eric."

"They didn't teach us about stuff like this. You were right behind me in class, Lex. If you hadn't copped out at the eleventh hour you'd be my boss by now."

"Police work wasn't for me. Just like personnel isn't for you."

"You could have made a damn good cop. I bleed whenever I think about it."

"Gentlemen," Dayton interrupted, "this isn't getting us anywhere. We have to decide on a course of action. Since you want me to get involved, it's imperative that I talk to the girl. Not that I'm giving credence to her statements about being precognitive. As I see it, she may know something about the bomb threat. If she didn't send it herself she might know who did. Then again, we might just be traveling up a blind alley. You say this is the third such threat? Did the papers report on the others?"

Eric squirmed. "Yeah, we had a leak somewhere."

"Then it's just possible that the whole business is a coincidence. Angela, having read about the previous bomb threats, could just be making a bid for attention, little realizing that she would be backed up by this latest missive."

"That's what her psychiatrist told her mother – that she was making a bid for attention," Eric said. "Maybe she is. I don't know. But that's why we want you to talk to her."

"Well, where is she?" Dayton's smooth tone and slightly raised eyebrows challenged him.

"What's your opinion, Harold?" Summers looked at the chief of security who was sinking lower and lower into the sofa, his empty glass clutched in his hand.

"I don't know about Angela. I haven't met her or heard what she has to say. But as far as the mall goes, I don't think we have any choice. It should be closed. Lassiter agrees. Any risk is too big a risk as far as I'm concerned."

"That's why Richards fired you, because you told him to close the mall." Eric laughed, "He fired you for the most sensible thing you've ever said."

"I'm no fool," Harold continued, "but what if this is some kind of trick? What if the kid is doing it for attention? If we do close the mall, do you have any idea what it would mean to sales? In Christmas week! Jesus, I need a refill. How about you guys?"

He hefted himself up from the sofa and headed towards the bar where he fixed himself a double Scotch.

"Right now we need to find the girl," he continued. "And I don't need to remind you, Lex, that the kid is still a minor so we can't haul her in here without parental permission. And you don't think we're going to get that, do you?"

"No. But Mrs Steinhart is one of the reasons that I don't believe all this stuff with Angela is a coincidence. The woman is scared, scared because she knows something is going on with her daughter, that she's somehow connected to all of this. And that's reason enough for me." He turned to Dayton. "You'd have to meet her," he said, "but it seems to me that Angela is an embarrassment to her. She was absolutely livid because she knew Angela had caused the flooding throughout the

85

house. The whole place is ruined – ceilings, floors, the works."

"She flooded the house?" Harold asked, unbelievingly. "Why?"

"How the hell should I know? Maybe she thought she was getting back at her mother. Mrs Steinhart started out by saying she'd had an 'argument' with Angela, then changed her choice of words to 'discussion.'"

Dayton listened with interest. He turned to Eric, "Have her hauled in. You've got enough to go on. How much does the department know?"

"Only about the bomb threat," Summers said sheepishly. "So much has happened and so fast."

"Good. Let's keep it that way for the time being," Dayton suggested. "Give the department one good lead and they forget everything else. If it really is a blind alley, too much time will have been wasted. We need to find out what the Steinhart girl can tell us. In the meantime, let the police attack the problem from the other end – the letter."

Eric reached behind the sofa and pulled out a shiny black phone. He dialed a number and motioned for the other men to be quiet. "John Wharton, extension 232." He waited, tapping strong square fingers. "John, old buddy. How's it going? . . . Not bad. Listen, you owe me one and I need to collect. I want you to pick up a kid named Angela Steinhart . . . No, there's no file on her, at least none that I know of. Go ahead and check it out. I need her yesterday, Wharton . . . You can reach me here, at my house. Or at Timberwoods Mall. Not downtown. If you can't get me, try for a guy in personnel at Timberwoods, Felex Lassiter . . . Yeah, he'll know where to reach me."

As soon as Eric replaced the receiver, Noel stood and

checked his watch. "Look, Eric, I'm not sorry I came over. I'm only a half-hour away and I'll come running when you need me. Okay?"

"Fine, Noel, but you're not running out yet. You haven't seen Amy. She's as big as a house!" Eric laughed affectionately.

"Sure is, and she's bringing out a pan of brownies," Harold beamed. "With lots of nuts."

The persistent wind beat against the north side of the Summers' house. Within its brick walls Eric and Amy nestled beneath the bed covers, warm and content to be in each other's arms.

"Amy?" Eric ventured.

"Hmmm?"

"You're uncomfortable, aren't you?"

"A little, but it'll be over soon enough and it'll all be worth it. Imagine, a child of our own, Eric. Our own baby."

Eric put his lips against the warm scented skin at the back of Amy's neck. He loved her like this, warm and loving and looking forward to the future. Sexual desire had little to do with the feelings right now; this was more basic. It was the deep abiding love a man felt for his wife.

"I love you, Amy," he said.

"Both of us?" Amy smiled, snuggling closer to Eric's warm body.

"Both of you."

The sound of the bedside phone was a rude intrusion into the warm dark room. Amy reached for the receiver but Eric stopped her. "Go to sleep, honey. I'll take it in the living room."

Eric padded out to the living room and picked up the jangling phone. "Yes?" he asked wearily.

"Detective Summers? Pete Hathaway here. My chief told me to report to you. You're looking for Angela Steinhart?"

"Right."

"Wharton told us to keep an eye out for her. I spotted her out on the highway and pulled her over but she got smart with me and – well, I rousted her a little bit. I hate to admit it but she kicked me in the groin and got away. She asked me something funny though – she wanted to know who was paying me, her mother or Timberwoods Mall. Say, ain't that where you're assigned for the next couple of weeks?"

"Yeah. Go on."

The officer's tone became belligerent in the face of Summers's coldness. "Look, Wharton warned me this ain't police business and I ain't got no reason to stick my nose in. But I was told to report to you. Consider it done."

"Okay, okay. Get back to your beat. Remember, I want that kid."

"Yeah, yeah, and I want to go home," Hathaway muttered as he hung up the phone.

Six

Timberwoods Mall was ablaze with Christmas cheer. Busy shoppers fought their way from store to store with good-natured directness, garlands of evergreen hung from the ceiling, artificially scented to add to the delicious atmosphere of the holidays. The glittering displays, the noisy fun of the puppet shows, the Christmas train that carried its young passengers in a wide circle around the promenade level, and the general feeling of good will and peace on earth were all enhanced by the piped-in Christmas carols.

Heather was suffering the afternoon blahs. She walked on lagging feet to her office and forced herself to make a pot of coffee. Dark lavender circles under her heavily fringed eyes gave her a waif-like appearance. When Lex came into her office, he was shocked at her appearance.

"Heather," he said, walking up to her, his dark blue eyes troubled. "This is going to turn out all right. Please don't let it get to you like this. If you want to go home, we'll understand. You don't look well."

He ushered her to a chair and handed her a cup of steaming coffee.

"I'm fine, Lex, really I am," Heather said as she gratefully accepted the coffee. "My spirit may be dead but my body is here. I didn't sleep well last night. Besides, I have a job to do like the rest of you. You can count on me to do my share. Don't worry, I'll be all right once I've finished this coffee."

Lex hunkered down beside her chair. "I wanted to call you last night but it was too late by the time we finished."

"I figured as much," she said.

"How about something firmer. Like tonight? We'll have a nice, quiet dinner. And we won't discuss work."

She was about to accept when Harold waddled into the office, fifteen minutes late. His eyes were bloodshot and he looked decidedly rumpled. Nevertheless he smiled and greeted them both heartily. He poured himself a cup of coffee and rolled his eyes in Lex's direction. The tall man grinned.

"Is Summers here yet?" Harold asked, cupping the heavy mug in both hands.

"His car is in the lot so I guess he's around somewhere."

"I think you should fill Heather in while I sit down and enjoy this coffee. May I say, Heather, this is the best coffee I've had in a long time."

Heather looked puzzled at Harold's tone. She glanced at Lex – what was the joke? The man seemed almost human this morning.

"This is the new Harold," Lex explained.

Heather's face was still blank. She really didn't care if this was a new Harold, an old Harold or a recycled Harold. All she wanted was to lose herself in a void somewhere and never wake up.

"I want a head count at four o'clock," Harold said over

the rim of his coffee cup. "The seventy-two hours will be up on Friday."

"You're forgetting that Friday is the parade and the start of Walden's half-price sale," said Lex. "There'll be a massacre in this mall if the doors don't open on time. Do you have any idea how much those cash registers can ring up in two hours? Richards will never buy opening late. Neither will Walden's."

"It's the only way," Harold said, getting up and pouring himself another cup of coffee. "The bomb squad and the dogs will have all night and Friday morning to go over this mall. If it checks out, the center will be clean when it opens. We just have to keep it that way, and that's the reason for the check at the doors."

"I agree. And don't forget they're predicting a heavy snowfall for the weekend."

"Oh Jesus," Harold groaned. "When did you hear that?"

"This morning on the way to work."

"Just what we need right now," Harold grumbled. "This center will be like a circus on Friday. People will be trying to beat the storm and shop early. Sales or not, they'll be here in droves. You'll have to alert the maintenance department for the second shift tomorrow. Jesus, I can see it now . . ."

The members of the bomb squad, along with officers from the Woodridge Police Department, were waiting patiently in Eric Summers's office for Dolph Richards to arrive. He stormed into the office ten minutes late, his face a mask of fury.

"What right did you have to call the police, Summers? You didn't even give me the courtesy of clearing it with me. We do have rules around here!" he shouted angrily.

"You seem to forget, Richards, I am the police. And the department's been in on this from the beginning because of the bomb threat. The safety of this center is in my hands, not yours," Eric said coldly. "My first concern is for the people who work and shop in this center."

"Your first concern is this center and the shop owners. And then me. I'm your superior – you have to check with me before you do anything!" Richards stamped his foot in childish fury. "That bomb threat is nothing more than a nuisance and you know it."

"I don't know any such thing and neither do you. Just what the hell is your problem, Richards?" Summers demanded.

"I thought . . . that is . . . the kid . . . Ah, forget it. You couldn't be that stupid." Richards turned his back on the lot of them. This damn center was a constant source of irritation. Every time he turned around there was a bomb threat or something else equally threatening but, to date, they had never come across anything that remotely resembled a bomb. As far as he was concerned, Eric Summers had dug in too damn deep. It always happened that way – give a minority a little power and it went straight to his head. He knew – and so did his security team – that no bomb would be found. All those men he'd had to pull off other assignments! And what the hell was he going to do come Friday morning when gung-ho Summers would be screaming for more cops with the snow that was predicted? Son of a bitch, why did it always have to happen to him? "Who the hell needs it?" he muttered under his breath.

He turned to the bomb squad. "Plain clothes and a full crew tomorrow," he said firmly. Their captain nodded and wearily took his leave.

As soon as he had closed the door behind them Richards said *sotto voce*, "One word about that kid and I'll personally kill you, Summers. This center isn't going to blow and you know it!"

"Put it in writing, Richards," Eric snarled as he pushed back his chair. "Why don't you go exercise your libido. I have a center to take care of."

"You smart-assed bastard. You'll sing another song when this center is still standing for the new year."

Eric moved around his desk. "On second thought, perhaps you need a frontal lobotomy," he said menacingly.

Richards stepped back from the black man. He had no desire to have $6,200 worth of porcelain caps destroyed. "The mall stays open!" he spat as he quickly closed the door behind him.

"A frontal lobotomy is too good for the bastard," Eric said, kicking the wastebasket across the room.

The two-way radio on his desk beeped. He pressed the button, "Summers." He listened quietly, a frown on his face. "Are you sure?"

"Of course I'm sure," the disembodied voice shouted. "They're gathered in groups on the mall. A couple of the smaller shop owners are on their way to see Baumgarten right now. The word is spreading and people are leaving in droves. I don't know what the hell it is, but . . . Christ, here comes Walden himself! Over and out."

Eric stuffed the radio into his pocket and took off on the run for Baumgarten's office. "Well, the shit's hit the fan now," he muttered as he narrowly avoided one of the secretaries from the chief's office.

*   *   *

Charlie Roman hoisted the bright red sack over his shoulder and clutched a bunch of candy canes in his hand. Something was wrong. His round eyes darkened as he watched the groups of people muttering among themselves. Some of the store owners had gathered outside their shops and were talking and gesticulating angrily.

Small gatherings of store owners were chattering angrily outside their storefronts.

Charlie walked up to a small group of young women and held out the candy canes. "Ho! Ho! Ho!" he chanted. The women ignored him, but it gave him the chance to listen to their conversation.

"I don't see any police," one of them complained. "They always have police if there's a bomb threat. I'm not leaving, I have too much shopping to do! Do what you want, I'm staying!"

Charlie walked away, stunned. It appeared the whole complex was on red alert. The woman was wrong – right now he could see several plainclothes men aside from the usual security guards. He was perspiring profusely by the time he rounded the corner to the stairway leading to the lower level. Bomb scare! He stumbled over to a bench and dropped heavily onto the hard wooden planks.

A little girl approached him and tugged at his sleeve. "Are you sick, Santa? Please don't be sick, you have to bring me my new dolly. Are you sick, Santa?"

Charlie brushed her off roughly, his red-rimmed eyes glaring. The child backed away, frightened by the malice in his eyes.

A young woman grabbed the little girl's arm and yanked

her away. "Leave Santa alone, Marcey, he's tired from all
this Christmas rush. C'mon, we have to find Grandma."

Charlie stared straight ahead, dimly aware of the woman
taking the little girl away. This was the best part – the
watching. Security and the police would crawl all over
the complex like ants at a picnic. They would look and
look and snoop and snoop and never find anything.

He thought of the many hours he had spent cutting
words and letters out of newspapers and magazines to
compose his latest letter. Common magazines, the ones
everybody got. Nothing fancy like *National Geographic*
or *Smithsonian*. He'd even used a few letters right out of
the sales circular from Walden's. They'd never trace it.
Besides, the dumb shits were looking for a regular bomb
– sticks of dynamite and an alarm clock. He laughed. This
was always the best part – the challenge. Soon everybody
would know that Charlie Roman was smarter than an entire
police force of wise guys.

His mind flipped back a couple of weeks ago to when
he had first put together his plan. The weather had been
cold, yet dry. Perfect for mending the roof. The maintenance crew had come down to the employees' cafeteria
for lunch and Charlie had overheard them discussing the
procedure for patching the roof where the rain was seeping
in. When the talk got around to using propane for heating
the tar vat, Charlie's ears had pricked up – propane? Up
on the roof? The information had lodged itself in his mind
and he had hummed along with the music being piped into
the cafeteria. There was the chance, finally, that he could
belong . . . if not in life, then in death.

Up to then Charlie had been contemplating suicide, the
last lonely act a man could perform. He was sick of being

lonely and Christmas was a particularly bad time – the worst of all. It seemed everyone had someone to love but him. He had no family, no friends . . . no one at all. The only people he talked to were the guys he worked with, and he hated their rotten sense of humor. They were always ribbing him, waiting for him to make a mistake, to lose his balance and fall down – anything was reason enough to ridicule him. But if he could rig something with that propane, the whole damn place and everyone in it could keep him company when the time came.

Tossing his half-eaten lunch into the garbage, Charlie had left the cafeteria and taken the three long flights of stairs to the roof. Puffing and panting, he'd opened the door and stepped out onto the flat black expanse, the cold air hitting him like a physical blow. A tour of the area led him to where the maintenance crew had left the vat of tar to cool. Thank God, he had kept the Santa suit on, he thought as he waved his arms around to keep warm.

The fifty-gallon, silver liquid-propane tank was attached to a burner-like system beneath the tar vat, its heat slowly melting the chunks of tar into a glossy black viscous liquid. Three spare tanks stood at the far end of the roof, well away from the open flame. Charlie's brain had ticked over with possibilities.

That evening, back at home, Charlie had dug through the air-conditioning plans stashed away in his basement. He'd found the blueprint for Timberwoods easily enough, and two hours later had lifted his head from the papers, a euphoric smile on his doughy face. It would work. He was sure of it.

The following day, in the late afternoon when the roofing crew had left for the day, Charlie had returned to the roof, carrying with him a variety of tools. First, he had pried open the side of the aluminum housing then, using a hammer he drove a length of pipe that he had sharpened to a wedge at one end through the blacktop. It bored easily through the layers of roofing into the space just above the fresh-air intake duct. Carefully Charlie had tapped the end of pipe until he could feel the top of the duct giving way. In his mind's eye he could see the one-inch cylindrical pipe protruding into the vent several inches above the duct's bottom.

Charlie had turned next to the spare tanks. Grunting with effort he had rolled one of the silver cylinders across the width of the roof to the main fresh-air intake vent. Struggling with its weight he had managed to stand it upside-down next to the aluminum housing which covered the blower motor. The cold air bit at his fingertips as he secured the cylinder against the housing with two steel straps and metal screws.

As he worked, he congratulated himself on his foresight. Had he left the tank upright, the propane gas would have emptied very slowly into the air duct, taking hours, possibly a whole day to filter through. But this way, upside-down, the liquid propane would empty much more quickly and dissipate into gas in a relatively short time. Six or seven hours at the most. Volatile deadly barely detectable propane literally being sucked into the main fresh-air duct before dispersing to every little shop, restroom and storage closet in Timberwoods Mall. And when the necessary proportion of gas to oxygen was reached . . .

Excited by the vision, Charlie had worked quickly to join the pipe he had sunk into the duct to another length of tubing, which he then connected to the propane tank by means of a ball valve. In spite of the frigid temperature he was sweating profusely. He could feel a damp trickle running down the length of his broad back. Within half an hour he had completed the rest of the mechanics: a heavy spring attached to the handle of the ball valve would, with heavy downward pressure, open it, while a length of piano wire was in place to offset the pressure.

Charlie grinned as he set about his final task. Removing a can of red spray paint from his kit he painted the silver propane cylinder so that it resembled a harmless fire extinguisher. The wind caught some of the miniscule globules of paint and splashed them onto his red velvet Santa suit. Stepping back to survey his handiwork, Charlie pulled a strip of printed tape from his pocket, stolen from the maintenance storeroom. Carefully he positioned it on the tank, making sure not to smudge the fresh paint. Stepping aside, he viewed its effect. He complimented himself and collected his gear, then walked back to the door leading inside Timberwoods Mall. There was a new lift in his step. Looking back he saw the bright red cylinder with its new red and white sticker proclaiming: EMERGENCY EXTINGUISHER.

Someone jostled him and, startled, Charlie quickly returned to the present. Mike Wallace from security was standing in front of him. "Roman, is that you under all that beard?"

"Yeah, it's me," Charlie answered flatly, pulling himself away from Mike's rough hand. Why did people have to react to him in a big way just because he was big? Big voices, big hands, big slaps on the back.

"Christ, you look scared to death," Mike exclaimed, not noticing that Charlie was shrinking from his touch. "Look, take it easy, fella. I guess you heard about the bomb threat, huh? It was a letter, same as before, but we're trying to take precautions."

Mike's walkie-talkie beeped shrilly and he stepped away from Charlie to answer it.

Charlie stood on shaking legs, expecting the floor to come up and hit him in the face. He turned and walked in the direction of his throne in the Toyland display. Over his shoulder he heard Mike call to him, "Hey, you okay?" but he kept going, too shocked, too angry to answer. What if there was a bomb and it wasn't his? Maybe somebody else had come up with the same idea! All his life he had been too 'something' – too dumb, too big , and now too late! One way or another, somebody was always there, ready to steal his thunder.

Eric beat the angry shop owners to Dolph Richards's office by mere moments.

"Here it comes!" He breathed raggedly as he regained his stance. "They're coming in droves. Word must have leaked out somehow. Mike says the customers are leaving as fast as they arrive. Get ready!" he gasped as the door was thrust open.

Heather followed Harold into Richards's office. Lex also inched his way past the angry shop owners. Richards remained seated, his movie star smile fixed on his face. "For heaven's sake, what is this?"

"You aren't sugar-coating this one, Richards. We heard," shouted an angry shop owner. "What's going on?"

"That is what I'm asking you. Why this parade? Why are you all so angry?"

"Angry?" shouted the owner of the crystal shop. "The

mall is almost empty. As fast as they come in, they leave. Word is out there's a bomb in the center!"

"Poppycock," Harold smiled. "If there was a bomb, don't you think you would have been told? Don't you think we would have evacuated the mall? Use your heads."

"If there's no bomb, get on the loudspeaker and say so. Now!" bellowed the owner of the leather goods shop.

"Detective Summers, why don't you explain the circumstances?" Harold said jovially, oblivious to Richards's scowl.

Eric cleared his throat and spoke quietly. "We did get a bomb threat yesterday. We get them regularly, as you know. This particular threat said the bomb would go off in seventy-two hours. The seventy-two hours will be up Friday morning. We doubled the security as soon as we received the threat. We haven't found anything so far. I can't speak for tomorrow or Friday. When this center closes tonight, the dogs and the bomb squad will arrive. By Friday morning everything should be A-okay. There isn't anything else I can tell you. You say the customers are leaving the mall. Did you stop to think that your own actions could have something to do with it? My men told me you were clustered in the mall discussing this among yourselves. What do you expect?"

"You only have yourselves to blame," Richards chastised, ending Summers's speech. "Go back to your stores and show a little confidence in this security. An announcement will be made over the loudspeaker in a few moments. And for God's sake, smile when you leave here."

The group of owners dispersed, muttering among themselves. Several mouthed sincere apologies while others looked doubtful. Richards followed them out, still uttering soothing phrases.

"I need a drink. Do you have anything, Harold?" Eric sounded exhausted.

"No, but I'm going to send my secretary out right now to get a bottle of Scotch. A man just can't get through the day without a little help." He picked up Richards's phone. "Margaret, go down to the Liquor Locker and get me the biggest bottle of Scotch they have. Take the money out of petty cash. This is a necessary expenditure."

He turned to Summers. "What kind of Scotch?"

Summers shrugged helplessly.

"What the hell, Chivas Regal," Harold blurted, "and make it snappy."

Replacing the receiver, he turned back to Summers. "That wasn't good," he said nervously. "That was only a few of the owners from the smaller shops. What happens later when they all get together? How did this leak out in the first place?"

"Don't ask me. You know this sort of thing always gets out no matter how you try to hide it. A cop is a cop. He looks and acts like one whether he's in uniform or not. And it only takes one man to tell his family to stay out of Timberwoods Mall and why. Harold, I still say we should close the mall and lay the whole thing before the merchants. If this center blows, so do we. I'm talking about Angela's vision."

Dolph Richards burst back into his office, his face a mottled purple. "You dumb stupid bastard! You almost blew the whistle!"

Eric swung around and shot Richards a piercing look. "I'm sick and tired of you, Richards. I'm doing what I have to do the best way I know how, and so is Baumgarten. If you cross my path once more today I'll do the frontal lobotomy myself."

"When I've finished with you, Summers . . . You too, Baumgarten . . . you'll both . . ." he sputtered.

"I'll stand on my record any day of the week. If push comes to shove, can you say the same?" Eric said harshly. Richards shook his fist in the air and muttered a few choice obscenities that followed Baumgarten and Summers back to Harold's office.

"He gives me an itch," Harold smirked. "Where is that girl?!"

"Here I am, Mr Baumgarten." Margaret entered the office with a large bag in her arms. "There were several people ahead of me and I had to wait. I also purchased some glasses since I knew you didn't have any. And," she said proudly, "I picked up some ice."

"You're a conscientious girl, Margaret. Why don't you take an early lunch. Don't hurry back. Take a little extra time in case you want to shop."

"Oh, thank you, Mr Baumgarten. I appreciate it, really I do."

Harold beamed as Eric handed him a double Scotch. "To fear," Eric said, holding his glass aloft.

"I'll drink to that," Harold chuckled and promptly drained his glass. He capped the bottle and laid it to rest in the bottom drawer of his desk. When the drawer closed, he felt more confident than he had in a long time.

"Progress reports on the hour, Summers," he said briskly.

"Yes, sir." Eric saluted as he closed the door behind him.

*   *   *

102

Split Second

Charlie Roman almost fell off his throne when he heard the announcement.

"Ladies and gentlemen, may I please have your attention. There is no bomb in this shopping center! I repeat, there is no bomb in this shopping center. You can all shop with a clear mind. Enjoy the displays and have a happy holiday."

Seven

Angela steered the Porsche down the dark winding road, peering intently through the windshield. Was it safe to put the lights on yet? The dull roar of the engine was enough to wake the dead. What time was it? The digital clock on the dash read two-twelve. Almost the middle of the night. It didn't look as though there were any cops on her trail. She was going to be a lot more careful in the future. The Porsche was a dead giveaway; there wasn't another like it in the area.

Her nerves were still rattled from a few minutes earlier when the police car had blared its siren and pulled her over. She had known immediately that this was no ordinary speed check. The young officer hadn't asked for her license or registration, and he had called her by name. It was when he had physically tried to remove her from the car that she had panicked and begun to struggle against his grip. The proverbial well-aimed knee at the vulnerable crotch had worked its magic.

Angela had scrambled back into her Porsche and roared away. She pressed her foot down and the car took wing, up one street and down another. A good thing she knew where West End Avenue was. Cross over the highway, forget the light. There weren't any cars out anyway. Another mile or so and she would be at Charlie Roman's house. Did he live in the house by himself? He was a weird kind of guy but nice. He'd be more at ease once they got to know each other a little better. It was really strange the way she felt drawn to him, almost close. They were two lonely people who recognized one another, she guessed. Whatever, she was almost there.

The Porsche slowed as Angela looked over her shoulder, not trusting the rear-view mirror. The street was quiet, deserted at this late hour. A blue bulb burned high on a telephone pole at the end of the street, casting a kind of graveyard light over everything.

Angela cut the engine and coasted to the curb. Thank God he had a garage. It looked like a nice house. She slid from behind the wheel and ran up to the door. She jabbed her finger against the bell and waited, all the while casting quick looks over her shoulder. The street remained quiet, its occupants asleep.

A light went on inside the house and a few moments later Angela heard the quiet click of a dead bolt being eased. The door was opened a crack, the chain clearly visible. A single eye peered at her and then the chain was removed.

"Hi," Angela said. "I was in the neighborhood and I suddenly find I need a place to stay. Can I put my car in your garage?"

"Okay, go ahead. Wait a minute and I'll open the door for you. Be careful because the overhead light is burned out. Stay in the car till I come and get you."

Angela raced back to the car and turned on the ignition.

Charlie closed and locked the front door then put the chain back in place. He padded to the garage and opened the door, his pajama bottoms slipping down his hips as he reached up. He stood back, holding up his pajamas, as Angela guided the luxurious sports car into the space next to his old Chevy. Quickly he lowered the door and locked it. He helped Angela from the cramped quarters inside the sports car and guided her into the kitchen. He excused himself for a moment and left her sitting at the butcher-block table while he went up stairs for his robe and slippers.

When he returned, Angela had a pan of milk warming on the stove and was about to pour cocoa into it. "I'm making us some hot chocolate."

Charlie sucked in air. Now she was making 'us' hot chocolate. "Great," he grimaced as he sat down at the table to wait for Angela to place the heavy mug in front of him. He hated hot chocolate almost as much as he hated lukewarm coffee with no cream or sugar. Why was he doing this? Why didn't he just tell her to shut up and leave? Why had he let her put her car in the garage? Why was he letting her get to him like she was? What was there about her that made him feel so . . . ?

"Here you go." She handed him a mug of steaming chocolate. "I'm really sorry I woke you up but I didn't know where else to go."

"It's okay," Charlie answered without thinking.

"This will work wonders for you. Make you sleep like a baby. I learned it in my homemaking class at school." She turned around and gave the kitchen a final once over. "I've been looking around and you keep this place pretty neat for a guy," she commented.

Now she was complimenting him. She wanted him to sleep like a baby. She knew about homemaking. Shit!

Charlie brought the mug to his lips and sipped at the hot chocolate.

"Make all gone," Angela prattled as she drained her own cup. "Okay, point me in the right direction. Where do I sleep? We'll work out the money details tomorrow. Right now, I'm so bushed I could sleep standing up."

"Upstairs, second door on the left. The bathroom is across the hall," Charlie said testily.

"Okay, see you in the morning." Angela bent over and dropped a light kiss on Charlie's forehead. "That's because you're so nice," she said softly before she fled the kitchen.

Charlie watched her go. He felt a strange glow encompass him. He rinsed the mugs and put them on the draining board, then sat back down on the kitchen chair. He fingered the spot on his forehead where Angela had dropped the light kiss. The strange glow stayed with him for a long time. When he looked at the kitchen clock it read four-thirty. He finally climbed the stairs to go to bed.

Angela was right; he slept like a contented baby.

Angela dozed fitfully as dawn broke over the quiet street outside her window. She rolled over and assumed the fetal position. She heard a noise and burrowed deeper into the covers. She half-felt and half-heard Charlie creep into the room. A deep sigh escaped her. She wasn't the least bit alarmed; Charlie would never hurt her. She didn't know how she knew that, she just knew. She was safe with him. As long as she stayed in this bed in this house, she would be safe. One sleepy eye opened when she felt a feathery light touch on her cheek. In the twilight of her sleep, she smiled.

Charlie returned her smile. He didn't know why he'd felt the need to check on her. But he was glad he had. Real glad. Damn, he felt good, and it had nothing to do with sex. It was going to be a hell of a good day; he could feel it in his bones.

Angela rolled over onto her stomach, another sleepy sigh escaping her as Charlie tiptoed from the room. He turned and stared at the sleeping girl. Tonight he would have something more than an empty house to come home to. He would have a friend. He promised himself that he would try to be more charismatic or at least more talkative. Now that he had decided he liked her, that she could be trusted, he could let his defenses down a little. Relaxed in sleep, she was almost cute.

It was five minutes before noon when Angela became fully awake and aware of her surroundings. She lay for a moment, staring at the ceiling. She felt wonderful, better than she had in months. Years, when it came right down to it. Her eyes scanned the small bedroom. The furniture was hard-rock maple and held a high gloss, as though it had just been polished with lemon oil. The tiny floral print of the wallpaper, though faded, was pleasing to the eye. The maple rocker with the green velvet cushions looked so inviting that Angela hopped from bed and raced over to it. Mothers rocked their babies in chairs like this when they nursed them or gave them a bottle. It was an old chair but it felt good. She rocked a few moments, savoring the feeling as she wondered if Charlie's mother had rocked him and fed him in this very chair.

She remembered that Charlie had come into her room earlier. She remembered because it was the first time she'd seen him smile. He wasn't a handsome man by any stretch of the imagination but he had a nice smile, a warm smile. And she would be willing to bet that not too many people had ever seen it. He struck her as being a generally unhappy man and a loner, much like herself. She wondered what had happened to make him that way. Maybe one of these days he would tell her.

Angela showered in the surprisingly clean bathroom and then carefully made her bed. She smoothed the rough chenille till there was no sign of a wrinkle. Then she trotted into Charlie's room and made his bed. She looked around at the room and was not surprised to see how spartan it was. He hadn't struck her as a collector of anything. His dresser was bare except for a brush and comb. She lined up his scuffed slippers and hung his robe on the back of the door. She took a quick peek into the closet and again was not surprised at the sparseness of the contents. One suit and one sports jacket. Two pairs of trousers on separate hangers. One heavy sweater with leather patches on the elbows – these were all that were hanging on the long rod. A pair of dress shoes, a pair of work boots and a tattered pair of sneakers were the only things on the floor. The overhead shelf was bare. No sign of a carton or box and no suitcases. All of which told her he didn't do much socializing or go on vacations. How lonely this man must be. Even lonelier than her.

Making her way down the stairs, Angela sniffed at the aroma of coffee. Charlie had left her coffee; the machine was on warm. It would be bitter by now but it was a nice thought. A note rested next to the machine. Angela stared at it, trying to make out the squiggly lines. "I'll call you on my break. There's plenty of food in the refrigerator." It was signed with a large scrawled 'C.'

Angela peeled a large orange and sat at the table with the juice dribbling down her chin. She really wasn't hungry. A cup of microwaved coffee finished off her meager meal. When she was through she rinsed the glass coffee pot. Perhaps later she would make a fresh pot. She wondered what time Charlie's break was. What would she say to him when he called? She hoped he would have something to offer to the conversation. It was hard going trying to make conversation with Charlie Roman. Maybe he didn't have anything to say because he never did anything but work. What a shame. She smiled, remembering the light touch on her cheek when he thought she was asleep. He was probably just bashful around girls he didn't know.

The kitchen floor was dirty. That was something she could do. She wasn't worthless like her mother thought. She had paid more attention than anyone knew in the homemaking class. If she had to, she could run a house as efficiently as Martha Stewart. Well, maybe not that efficiently, but then Martha had an army of helpers. She even knew how to shop for food, what to look for and what to stay away from. She would clean out the refrigerator, scrub the floor and make a cake. And of course she would cook dinner for Charlie. Just the two of them. Real cozy. If she had it all ready he could come home for his supper break and still get back to the mall on time.

Angela had just finished putting a coat of wax on the kitchen floor when the phone in the hallway rang. Cautiously she answered it, "Hello."

"This is Charlie."

"I know. I just scrubbed your kitchen floor," Angela blurted.

"Thank you." Charlie was nonplussed at Angela's statement.

"I waxed it too."

"I always wax it after I scrub it," Charlie said, not knowing what else to say.

"Thanks for the coffee, it was real good. What time is your supper hour? I thought I would cook dinner and have it ready for you. That way you could come home, eat and still get back on time for your evening shift."

"That sounds good. Yes, that's fine. Why don't you do that? I can be home by six-fifteen," Charlie said happily. "What else did you do?

"Not much," Angela said, warming up to the voice on the other end of the phone. "I got up kind of late and then I rocked for a while in the rocking chair upstairs. I took a shower and made the beds and then I ate an orange and scrubbed the floor."

"Oranges are good for you, especially if you have low blood sugar," Charlie volunteered.

"I didn't know that. Is there anything in particular you would like for dinner?"

"I'm not fussy, but I would like some hot coffee to go with whatever you make."

"Okay. I guess I'll see you later then. Goodbye, Charlie."

"Goodbye, Angela," Charlie said, a wide smile splitting his face. He'd been right. It was a good day and it was going to get better.

Angela danced her way around the kitchen as she set a package of chicken breasts out to thaw. She wiped down the stove and refrigerator with a solution of baking soda and vinegar and was pleased with the high shine her efforts produced. She wondered if Charlie would notice. She scrubbed two oversized yams and deftly cut up vegetables for a salad. She found some fresh string beans that were limp but still useable, cleaned them and set them to soak in a bowl of ice water. They'd crisp up in an hour or so.

Now for the cake. She looked around, pushing jars and boxes to the back of the cabinet as she searched for the ingredients. Charlie looked like the chocolate type.

Everything in front of her, Angela dusted her hands together dramatically in preparation for her first homemade cake. The cake batter prepared and in the oven, she set the timer on the stove and then settled herself to watch the soap operas. An hour later she was disgusted with the idiot box. And she thought she had problems!

The soap operas and their daily drama gave way to the four-thirty movie. Before long Angela became engrossed in the story. She raced to the kitchen during the commercial break to set the table and mix the salad dressing. Since there wasn't enough sugar in the house to make frosting for the cake, Angela whipped up some instant pudding and then poured it over the cake. Later she would add the whipped topping she had seen in the refrigerator. Charlie must like the creamy white stuff because there were six containers resting on the back shelf. She drained the string beans and tested one by snapping it to see if they had crisped the way her homemaking teacher said they would. They had. She added fresh water and set the pot on the stove. She peeked at the roasting chicken and grinned. It was browning nicely and the dressing inside would surely add to its flavor.

Boy, the kitchen smelled good. Charlie would be pleased. Men liked to come home to a good-smelling house and know that all they had to do was sit down and eat. It must be a good feeling, she mused. For some reason there were never any delicious aromas in her own house. Was it because the cook always made low-calorie things like salads and bought everything else frozen and just thawed it out? Even the cookies she baked were from a box and the cakes were always ready-made or frozen.

Coffee – she had to make coffee. God, how she hated those automatic coffee-makers. Old fashioned perked coffee was the only kind to make. Irma, her mother's housekeeper, had taught her that. Angela stared at the coffee-maker and decided it must be fairly new since there were no coffee stains on the white plastic. Charlie probably used it because it was quick and he didn't have much time in the morning. She pulled out a stool, climbed up and started to search the cabinets. Charlie looked like the type to save things if they weren't worn out. She finally found the aluminum percolator in the back of the third cabinet she searched. Industriously, she scoured the small pot till it gleamed. It was the kind you perk on the stove and now not only would there be dinner aromas but also the fragrant smell of real brewed coffee to greet Charlie. Boy, was he going to be surprised. She measured out the coffee, added cold water and set the pot behind the string beans. Both would be turned on at the same time.

Satisfied that everything was under control, Angela trotted back to the living room to the movie. She had missed too much of it and her interest waned. Oh, well. Another half-hour and Charlie would be home. They would sit down and eat and talk. It had been a long time since she had talked to anyone, really talked. Offering explanations and arguing didn't count. When Charlie went back to work, she would clean up the kitchen and give herself a big A. She couldn't wait to hear Charlie's compliments and praise. She hadn't had a compliment or heard praise since . . . since . . . Had she ever heard any? Only from her childhood nanny and her teachers. But not from the people who really mattered. Her mother. Her father.

God knows she'd tried to please them. As a small child she'd been sickeningly obedient and all through elementary school and junior high she'd studied her heart out to get good grades, but her mother hadn't even batted an eyelash. And her father – he'd noticed, but only for about five minutes. And then he'd pulled out his money clip, peeled off a few dollars and given her a pat on the back.

She would have preferred a hug.

Tears stung Angela's eyes; she impatiently wiped them away with her shirt sleeve. Only babies cried. But what did she know? Since she had never been a kid she had never been a baby either. If you were to believe her mother, she had been hatched from an egg. A rotten egg. The tears burned again. This time she let them gather on her lashes and then trickle down her cheeks.

Emotional cripple. She had heard her mother say that to her father. If she was, then it was because they had made her one. God knows she hadn't become this way on her own.

Charlie walked into the house promptly at sixteen minutes after six. Angela's face lit up like a candle as she watched him sniff the air. Her thin gaunt face exploded into a

114

delightful grin that matched his when he said, "It smells just like Sunday dinner the way my mother used to make it. Roast chicken, chocolate cake and all the works."

"Right, right. And I found your old aluminum coffee pot and perked some real coffee for you. I know you like coffee," Angela said, suddenly shy.

"I love perked coffee," Charlie said exuberantly. "Is it ready?" he asked hopefully.

"All you have to do is sit down and eat. Come on." Angela took him by the arm. He didn't pull away from her as she thought he might.

Quickly and deftly, she served him – a regular June Cleaver out of the old TV show. Charlie ate ravenously, making comments like, "This is delicious. Where did you learn to cook? This is every bit as good as my mother used to make. More, one more helping." And then, finally, "How did you know my mother used to pour pudding over the cake?"

"I didn't know." Angela could feel herself smiling from ear to ear. "There wasn't enough sugar to make frosting so I improvised. I'm so glad you like it and that I did it right. More coffee?"

"Sure, and another slice of cake. Aren't you having any?"

"Charlie, I already had three pieces," she giggled, rolling her eyes.

"Oh, I've been so busy eating, I didn't notice." Charlie leaned back and patted his stomach. "God, I ate too much. If I ate like this all the time I'd be as fat as a pig. People shouldn't eat so much. I know. I used to be really fat and people made fun of me, but I couldn't seem to stop eating," he said honestly.

"How would you like to be as skinny as I am and hear people say you look like a scarecrow or a skeleton? I eat all the time and really pile on the food, but I just can't gain weight. It might not be so noticeable if I didn't have such irregular features."

Charlie stared at Angela. "I think you have interesting features, Angela. You're no beauty queen, but most girls aren't. You're . . ." He searched for just the right word that wouldn't hurt her feelings. For some reason he really cared about this peculiar looking girl with the too big teeth and strange nose. "You're just ordinary," he said sincerely, knowing he meant every word he was thinking and saying.

Angela's face brightened. "Do you mean it? You really don't think I'm ugly? How about homely?"

"Ordinary," Charlie said firmly as he held out his coffee cup. "Which is a lot better than being awkward like me."

"You're just big," Angela said, leaning her elbows on the table. "Big people are always awkward. It comes with the territory. What really matters is that you have a likeable face. A pleasant face actually," she said, leaning closer. "And you have a great smile. It lights up your whole face."

Charlie felt a surge of something, and it had nothing to do with his libido. Protectiveness. He wanted to wrap himself around her and hold her tight. The feeling startled him. "Are you putting me on?"

Angela stared at Charlie for a full minute before she replied. "You'd better know something about me, Charlie Roman. If there's one thing I'm not, it's a liar. What you see is what you get."

Another strange surge coursed through Charlie. He

116

would figure out what it was later. Now he had to leave or he would be late and Dolph Richards would have his head. He nodded. "Okay, you don't lie. I gotta go. I'll see you later. That was the best dinner I've had in years. Thank you," he said shyly.

Angela blushed. "Hurry up or you'll be late. When you get home I'll make some popcorn and we'll sit on the couch and watch television together."

Charlie beamed and nodded as he closed the door behind him. God, was he ever lucky to have run into her. And to think he'd almost blown it. He shook his head and laughed.

Charlie returned from work anticipating a relaxed hour or two with Angela. She was as good as her word. A large bowl of hot buttery popcorn rested on the table. Frosty glasses of beer were set on napkins on the end tables. For over an hour she sat next to him on the sofa in companionable silence, munching, sipping and watching TV. Reluctantly Charlie finally had to call it a night. He needed his sleep. Angela yawned and agreed.

"You can have the bathroom first," Charlie said gallantly.

"Okay, I'll see you in the morning then. Good night, Charlie," Angela said quietly. "Oh, I forgot about the dishes. I'll do them before I use the bathroom. You go ahead."

"Oh no. You cooked dinner and made the popcorn. I'll clean up. You go to bed. You look tired. Go on, now," Charlie said sternly as though he was talking to a child. "Angela," he added thoughtfully, "if you don't mind my asking, how old are you?"

She turned to face him. "Is it important? Age is just a number, after all. It's what in here and here that counts." She tapped her heart and head.

Charlie nodded. If she didn't want to tell him he wasn't going to pry. She hadn't quizzed him and she hadn't made any unkind remarks. He would show her the same courtesy. He knew he was older by a good many years and thought maybe that was what made him feel so protective of her. He bent over to pick up the bowl and the glasses.

"Angela," he said quietly, "you aren't just ordinary. You're special ordinary."

Angela was stunned. She stopped in mid stride. She knew – she didn't know just how she knew, but she did – that Charlie Roman had never said that to another human being. She was touched. Really touched.

"Thank you, Charlie," she said with all sincerity. "I know you mean it and I think you're pretty special too. Good night." She turned to go up the stairs.

Charlie followed her over to the foot of the stairs and watched her as she climbed the steps. She stopped on the fourth step and looked back at him over her shoulder. "You know, Charlie. That was probably the nicest thing anyone has ever said to me." She sighed heavily.

Charlie felt something burning inside him. "Listen," he said impulsively, "I'm off on Sunday. How would you like to do something? Go somewhere?" He waited, hardly daring to breathe, for her answer. The invitation was the only way he could think of to find out if she was going to stay with him beyond tonight. He had learned the hard way from past experiences that when something was especially good, things started to go wrong. He willed her to say yes with every fiber in his body.

Angela smiled. "I'd like that, Charlie. Hey," she said excitedly, "we never discussed me paying you rent. I meant to bring it up at dinner time, but we were so busy talking and eating that I forgot."

Charlie's face went blank and then he flushed. "I don't want any money from you. I thought we were friends. You said we were friends." His voice just stopped short of being accusing.

"Okay, okay, don't get upset. I just like to pay my way, that's all. I'm not a freeloader." Angela could sense him drifting away from her suddenly. He had done the same thing at dinner and then again when they were watching TV. It was almost as if he went to some other world for a few moments – a world he didn't particularly like. She thought he must have something on his mind, something he had to work out. "Charlie," she said hesitantly, "whatever it is that's bothering you, do you want to talk about it?"

"It?" Charlie pretended not to know what she was talking about.

"Yeah, it. From time to time you sort of fade off into the distance, if you know what I mean. Like you have something heavy on your mind. Do you want to talk about it? If you do, I'm a good listener and I don't flap my mouth. What I'm saying is, if it's a secret you don't have to worry about me blabbing it." She could see that he was getting agitated. "It was only a suggestion," she said hastily.

"No, it's okay." And it was okay. His mind was made up now. He knew what he had to do. Relief washed over him and he felt like he was drowning in his own perspiration. He had decided not to blow up the mall and Angela had helped him make the decision, even though she didn't

119

realize it. "I'm sorry if I was rude to you," he apologized. "I didn't mean to be."

"You weren't rude," Angela said, towering over him from her position on the fourth step. "Everybody has his private moments. I just wanted you to know you could bend my ear if it would help. And, hey," she cried excitedly, "I'm going to look forward to Sunday."

Charlie grinned from ear to ear. His world was right side up again. "Good night, Angela," he said, trotting out to the kitchen. He was happy and content. He did not feel sexually aroused, he felt friendly. It was a new experience. All the anger and hostility of yesterday evaporated and was replaced with a kind of euphoric bliss. He felt slightly puzzled about his lack of sexual excitement but he had no desire to tamper with this strange new relationship. He hummed a few bars of 'Jingle Bells' as he washed and rinsed the dishes and set them in the dish strainer to dry. He filled the coffee filter with coffee for the morning and set a pitcher of water next to it.

He was asleep the minute his head touched the pillow. His sleep was deep and peaceful and in the morning his covers were barely disturbed. Usually, he slept fitfully and his bed had to be made from scratch.

Two cups of coffee and three English muffins later, Charlie tiptoed back upstairs to Angela's room. She looked small and fragile in the big double bed and she had kicked off the covers. One long skinny leg was actually dangling over the side of the bed. Gently, so as not to wake her, Charlie pulled up the coverlet and stood staring down at her. Her curly hair was sticking up around her face in stiff points. His eyes went to her hands and for the second time he noticed her fingernails, or lack of them. They looked raw and painful. She must have really strong teeth to chew the nails down as far as she had. It bothered him, those chewed-down nails, and he didn't know why. Maybe he should rub some ointment or something on them. But if he did that she would wake up and think he was taking liberties with her. Immediately he backed off a step. He would mention it later in the day when they were talking. That's what he would do. He'd even buy a fresh tube of ointment while he was on his break.

An overpowering urge to touch the spiky curls came over him. Before he could think about it, he moved closer to the bed and reached down. Gently he tried to brush them from her cheeks. Maybe she needed a hairbrush. He turned and went to his room, fetched a brush and placed it on the night table next to her bed. He wanted to kiss her nose. He bent over and stared at her a second longer before he gave her a quick peck. It was a strange nose, just like the rest of her. He frowned. She didn't look like she was put together right. In the end he decided it didn't matter how she was put together. He liked her just the way she was. And the best part of all was that she liked him; he could tell. Looking regular wasn't all that important, not to him anyway.

Charlie went through his day in a state bordering on euphoria. He called Angela on his break, then managed to buy some ointment for her fingers and still make it back to his throne on time. Dinner was the same as Wednesday night, only this time Angela had made spaghetti and meatballs. All evening long he prayed silently, as the line of children dwindled, for God not to change his mind. Please, he pleaded silently, don't let things change. Let me have this. I never asked you for anything before. Just this. Please, let me keep it.

That evening Angela suggested they watch an old movie called *Back Street* with Irene Dunne. She said she liked old movies better than the new ones, that the actors and actresses were better and the plots more interesting. Charlie agreed. All of today's movies were about drugs and high crimes. He hated them.

Angela made a huge batch of French-fried onion rings and they drank beer out of the bottles. She might be strange, and she might not be pretty, but she was a great companion. Charlie couldn't remember being so happy in his entire life. He hadn't really been happy since the year he got an electric train set. His father had given it to him and then said he was too young to play with it, that he might get electrocuted, but that if Charlie was a good boy he could watch Mommy and Daddy play with it. Damn, now what made him think of that? He smiled inwardly. He would get it down out of the attic and he and Angela would put it together and play with it. He'd even let her turn the switch on and off. She'd like that.

He'd get a Christmas tree too. A real live tree in a pot that you could plant in the yard later. A big one with strong branches so it could hold all the ornaments packed away in the attic. He and Angela would decorate it together, hang lights on it, glittering red balls, popcorn and tinsel. He would put on some Christmas music, choir music. And they would drink apple cider. Maybe he would even unearth his mother's old manger scene. Angela wouldn't object because she was Jewish, would she? Jesus, how had he gotten so lucky? God was being good to him and he would put out the manger scene even if she didn't like it. He would just explain to her. Angela had said she was a good listener, that she had a willing ear.

It was early according to the small clock on the night table. Angela stared at the luminous dial, not believing her eyes. Why had she woken up at five-ten in the morning? She lay back and listened to the driving rain (or was it sleet?) that was pelting the windows. She snuggled deeper under the covers, willing sleep to overtake her again. It didn't work. She was wide awake. She might as well get up and go downstairs. At least she could turn on the TV in the living room and get the weather report off the local new station. Was this the storm the weatherman had spoken of the night before? He had predicted six inches of snow by morning but, as usual, they were getting rain.

Quietly, so as not to disturb Charlie, Angela dressed and crept downstairs. She reached for the aluminum coffee pot and filled it with the water Charlie had left out. Within minutes she had bacon frying on low and was mixing a batch of pancakes. On a day like this Charlie needed more than coffee to see him off.

Her mind whirled as she stirred the pancake batter. What would she do with herself all day? Water the plants, clean the already clean bathroom. She could strip both beds and put on fresh sheets. The towels needed to be washed. She could dust and vacuum and read the paper. After that, television, and then time to make dinner. Some day she would make someone a good wife. She liked to potter around the house and take her time doing small things. She liked clean things and everything neatly in its place. She particularly liked watering Charlie's plants with the yellow watering can with the orange flowers painted on the side.

It made her feel very domestic. She was enjoying every minute of her stay here with Charlie. But how much longer could she stay? Sooner or later she was going to have to confess all to Charlie Roman. If good old Mummy ever found out where she was, poor Charlie would be dragged into court for contributing to the delinquency of a minor. She couldn't allow that to happen to him. He was just too nice. She would kill before she squealed on him. Her face was fierce as she stirred the batter with a vengeance.

"What's wrong?" Charlie asked, alarmed at her strange look.

Angela looked up. "Nothing," she said calmly. "I was just thinking of something unpleasant there for a minute. Sit down, I'm making you pancakes and eggs and bacon. You need something besides coffee before you go out on a day like this. Didn't I tell you that weatherman was all wet last night?" She giggled.

Charlie laughed. "Those were your exact words, all right. Do you know what woke me up?"

"The smell of coffee perking?"

"All the way upstairs. It's a great smell. Do you like to smell gasoline when you're getting your tank filled up?"

"I love it. Did you ever sniff glue?" Angela asked as she poured the batter onto the square-grilled pan.

"No. I like the smell of pine, though, especially at Christmas time." Charlie paused. "I was thinking, Angela, on Sunday would you like to take a ride to Cranbury and buy a real Christmas tree? We'll bring it home and decorate it together. There are boxes and boxes of decorations in the attic."

"Oh, Charlie! Really? Oh, I would love that!" Angela cried, her eyes like round saucers. "I've never decorated a tree before. For a few years we had one of those artificial things that came decorated. Don't ask me why since we're Jewish. My mother must have thought it was the thing to do, I guess."

"You've never decorated a tree before?" Charlie asked incredulously before remembering that she was Jewish.

"No, but I've always want to. So do you have a star for the top?"

"Better than that. A gossamer angel!"

"I can't wait to see it," Angela said, sliding a stack of pancakes onto his plate. "Your eggs are coming right up."

Charlie ate like there was never going to be another ounce of food put before him. He savored each and every mouthful, not because he was that hungry but because Angela had made it especially for him. He knew she would be pleased if he ate it all. When he'd finished, he leaned back heavily on the stout wooden chair. "I hate to eat and run, but I'd better get an early start. The weatherman said the roads were freezing over and there were traffic jams. I'll call you on my break and, if I get a chance, I'll stop at the grocery store on my lunch hour. Make up a list of things we need and you can read it to me on my break."

"Okay, Charlie. Drive carefully."

Drive carefully. No one had ever told him to drive carefully before. Did that mean she cared if something happened to him? Charlie wished he had more experience with women. Women were supposed to be a mystery to men. He frowned as he steered his car through the streets at a crawl, watching any and all traffic. This was no time to get himself in an accident. Angela was no mystery though. When a girl said, "What you see is what you get," how could there be a mystery? He had never liked

125

mysteries anyway – they always had unhappy endings, the characters always got found out on the next to last page. But he didn't have to worry about that now that his decision was made.

Eight

Eric Summers's head pounded as he clenched and unclenched his brown fists. His stomach was in one big knot. He watched Heather Andrews walking by with short jerky steps; every so often she glanced over her shoulder. Fear. It was a living thing touching all their lives. How could those asinine shoppers below be so oblivious to what was going on? And the damn merchants were so greedy for a few dollars extra that they were willing to discount their own lives as well as everyone else walking through the monstrous center. It was true – money was the root of all evil. That's what the feeling was – evil. It was everywhere.

Lex came into his line of vision, his face grim and tight. Business as usual. You got paid for eight hours or you were without a job. Bomb threats came under the heading of nuisances and they were something you took in your stride while you put in your eight hours. Dedicated public servants, be damned. Christ, he was edgy and he had every right to be. Downright frightened, if he wanted to be honest. How many hours were left of the seventy-two that the bomb threat referred to? Not many. Was he going to die with all of these people here? It wasn't the dying so much that he minded; it was the absolute helplessness he felt. He should be doing something instead of this aimless wandering around. Another half-hour and the Christmas parade would start. Was that when it would happen? When all the people were clustered in one area?

He turned at the touch on his shoulder.

"No, I don't know anything and no, we didn't find anything," he said curtly to Dolph Richards.

"That's because nothing is going to happen and there's nothing to find. When are you paragons of law and order going to get that through your heads? The fool hasn't been born who would have the nerve to blow up my center. Relax, Summers, and enjoy the parade," Richards responded urbanely.

"You know, Richards, you're a first-class, grade-A, number-one fool," Eric said, stomping away. He couldn't look at the man's face another second.

"Takes one to know one," Richards said softly to Eric's retreating back. If ever there was going to be one black-faced idiot with his ass hanging out it was going to be Eric Summers when this center didn't blow. It annoyed Richards that the mall was full of plain-clothes police and his own security people. What could possibly go wrong? There wasn't so much as a hint of anything out of the ordinary. If the amount of packages and shopping bags the customers were carrying were any indication, then his projections were on target.

Spend! Spend! Spend! he thought happily as he made his way to the make-believe North Pole where the parade was to start. It really was a stroke of genius on his part in agreeing to hire Charlie Roman to play this year's Santa. He was perfect. Maybe if everything went off well he would give the man a small bonus. It did pay to show gratitude from time to time. Just look at him. Richards grinned.

Charlie was ho-ho-ho-ing with all his might. He waved his arms to signal that the parade was about to begin then climbed into his sleigh. Its wheels were camouflaged by white bunting and it was being pulled by eight robust college boys dressed in reindeer costumes. Charlie tossed out candy canes as the sleigh cruised through the mall. "Ho, Ho, Ho," he shouted to one and all. "Be good boys and girls and I won't forget you."

The laughing wide-eyed children scrambled to pick up the gaily wrapped coloring books and crayons he was tossing them along with the candy canes. Flash bulbs popped as the newspaper reporters snapped his picture. Charlie knew he would be on the front page of the second section of the morning paper. He hoped they managed somehow to capture his happy spirit as he made his rounds.

The strained faces of the police and security were not lost on Charlie as he continued on his sleigh ride through the mall. He felt the urge to tell them to relax and not to worry, that he wasn't going to blow up their precious center after all, that he had put all his grudges and anger behind him. And it was all due to Angela Steinhart – his first and only friend. Because of her he wasn't lonely anymore and life was good. Damn good!

No need to go overboard, he thought. They would know soon enough. The seventy-two hours would be up in another hour and the mall would still be standing. Meantime, they must be sweating their balls off. He chuckled again. He had made them sweat. He had caused all this commotion. He, Charlie Roman. He was almost sorry for their agitation. Almost but not quite. It wouldn't hurt them to be agitated for a few more hours. He had been in a constant state of agitation all his life. Now it was their turn.

Charlie squirmed inside the heavy suit. Had they turned up the heat in the mall or what? Why did he feel so hot and sweaty all of a sudden? For a few moments the brilliant Christmas trees with their winking lights and bright tinsel blinded him. The garlands of greenery swam before his cloudy gaze. He felt lightheaded as the strains from 'Frosty the Snowman' rang in his ears. And then he was all right. It was just tension and the relief, he told himself. The parade continued.

Eric Summers fixed his gaze on his watch and stared at the hands until they passed the seventy-two-hour mark. He waited another five minutes before he let the cuff of his shirt slide back down his wrist. It hadn't blown! Cold sweat dotted his brow. He was as near to fainting as he had ever been in his life. He released his breath in a long drawn-out sigh.

Richards passed him on his way back to the office. His smirk left no doubt in Eric's mind as to what he was thinking. There was no need to say 'I told you so' aloud. Richards's eyes said it all.

Heather wrapped her arms around Lex's neck and waited for the clock to strike the hour. The seventy-second hour. Silent tears ran down her cheek. "Lex . . . if something does happen . . . I think you should know . . . I mean . . . I want you to know that I care a great deal for you. I meant to tell you sooner but . . . well, you know how it is."

"Yeah," Lex said, pulling her close. "I know how it is. For the record I feel the same way about you. I just wish to hell we hadn't waited so long to tell each other how we feel. I wish . . ." He stopped abruptly when he saw the hour hand and the second hand come together on the wall clock.

Five minutes later they were still locked in each other's arms, their fear having lessened only slightly.

"This is a reprieve," Lex said. "Nothing else. We still have the rest of the day to get through. Another twelve hours to go before the center closes for the day. All we've done is shift positions on the dynamite keg."

"Take me away from here, Lex," Heather said. "Take me anywhere. I don't care where just as long as it's away from here."

"You got it, babe. You got it."

The Christmas tree lot was full of parents and kids, last-minute tree shoppers like themselves. The best trees were already gone but Angela didn't care. Any tree was good as far as she was concerned. She would have even settled for an artificial one.

"What about this one, Charlie? Its backside is a little bare, but no one will see it because it'll be in the corner."

"Looks good to me," he said, giving the tree an all-over inspection.

"Oh, Charlie! This is so exciting. My very first live Christmas tree!" On impulse she flung her arms around his neck and kissed him. It was a smacking kiss, hard and quick and over almost before it had begun. "I'll go get someone to ring it up," she said, dancing away from him.

Charlie stood staring at the tree but not really seeing it.

She had kissed him. Kissed him! Charlie Roman. Now there was no doubt in his mind that she liked him. Really liked him. He didn't quite know what to make of it. But he liked it.

They put the tree in the car trunk and tied the lid down. Charlie drove slowly all the way home, taking the curves carefully so as not to disturb the tree. Angela chattered like a magpie, telling him how excited she was, that she'd never celebrated a real Christmas before.

"I'm going to bake you some Christmas cookies. You know, the iced cookie-cutter variety. You do like Christmas cookies, don't you, Charlie?"

"Are you kidding? I love them."

"All right then, tonight we'll decorate the tree and tomorrow while you're at work I'll bake a big batch of cookies and I'll cut them into Santas and sleighs and stars." Angela paused in the middle of her happy chatter. "You know what, Charlie? I just had a terrific idea. Christmas Eve I'll set out a glass of milk and a plate of Christmas cookies on the coffee table and you can put on your Santa suit and we can eat them."

Charlie started to say that he couldn't bring the suit home, that it belonged to the mall, but he didn't want to disappoint her. He would find a way to sneak it out then sneak it back in. No one would be the wiser and Angela would have her Christmas wish.

It was past midnight when they finished decorating the tree and turned off the overhead light. Hand in hand Angela and Charlie stood back and admired their work. The cassette player switched to a new song and the Mormon Tabernacle Choir sang an angelic version of 'Joy To The World.'

"As long as I live I'll always remember this night," Angela said, squeezing Charlie's hand. "Now I know what they mean when they talk about the magic of Christmas."

"You're the magic, Angela. You made all this happen."

"Oh no, Charlie. You're wrong. It was you. It was all you."

For the first time in his life, Charlie Roman felt the stirrings of love.

Heather Andrews slowly opened her eyes and was surprised to see Lex's face above hers.

"Hi there, sleepyhead," Lex said.

Heather raised up on one elbow, the sheet slipping down to reveal the tops of her breasts. "Oh my God, what time is it?"

Lex pointed to the clock on the bedstand beside her. "It's early yet. We've got plenty of time," he said with a mischievous smile.

Heather breathed a sigh of relief, then lay back down and snuggled up close to him. After leaving the mall, Lex had taken her straight back to his house and fixed her a couple of strong drinks to calm her down. They'd talked and talked and one thing had led to another until they had found themselves in bed. Memories of last night's wild lovemaking washed over Heather, arousing her all over again. "Okay, if you say so," she laughed.

Angela worked non-stop, taking a break only long enough to read off another grocery list for Charlie. It was three-thirty when she finished all her chores and her cookie baking. She was so tired she had to drag herself up the stairs.

She took a bath and soaked for over an hour in a

home-made bubble bath of dish detergent and baby oil. When the water had cooled, she stepped from the tub and lay down on the bed. Within seconds she was asleep.

It was dusk when she woke. She lay for a few moments, trying to orient herself, then relaxed as she remembered where she was. She crept from her cocoon of blankets and started towards the bathroom. For some reason she felt disoriented as she staggered down the hall. A bright flash of light suddenly spiraled across the hallway, lighting it up like a fireworks display. "Oh, no," she moaned, "not again, not now. I won't look, you can't make me look." She slid to the floor, her hands covering her eyes.

Colors swam before her, spinning her, catching her and pulling her into the dreaded vortex of one of her visions. Around and around her consciousness spun, gripped by the maelstrom that wrung every fiber of her being until it left her weak with exhaustion. Helpless, incapable of movement, she felt her perception sharpen. In one dazzling split second she saw and heard it all. Not buildings collapsing but a steady drone, the sputtering of an engine. A small plane . . . writing on the side . . . P-654RT . . . fire . . . plane on fire . . . sky on fire . . . explosion . . . little girl . . . so still . . . dead . . . asleep. So pretty. Dead? Asleep? Not that little girl. She's too pretty to die. Her mother will be so sad.

Angela struggled to her knees, her arms outstretched in an attitude of prayer. Why does it have to be me? she thought. Why do I have to see all this death? Why do people have to die? I try but I can't do anything. She's such a beautiful little girl with all those dark curls and her tiny gold earrings. Someone must care a great deal about her to put those pretty little circlets in her ears.

Please don't let her die. "Where is it? Where is it?" she screamed to the empty room. "Take me, no one cares about me. Take me!"

Angela burst into heartrending sobs. She cried until she was exhausted, knowing she would find no answers sitting on the floor. There were never any answers. Sobbing, she got to her feet and dressed.

The icy air hit her like a blast from the Arctic as she walked on numb legs around the driveway to the garage door. Her tears tingled on her cold cheeks. She backed the orange Porsche out of the garage and turned it around, the wheels spinning on the icy road.

"This is it. I'm going to drive this car till it runs out of gas, then I'll get out and walk until I drop. I don't want to see that little girl. I don't want to know what happens. No more. I've had it. This is the last time I'm going to allow this to happen to me. I don't care about this vision and I don't care about Timberwoods. I don't care!"

The traffic was terrible, bumper to bumper. She could get to where she was going faster by walking. There was no doubt in her mind as to where she was going. To Timberwoods Mall, to Charlie. She would tell Charlie about her latest vision. Charlie would listen.

She needed something to drink, a beer, a hot chocolate, something soothing. Until then a cigarette would have to do. She opened the window and lit up. The minutes dragged by as she fought the traffic. After a while time seemed to lose its meaning and the urgency she'd felt melted away. She realized there was absolutely nothing she could do about what she'd seen. Nothing. The plane would crash. The little girl would die. And that was that.

The mall parking lot was full, as she'd known it would

be. I'll double-park and hope for the best, she thought. She flipped the butt of her cigarette out the window as far as it would go then slid out of the car. Immediately she slipped on the ice. She was all arms and legs as she grappled for a hold on something. Her hands reached for the bumper on the back of a small foreign car and she managed to swivel quickly enough to avoid doing damage to herself by falling. She had a fear of traction and hospitals.

Righting herself, she made her way to the front of the center and was barely through the door when she spotted a cop. She turned to run back the way she'd come when a long arm jerked her backward. "Make it easy on yourself, kid, and don't give me any trouble."

Angela muttered a curse as her arm was wrenched behind her. "Let me go, I didn't do anything."

"That's what they all say. Come on now, we're going for ride."

"Maybe you're going for a ride but I'm not," Angela said, jerking free of the young officer. They always traveled in twos, she remembered. But where was his partner? Probably waiting outside to nab her when she went through the door. Or maybe not. This one looked a little edgy. Onlookers stopped and stared then went about their business. You didn't interfere with the law.

Angela crouched low, the cop circling her, his arms outstretched. God, what did he think she was going to do to him? Angela's own arms were outstretched to ward him off should he make a sudden lunge for her. She backed up slowly and felt the door give behind her. A body, a soft pliable body, was against hers. Angela straightened up and was off and running before the young cop could move around the plump matronly woman. Slipping and sliding over the slick parking area Angela raced. She couldn't possibly make it to her car and hope to get away. She would have to make it on foot across the open fields where they were planning the annex to the mall. It was her best bet, her only bet at this time. She would be able to outrun the cop in an open field.

Her long coltish legs pumped furiously as she made her way up the slight incline and leaped over the guard rail. Open ground. She risked a quick look over her shoulder. He was right behind her. Her feet sunk down into the crunchy grass with its coating of ice. Mud oozed into her shoes as she ran, her breath coming in quick hard gasps. What the hell were they doing chasing her anyway? There must be some real criminals out there somewhere that they needed to go and catch. She hadn't bothered anyone so why was he after her? If only Charlie was here, he would make the cop leave her alone.

God, Charlie. She had forgotten about him. What was he going to think when he got home to see no dinner and no Angela? Poor Charlie. Well, she couldn't worry about that now.

She didn't see the hole and went face down into the crusty mud. She was up and running again straightaway but she'd lost valuable time and momentum. The damn cop was gaining on her. She slipped again on the icy ground and went down. This time the cop tackled her and they rolled around on the ground, Angela intent only on freeing herself, the cop intent on making her his prisoner.

He jerked both her arms backward and handcuffed her. "I wouldn't have done this back at the mall, but you forced me into it." It sounded almost like an apology.

"Screw you," she spat.

The cop ignored her. He heard worse a million times a day. "Look, all we want to do is talk to you. Take it easy. I'm not arresting you." Again, the tone was defensive.

"Look, you turkey, do I or do I not wear a pair of bracelets that prevent me from fleeing your charming person? I want a lawyer and you can tell your story to a judge."

"For the last time, I'm not arresting you. Someone wants to talk to you and I'm taking you to him. Now get moving, or do I have to carry you?"

"Do you know who I am?" she demanded.

He ignored her and kept her moving.

"I'm Murray Steinhart's daughter," she shouted. "Steinhart, you oaf, as in the Steinhart who owns half this town . . ."

"I know who you are and you don't scare me. So shut up and keep moving."

"The least you could do is tell me who it is who wants to talk to me." Angela was shivering uncontrollably now, wet mud and ice particles clinging to every inch of her clothing.

"You'll know soon enough."

"Then I'm not going anywhere and you can't make me." Angela dug her heels into the slushy ground and braced herself. He was bigger and stronger but she wasn't going without a fight.

The young cop squared off, sensing her intention to dig in and fight him. "Listen, kid, I don't like this any better than you do. We both know you're gonna come with me so why don't you make it easy on the both of us. Besides," he pleaded, "I'm cold. And you look like you're half frozen."

"I can last a lot longer than you can out here," Angela shouted as she dug her heels deeper into the semi-frozen mud.

The cop circled her, his handkerchief held out in front of him. He was quick and thorough and had Angela around the neck before she could move. He tied the cloth around her mouth and shoved her forward. "Move!"

She was defeated. A fool she wasn't, but she made the cop work for his money. He dragged her every step of the way, both of them slipping and sliding in the mud till they resembled creatures from some dark swamp.

Angela stared at the cream-colored Dodge the cop was steering her towards. If she hadn't been gagged she would have howled with glee. Cream-colored with fabric seats. For a brief moment the cop paused, slapping his forehead with a muddy palm. But he had no choice. "Get in and sit in one spot. Do you hear me?"

Angela turned slightly and, even though her hands were bound, managed to hit him with her shoulder and knock him off balance. The cop held back his fury as Angela climbed into the back seat of the car. The first thing she did was to sprawl full length on the seat. The cop slid behind the wheel, watching Angela dig her muddy heels into the rich fabric of the upholstery. Jesus H Christ, he had sweated to buy this car and now this punk kid had ruined it in three seconds. Someone was going to pay for this and it wasn't going to be him. And this wasn't even department business. A $25,000 car with only 10,211 miles on it. Shot to hell! His shoulders slumped as he steered the quiet car from the parking lot on his way to Eric Summers's house.

Nine

C harlie glanced in the back seat to make sure the groceries hadn't been stolen. He had shopped during his lunch hour and left the food in the car. By now everything must be frozen solid. He hoped Angela wasn't going to be upset.

Angela.

Icy treacherous roads permitting, he would see Angela in less than twenty minutes. Everything was so perfect, just like in the movies or a romance novel. Happy endings really did happen to people like him.

His eyes glued to the hazardous highway, Charlie fumbled with the radio. Storm warnings and dangerous driving conditions. "Tell me about it," he snorted as he watched a car in the next lane swerve, slide and then right itself.

The traffic slowed to a near halt and Charlie shifted the car into low gear. Right now his top priority was Angela and their relationship. For the first time in his life someone had bothered to look inside him, to see that he really did have a heart and a sensitive soul. And Angela was responsible for all of that. Angela was responsible for his feeling the way he did at this moment. His face darkened momentarily. Once in a while he was stupid; not often, just once in a while. Wanting to blow up the shopping center had been a stupid idea. His mood lightened again and he felt almost giddy. If – and the if was a big one – he ever told Angela about his stupid idea she would be so proud of the fact that he had come to his senses in time. And when he told her that she was the one responsible for his giving up on the stupid idea, she would positively beam with good feeling. She would radiate towards him like the sun. He knew it; he could feel it.

At first he thought he'd made the wrong turn. Or was it the wrong driveway? Had he missed his own house? With all the rain and sleet anything was possible. But no, that was his house; he could tell by the mimosa tree on the front lawn. His was the only house on the street with a mimosa tree. But the front light was off and there was no sign of life anywhere. Why was the house so dark? Of course, he reassured himself, Angela must have worn herself out from all that baking and fallen asleep watching television. What other reason could there be? He would forgive her. She had problems. And if there was one thing Charlie knew about, it was problems.

His gut churned as he shifted the heavy grocery bag and worked the key in the lock. There was no scent of perked coffee but there was a lingering aroma of cookies. He looked toward the living room, toward the long sofa. She wasn't there. The television wasn't casting shadows in the dark room. Something akin to a primal moan in his soul struggled to the surface. He dumped the groceries on the nearest chair and lumbered toward the kitchen. Empty and dark. He flipped on the light and saw a couple of dozen Christmas cookies on a plate next to the refrigerator. They were in various shapes and decorated with different colored icing.

But where was Angela?

In his haste to get to the stairs Charlie tripped and sprawled full length across the potted rubber plant standing by the wing chair. Large tears flooded his eyes as he crawled up the steps. He already knew there wasn't going to be a skinny scrawny girl lying across the bed. She was gone! She had baked the cookies and left. Why? God, why?

He made it to the top of the stairs and struggled to his feet. It was such an effort to remain standing. He wanted to bang his head against the papered wall and scream down the heavens. What had he done? The light switch inside the doorway cast the small bedroom in a cozy dim light. The bedspread was neat and unwrinkled. A sob rose in his throat when he saw his hairbrush lying where she had left it. Angrily he tossed it onto the bed. He would never use that brush again. Never.

Great wracking sobs tore through his body as he stared at the brush on the white counterpane. He could have sworn that she cared, that she had seen what other people refused to see: that he was a sensitive caring person with a heart full of love that was as big as he was. And he had given up his dream for her. He hadn't blown up the shopping center. He should have known; he shouldn't have been so stupid. He had believed her, wanted to believe she cared for him. He had cared for her so deeply that he had given up the dream he had worked on for over a year. And for what?

He wrung his hands in a frenzy as he made his way back down the steps. He went from room to room, turning on all the lights. He didn't want the shadow of Charlie Roman stalking him, seeing his bitter humiliation, his degradation.

She had betrayed him. He had given her sanctuary when no one else would. He had fed her, cared about her, confided some of his innermost secrets to her. He had let her see his vulnerability – and wasn't that love? Letting your mate or partner see that you weren't perfect, that you were vulnerable, and that you could bleed like everyone else? His heart was broken; his soul and spirit were crushed.

Furiously Charlie lashed out at the cookies on the kitchen counter. Why had she put them there and then left? She had added insult to injury, letting him know the party was over. A bright light started at the back of his eye sockets, burning slowly at first then blazing into flame. His body trembled and shook and his thick lips pulled back from his small white teeth. An unholy bellow of insane rage erupted from him and shook the room. He calmed then, the roaring flame subsiding to smoldering ashes. He was still, not a muscle twitched. It was over. He was back to square one. It was a simple matter, really, when you thought about it. All he had to do was move on to square two and from there to square three, where it would all end.

Charlie settled himself into his chair in front of the television. He planted his feet firmly on the carpet and laced his fingers across his stomach. He waited. The dark night crept into dawn and still he waited. At six in the morning he maneuvered himself from the deep comfort of the well-worn chair. He stared a moment at the blank screen in front of him, then at the spilled cookies. Nothing moved him. The bright lights didn't bother him at all. He put on his jacket and walked out the door. What did anything matter now? The only thought in his head was moving from square one to square two.

Charlie sneezed twice as he fumbled with the ice scraper to dislodge the thick crust from his windshield. By the time he had it cleared his body was aching. It must be from sitting up in the chair all night, he told himself. He didn't bother with the heater in the car. He would never feel warm again, so what was the point? He drove with mechanical ease to the center and clocked on to begin his work day.

Amy Summers watched her husband pick at the food on his plate. She had taken extra pains to make his dinner attractive: sliced roast beef, cut extra thin as he liked it, and bright orange carrots next to the emerald peas and the mashed potatoes. At the last minute she had placed a small sprig of parsley on the square of bright yellow butter nestling in the mound of mashed potatoes.

"What is it, Eric? Is the roast too well-done?" she asked, her soft brown eyes reflecting her concern.

"No, it's perfect. I guess I'm just beat. I had a hell of a day. The drink I had must have taken the edge off my appetite. I'm sorry, honey." Eric had no sooner finished speaking than the doorbell chimed.

Suddenly he was off his chair and running to the front door. His gorge rose. He fully expected it to be someone coming to tell him that Timberwoods Mall had just blown. He realized that unconsciously he had been listening for a thunderous boom. That was silly – Timberwoods was nearly five miles away. Besides, if anything had happened he would have been notified by phone. But he couldn't help it – the nightmare wasn't through yet.

Amy stared at her dinner, then attacked it with gusto. After all, she was eating for two. Eric was back in a few minutes, his face blank. "Stay in the kitchen, Amy."

"Stay in the kitchen? What are you talking about? Hey –" she said, getting up from the chair, her dinner forgotten, "haven't you heard of the Emancipation Proclamation? What's in the living room you don't want me to see?"

"Amy, this is mall business. Now, stay out here in the kitchen. I mean it," he said firmly.

"I don't like the way you're talking to me, Eric. I've never interfered in your business before but this time it's different. There's something strange going on and I want to see for myself. This is my house, too, you know."

"Amy, honey . . ."

"Don't you 'Amy honey' me. This is my living room," she said going through the swinging door.

"Oh, my God!" she squealed. "Put that child down. What is this?" she snapped at her husband. "You tell me right this minute what's going on. Untie that child," she demanded. She waddled over to Angela. "Be careful with her. It's okay, honey," she soothed as eight long years of suppressed motherhood rose to the surface. "No one in this house is going to hurt you, and certainly not this big ox I'm married to. I'm Amy Summers. You'd better work faster than that, Mr Policeman," she said sharply. "What if you cut off her circulation?"

"She's fine, Mrs Summers. I had to do it this way," the cop said defensively. "She's a hell-cat."

The handcuffs removed, Angela massaged her wrists then wiped her lips with the back of her hand. What was she doing here, she wondered as she looked around warily. Why had the cop brought her here? Cool. Keep cool and let them talk. At least dear old Mummy wasn't here. Surely they didn't mean to kidnap her. No, not the pregnant lady, she wouldn't have anything to do with a kidnapping.

"Are you all right, honey?" Amy asked anxiously.

Angela nodded.

"Would you like a drink?" Again Angela nodded as she licked her dry lips.

"Are you hungry?"

"Yes, I'm starved."

"Oh, my God," Amy said, wringing her hands together. "She's starved. You come with me right now. I'll fix you some dinner." She fixed a bright, brown gaze on her husband and said sharply, "Just look at this poor child. How could you? Grown men! They didn't hurt you, did they?" she asked worriedly.

"No."

"Come on, Amy, we've only had her for half an hour," Eric muttered.

"Half an hour! Then why is she starved and why is she so filthy? No-account black man," she hissed. "I should have listened to my mother. Come on, honey, I'm going to feed you and then you're going to take a nice herbal bath. I grow the herbs myself," she chatted as she led the docile Angela into the kitchen. "You sit right there and I'll make you a nice plateful of supper. Do you like roast beef?"

"I love roast beef."

Within minutes Amy had a heaped plate before the girl. Angela wolfed it down and sat back in her chair. "That was delicious, Mrs Summers. I think that was the best dinner I ever ate."

"Why, thank you, honey. Would you like some peach cobbler and a glass of milk?"

Angela nodded. Amy watched her devour the rich cake and felt sad. The girl looked so defenseless.

"Everything was delicious, Mrs Summers. I really enjoyed it. Thank you."

"I don't know why you're here or what happened, but I want you to know that there isn't a more gentle man in this whole world than my husband. He won't hurt you, I promise you. Now, you come with me. I'm going to fix a bath for you that you'll remember for a long time."

Angela followed the waddling Amy down the hall into the bathroom. "See these little net bags of herbs? Take one, tie it under the faucet and let the water run through it. When the tub is full, untie it and let it float in the water. After you've soaked for a while you'll feel like a new person. I grow the herbs on my window sill in the kitchen. I have scented soap and Ivory. Which would you like?"

"Ivory will be fine, Mrs Summers."

"Here are the towels," Amy said, opening the bottom of the cabinet sink. "Bath powder and shampoo are in the medicine cabinet. I just might have something from the old days that would fit you. I didn't always wear these tents," she laughed.

She was back in a few minutes, her arms full of clothes. "You take your time now, soak as long as you like."

As soon as Amy Summers closed the door into the hall, Angela scampered into the bedroom to use the telephone. She had no idea how long Eric Summers planned on keeping her here but she didn't want Charlie worrying about her or thinking she'd run out on him. If there was one thing she'd learned about Charlie in the short time she'd known him, it was that he could jump to conclusions. She wasn't sure what she was going to say to him when she got hold of him, but something would come to her. She hated the thought of lying to Charlie but she had no choice. If she told him the truth about herself he might not like her anymore.

She felt a twinge of guilt at using the phone without asking but it wasn't as though anyone had asked her to come here. She'd been forced. Practically kidnapped.

She had memorized Charlie's number, which was the same prefix as her own and then all threes. She counted the rings – two, three, four, six. He wasn't home and without an answering machine she couldn't leave a message. Maybe she could try again after her bath.

When Amy settled herself in the living room the young police officer was gone. She stared at her husband with wide eyes.

"I don't want you to interfere, Amy. There will be other people here shortly and I want you to stay in the kitchen or bedroom. Do you understand?"

"I understand you," Amy said quietly.

"But you have no intention of doing what I ask, is that it?"

Amy nodded.

"This kid is different, Amy. She has information we desperately need."

"The girl is frightened, Eric. Where are her parents? Why was she brought in here trussed like a chicken?"

"Look, Amy, believe me, it's better you don't know. You're going to have to trust me. You have my word that nothing is going to happen to that kid. All we want to do is talk to her. Talk, Amy, that's all. Why don't you let me make you a cup of tea? You look tired."

"I don't want any tea and I'm not tired. Why are you trying to sidetrack me? How long are you going to keep her here?"

"She can leave any time she wants after she talks to us."

"All right, Eric, I'll go into the kitchen, but I want to see that girl before she leaves here. Promise me," Amy said firmly.

"I promise," Eric said shortly.

"I'm going to clean up the kitchen and then I'm going to bake a cake."

"Fine, fine, why don't you make two cakes," Eric said absently.

"Great idea and I'll lace them with arsenic. How would you like that?"

"Fine, fine, whatever you say. You know I like cake," Eric replied, his mind on other things.

The doorbell chimed. Eric opened it to admit Noel, Lex and Harold.

"You really found her?" Lex asked, amazed. "Where is she?"

"Taking a bath," Eric said disgustedly. "A herb bath, no less. Amy decided on a little advance mothering. After she takes a bath she's going to wash her hair and then God only knows what else. She's been in there a long time; she should be out soon. How about a drink while we're waiting?"

"That sounds good to me," Harold beamed. Noel and Lex nodded in agreement and watched Eric pour the amber liquid into tumblers.

*   *   *

Angela waved the blow dryer a few times around her springy curls and looked in the mirror. She would do. Mrs Summers certainly was nice. And wow could she cook! She wondered vaguely when the baby was due. She would buy a present for the new arrival. That is, if she weren't locked up somewhere. She tidied up the bathroom and put everything back the way she found it. Before leaving the bedroom she tried Charlie's number again. After ten rings she hung up. Where was he? He should have been home long ago. Or maybe he was home and just not answering the phone because he was angry at her. If only she'd left a note, but at the time she hadn't been thinking about anything except getting out of there and ridding herself of the vision.

If only he had an answering machine!

Angela went back to the kitchen and smiled at Amy, a sad winsome smile that went straight to Amy's heart.

"You were right, Mrs Summers, that was the best bath I ever had. I cleaned out the tub and returned everything the way I found it."

"You didn't have to do that."

"I didn't want you to have to clean the tub. I mean with . . . you being . . ."

"As big as a mountain. Thanks, honey."

"When is your baby due?"

"Right around Christmas Day. Won't that be a magnificent present?"

"The best," Angela grinned. "I wish I could stay here and talk to you but I have to go inside. Your kitchen smells so good. I love it in here."

Tears blurred Amy's eyes. "When you've finished your talk you come back here and we'll have some fresh chocolate cake and talk about my baby. Is it a deal?"

Angela nodded and walked through the swinging door into the living room.

Eric was shocked at the girl's appearance. Christ, she almost looked normal and she smelled like Amy, just like an herb garden. Lex raised his eyes and grinned at Harold. It was obvious the chief had a little trouble recognizing Angela for a moment. Soap and water certainly worked miracles.

"Angela, this is Dr Noel Dayton," Lex explained. "He wants to talk to you and so do we. I apologize for the way you were brought here, but you have to understand that we really had no other choice. Once we've talked to you, you can leave any time you want to. All we want to do is talk. Is it a deal?"

Angela looked at the faces surrounding her. They looked harmless enough and they hadn't called her mother over. Maybe they did just want to talk.

Lex went on, "I've explained the situation to Dr Dayton but I want him to hear it from you. So far Mr Baumgarten has only my word, as does Mr Summers, about what you saw. Don't be afraid. We only want to talk to you."

Angela waited. Let them say everything they had to say and then she would decide. Where was Heather? She felt better when the pretty woman was nearby. She willed her face to total blankness and Lex cringed. Jesus, what if she refused to talk?

Eric looked directly into Angela's eyes. "Your going to Miss Andrews and telling her about a potential explosion at Timberwoods Mall has caused us a great deal of concern. I'm going to ask you straight out, Angela, do you know anything about the bomb threat that you haven't told us? Did you send it? Do you know who did?"

Angela involuntarily took a step backwards, wanting to put some distance between herself and the man who was glaring into her eyes, trying to peer into her very soul.

"I . . . I only know what I've already told you. I don't know anything about the bomb threat. I don't know who could have sent it." She could feel herself beginning to tremble. Her gaze fixed on Dayton.

"You said he's a doctor. What's he doing here? Did my mother send you?" she demanded suspiciously.

"I'm a psychiatrist, Angela, and I want to help," Dayton said flatly.

"Help who? Me or the police?" she snapped defiantly.

Surprisingly Harold spoke up, his tone gentle. "We're here to discuss the possibility of saving thousands of lives. If we're to believe what you say, then you have to help us. We aren't going to laugh at you and we aren't going to ridicule you. I don't pretend to understand these things; that's why Dr Dayton is here. Summers and myself are responsible for the safety of the people who shop in the mall. Lassiter is here because Heather called him into the situation. We want to help, but before we can do that you have to help us."

Angela's face remained blank as she stared at first one man, then the other. They said she could walk if she talked. If she wanted out of this house she would have to play. It didn't make any difference; they wouldn't be able to do anything. "What do you want to know?"

She heard the audible sigh of relief from one of the men. So, they were worried.

Noel questioned Angela for over two hours, making notes on a small pad he held on his knees. Not once, by voice or look, did he show belief or disbelief. Harold squirmed from time to time while Eric just sat, his face stony and hard.

"That's all there is to tell," Angela said flatly. She had consciously omitted any mention of Charlie. They didn't ask and she didn't tell. Charlie cared about her, she knew he did, and she didn't want anyone to spoil it by telling him she was a weirdo. She wanted this relationship with Charlie, needed it. It was as though she was connected to him somehow, and she fed on that connection. "You can't do anything about Timberwoods Mall. Nobody can do anything. Why are you trying?"

"If nobody can do anything, why did you go to the mall and speak to Miss Andrews? Why did you tell her the story?" Noel asked in return.

"I don't know why I did that. I just felt I had to tell someone. I suppose I thought that if I told someone it wouldn't be so bad. If I didn't tell someone, all those people . . . all that . . . those deaths would be my fault."

"What would you say if I told you we could close the mall during Christmas week and there wouldn't be anyone there to get hurt?"

"You won't be able to close the mall," Angela said flatly. "You can't change what I saw. What I see happens, just like the plane and the little . . ." Angela stopped, trying to gulp back her words.

"What plane?" Noel demanded.

Angela flushed. "Nothing. I was just . . ."

153

"Tell me, Angela," Noel said firmly.

"I don't want to talk about it. I told you, it's nothing. Leave me alone. You said that when I told you everything I could leave. Well, I've told you and now I want to leave," she said. She got to her feet.

"Wait a minute, Angela. The deal was that you were to tell me everything. Once you've told me everything, then you can walk. You gave me your word. Now, what about the plane?"

"The plane had nothing to do with the mall," Angela said, her face drained of all color.

"Everything," Noel said firmly. "Up to now you've cooperated beautifully. Why leave anything out? Whatever it is, it might help us. Let us be the judges."

"If I tell you can I leave?"

"You have my word, and I don't give my word lightly," Noel said, leaning across the coffee table, his face earnest.

Angela licked her dry lips and looked from one man to the other. "All right, but you aren't going to like it. I woke up, just before I went to Timberwoods, right before the cop picked me up. I saw the light, just like the other times. I screamed and wouldn't open my eyes, but somehow my eyes opened and there it was. I don't want to tell you," she said, getting up suddenly. "I changed my mind. I want to leave now." Her features were rigid with fear. She could feel herself shaking. The tremors reached her fingers, her toes.

"You have to tell me, Angela," Noel said quietly. "Sit down and take a deep breath and let it all out. Don't you feel better when you tell someone? Of course, you do," he answered for her. "When you talk about it, it doesn't seem

154

so bad. I want to know, Angela. I have to know so I can help you."

"You can't do anything about this either, so why do I have to tell you?"

"We don't know for sure that we can't do anything. All we can do is try. Isn't trying better than nothing?"

"Okay, okay. There was this plane . . . It was little, not like the big jets. It was white with black lettering. *The Mask of Zorro* was playing at some movie. I don't know if it was night or day because of the bright light. The plane was on fire; I heard the drone of the engine and then I heard the sputter . . . The sky was lit up and the plane was burning."

Angela's voice began to rise with the onset of panic. "I think it crashed. The little girl died. I hoped she was asleep but she was dead. She was so pretty and she had tiny gold circlets in her ears. She was tiny and so still. She had a lot of dark curls. I didn't want her to be dead."

Tears trickled down Angela's thin cheeks as she talked. Wearily she shook her head from side to side. "You see, you can't do anything about this either. No one can do anything. Why do I always see death?" she entreated, looking to Noel for an answer.

Noel was off the chair and kneeling beside her. "Right now I don't have any answers for you. But I want you to listen to me. You had this vision a few hours ago. Is that right?"

"Yes. I've already told you."

"Where was the plane? By that I mean, was it here in Woodridge or was it some place farther away? Could you tell?"

"I don't know. Just that there was a movie. I saw the name of the theater. It could be anywhere."

"These other visions, the ones you've had in the past – were they all more or less around here, let's say within a twenty-five mile radius?"

Angela nodded.

"And you couldn't tell if it was day or night?"

"No, because of the bright light. I couldn't see beyond the light."

"Did the plane crash or was it on fire?"

"I think it crashed because it was on fire and then the whole scene was fire."

"What color was the plane?"

"White with some red on the wings and black letters on the side."

Noel's voice rose in excitement. "Did you see the letters?"

"Yes, I saw them. P-654RT. Big black letters."

"The little girl – how do you know she was dead?"

"I just know. She was so still."

"How old was she, Angela? Do you know, could you tell?"

"Three years, maybe four. It would be hard to say because she was so tiny. And she had little gold circlets in her ears, almost covered by the dark curls.

"Angela, if the plane was burning, wouldn't she have burned too? Or was she thrown clear?"

Angela frowned. "There wasn't any fire around her. She wasn't burned at all."

"Where did she come from?"

Angela looked puzzled. "I don't know. At first I thought she was asleep."

"How do you know?"

Angela appeared confused. "I don't know. She . . . she was dead, that's all I know. Her mother was sad. And don't ask me how I know that either. I just know."

"Think. Was there anything else, anything you might have forgotten? Was there anybody else in the plane? What about the pilot? Were there any other passengers?"

Angela shook her head. "Just what I saw."

"Is there any way for you to know how soon these things happen after you see them, how – "

"I don't know!" Angela cried, jumping up. "A day, two days . . . I don't know! Sometimes just a few hours. I don't want to talk about it any more!" Her voice rose to a shriek. She'd had enough. More than enough. She'd told them all she knew and they still wanted more. But there wasn't any more. She buried her face in her hands and tried to erase the little girl's face from her mind.

Charlie! She wanted Charlie! She wanted to know that when she left here she could go to him and that he would be waiting for her with open arms and no questions. But now she didn't even know that because he wasn't home or he wasn't answering the phone.

Amy heard her pathetic cry and was through the swinging doors in a flash, wrapping her arms protectively around the girl.

"You stop it right now! Right this instant! Come on, honey, you come with me. We're going to have chocolate cake and milk, and you clods can sit here and drink. You aren't getting any of my cake."

"Chocolate?" Harold asked longingly.

"Devil's food," Amy said tartly as she led Angela into the bright, fragrant kitchen.

As soon as the swinging doors closed, Noel had the newspaper open to the movie section. "*The Mask of Zorro* is playing at three movie theaters near here."

"Hey, wait a minute. You believe her, don't you?" Eric stared at Noel, a peculiar expression on his face.

"From the look of you, you believe her too."

"Now, hold on. Yeah, I believe she thinks she sees these things. The kid's weird. Claiming to see people and disasters . . ."

Noel's serious expression stopped Eric mid-statement. "I want to know. Do you believe her?"

For a long moment Eric stared at the floor, unable to face Noel. Then his gaze went to Lex, who was looking at him, waiting for his answer. And Harold, who groaned and rubbed his face with short stubby fingers.

"It seems I'm not the only one who believes her. Christ. I don't want to. I don't want to think she's right. About the plane, about Timberwoods, anything."

"Timberwoods!" Harold exclaimed. "She wasn't right about the mall. Nothing happened today. The letter said seventy-two hours. That's over and the center's still standing."

Eric and Lex looked at one another and nodded. Harold was right. They could all take it easy. There wasn't any plane. There wasn't any danger to Timberwoods. Then Noel's voice cut through them like a knife. "The bomb threat said seventy-two hours. Angela didn't. She said the height of the Christmas season."

His words were calm, almost flat in the delivery, and yet Eric felt a spread of gooseflesh on his back. "All right, Dayton, what are we gonna do?"

"What time is it?" Noel snapped.

"Ten-fifteen," Lex volunteered. "If it happens, let's hope it happens after midnight. Wait a minute. The letters. Don't pilots have to file a flight plan? Wouldn't the letters Angela saw help us to identify the plane?"

Noel had the phone in his hand and was dialing as Lex finished speaking. He asked his questions, waited, then hung up.

Lex held his breath while Eric paced the room. Harold clenched and unclenched his moist hands.

At eleven-ten the phone shrilled and Noel, in his haste, managed to bump his shins on the coffee table. They had been waiting for a call from his contacts at the NYPD who had a great deal more access to this type of information than the Woodridge Police.

"Hello, Dayton here," he gasped as he rubbed his bruised leg. "Oh Christ, was that the best you could do? Of course, I understand . . . All right, then, I'll do that."

Slowly he hung up the receiver. "He couldn't trace the plane. It must be privately owned. Anyway, without a point of departure it was hopeless from the beginning."

"What did he tell you to do?" Eric asked.

"What?"

"You said you'd do something. What?"

"Oh. Yeah. He said if we knew the destination I could call the airport."

"Well, do we know the destination? Or are we assuming it's a nearby airport? For all Angela's told us it could be in Oshkosh." Eric was fuming with a feeling of helplessness.

"That's what we'll have to assume." Lex fumbled through the phone book, but on second thought gave it up and dialed information, asking for the numbers of

159

nearby airports. Harold, Eric and Noel supplied a list off the top of their heads.

It was Harold who then picked up the phone and, in his most authoritative voice, spoke to air control at each of the airports, asking to be notified if a small plane with the numbers P-654RT asked for permission to land.

Now all the three men could do was wait.

"We believe that girl. Look at us. We really believe her." Lex ran his fingers through his hair. "What are we going to do?"

"I wish to hell I knew. We'll have to find some way to close the mall, that's all there is to it. If anyone's got any suggestions, I'd like to hear them," Eric said, propping his feet on the coffee table and stretching his hands behind his head.

"Not me," Lex mumbled. Noel was scribbling in his notebook and didn't bother to answer. Harold fidgeted in his chair, his round eyes pools of concern.

"Our hands are tied. They're not going to let us close the mall and you know it. If this plane crashes – and it will, I can feel it in my bones, the girl was right. We can only hope she was wrong about Timberwoods." Lex's voice was dry and tight. He heaved a sigh and rubbed his eyes.

"We could always murder Dolph Richards," Harold muttered.

"And who is going to murder all three hundred and forty-one shop owners?" Eric answered. "All we can do is sit and wait."

It was twelve-twenty-one in the morning when the phone rang. Eric answered it. "Yes, I'm Detective Summers of the Woodridge Police. I inquired about the plane."

He swore softly at the information he was getting from the other end of line. Another minute and he hung up the receiver.

"A Piper Cub crashed into the Apex Theatre on North Washington at thirteen minutes after twelve. The pilot complained of chest pains at eleven-fifty-nine. Let's go."

While the others were putting their coats on Eric went into the kitchen. "Angela," he said softly, "your plane just crashed into the Apex Theatre on North Washington."

He laid a gentle hand on her shoulder. "I'm sorry. Amy will take care of you, won't you, Amy?" he asked his wife.

"Of course I'm going to take care of her. What kind of mother do you think I would be if I couldn't take care of this child? Do whatever you have to do and don't worry about us."

"In my gut I thought the kid was making all this up," Eric mumbled on the way to the car. "It didn't seem possible. I still don't believe it. I won't believe it till I see the little girl and the numbers on the plane. Maybe she knew the pilot, or the kid or something. Nothing about that girl surprises me. When I walked into the kitchen she was asking my wife to explain how you grow herbs. She was asking as though she really wanted to know."

"She probably did want to know. That's why people ask questions," Noel said shortly as he slid his station wagon out of the dark driveway. "I wish I had some answers for you."

The van careened down the road, heading north to the outskirts of Woodridge. The four passengers were tight-lipped and silent until Noel pointed through the

161

windshield. "Fire trucks." Even as they watched the black wintry sky grew bright with red flames.

Minutes later the van maneuvered through the mêlée. Its passengers alighted and over to the perimeter of the crowd of firemen and police. Eric flashed his badge at one of the firemen. "How'd you get here so fast?" he asked. "We only got the call minutes ago."

"Fire station's just down the road. We were having our annual Christmas party so most of the guys were already on hand. Got to keep our eyes on one another though. The wine was really flowing."

Eric pounded him on the back and reassured him. "Well, it doesn't show. Looks like you're getting things under control."

The plane had lost a wing and its engines were flaming. A rescue team, assisted by a rush of water from the hoses, was trying to make its way to the cockpit and survivors. The firemen worked with precision, carrying stretchers and hosing down the parking lot. Though the area was well-lit both by the flames, and by spotlights on the hook and ladder, Eric couldn't see the numbers on the side of the plane.

Moments later two stretchers were hurried to the waiting ambulances, both bodies covered. They were dead.

"Did you get the baby out?" Eric demanded of one of the rescue workers.

"What baby? There wasn't any baby aboard that plane. Just the pilot and passenger."

"There had to be a baby," Eric snapped.

"Look, buddy, there ain't no baby. The way I hear it, the pilot radioed in to the control tower and reported chest pains. He said there was one, repeat one, passenger aboard.

And there he is." The fireman lifted his eyes to the stretcher bearing a full-grown adult, the body covered to give death its dignity.

Summers spotted someone he knew – Detective Sergeant McGivern. Rushing over, he grabbed McGivern's arm. "Who was the passenger?"

"Get out of here, Summers. You're not on this. And you're sure as hell asking a lot of questions. Now get out of my hair!" McGivern turned back to one of the uniformed officers, ordering him to take the names and addresses of any eyewitnesses.

Eric went back to his colleagues who were watching the frenzied proceedings in amazement. "They're dead. The pilot and the passenger. It was the right plane. But no little girl, thank God," he heard himself say. "Angela was wrong." He realized for the first time how relieved he was. If Angela had been wrong about the little girl, she could be wrong about other things too.

"There's just one thing I want to do before we call it a night. I want to go down to the hospital and find out the identity of those poor guys they pulled out of that wreckage."

"Both bodies are pretty badly burned," the morgue attendant said clinically. "Take a look if you want." He pulled back the sheet.

"Is there any way we can find out which is the pilot and which is the passenger?" Noel asked with authority.

"Sure thing. This one here, the little guy, was the pilot. Ephraim Evans was his name, and this man was Dr William Maxwell. There was a lady and gentlemen here a few minutes ago and she identified the doctor. She knew

Fern Michaels

the name of the pilot but had never met him. Seems she
heard the broadcast on the radio shortly after it happened.
She's been here waiting in the hospital for Maxwell to
arrive. Said he was a surgeon from Leahy Clinic in Boston.
He was supposed to operate on her little girl tomorrow –
actually today," he said, glancing at his watch.

Summers tensed. "Where are these people? The ones
who identified the doctor."

"Upstairs on the surgery floor, unless they went home,"
the attendant said, pulling up the sheet.

Eric led the way from the basement to the lobby and
scanned the nearly empty room. A woman, her head bent,
was crying into her hands while a tall heavyset man stood
awkwardly beside her, patting her shoulder.

"I'm from the police," Eric said as he tapped the man on
the arm. "I wonder if you would mind stepping over here
for a moment. It's about the plane crash."

"Of course," the man said, looking relieved. "What can
I help you with?"

"They told me in the morgue that you identified Dr
Maxwell."

"Yes, I did. My wife and I were sitting here waiting
for his plane to get in. He was supposed to operate on
my daughter this morning. She's too sick to be moved to
Boston."

"What do you mean?" Eric asked sharply.

"Without Dr Maxwell to operate on our daughter,
there's no hope. She'll die," he said huskily.

"There are other surgeons, other doctors . . ."

"No, he was the only one who would even consider the
operation. He was our last hope. Maxwell said he would
try. Now it's all over."

164

"Where is your little girl?" Eric managed to ask as a hard lump settled in his throat.

"In room thirty-four down the hall. They have her in a private room with a nurse. They didn't want her in the pediatric ward with all the noise and commotion."

Eric walked back to the small group and motioned them to follow him. Quietly he opened the door of room thirty-four and motioned to the nurse to remain seated.

The little group tiptoed around the small bed. Dark curls framed a tiny exquisite face that was wan and pale as death. The child's breathing was ragged and harsh. Noel bent over the small bed and gently moved a dark curl. A tiny gold circlet gleamed in the soft yellow light.

Eric Summers felt like screaming with frustration. Here it was, Saturday afternoon, and he had so much on his mind. It was at times like this that he hated his profession. He watched the happy shoppers surging through the mall and fear tugged at him for each and every one of them. Thank God Amy was safe at home. And, while he didn't actually dislike or like Angela, he was thankful she was staying with his wife. At this stage of the game the girl was better than no company for Amy.

Angela. He believed her one hundred per cent after last night. So did the others. Poor kid. Imagine having to live with stuff like that. When he was a child, he had always wished he could see what was going to happen in the future. No more.

There was an air of imminent destruction hovering over the mall. It was there, he could feel it stalking him from spot to spot. This center was going to be wiped off the earth, and soon. There was nothing he or anyone else could do to stop it. It was going to happen. At this point he was numb, almost beyond feeling. But he couldn't ignore it. How could he? All those thousands of people. Suddenly he wished he wore glasses so he could see the people better. He had to remember them.

Tomorrow was Sunday and the mall opening hours would be shorter. He would do everything in his power to make sure the center was searched from top to bottom one more time. It was always one more time. Dogs, the entire squad, the head of the bomb squad himself helping the dogs sniff. Every security man called in for overtime. Eric knew in his gut that it wasn't good enough though, they could search till hell froze over and they were never going to find anything. The bottom line was that the center was going to blow. Nothing and no one was going to change a thing.

Ten

Charlie Roman walked into the garage, his eyes immediately going to the shelf on the far wall where the remains of his experiments were hidden. He felt pleased with himself. It took a smart man to hit on just the right balance of modeling clay impregnated with acid to eat through the sample of piano wire. He had even tested it outdoors to see what effect the cold would have. Each time it had taken the acid approximately thirty minutes to eat through the piano wire, the same wire which now prevented the spring from snapping open the ball valve on the liquid propane tank.

Later on he would take a ride past the center just to satisfy himself. Somehow he knew the police would be there. They would have the dogs and they would be checking the center inch by inch. He looked at his watch and shuffled back into the house, his bedroom slippers making slapping sounds on the concrete floor. Time to take some cough medicine and more aspirin. Maybe he would take a cold tablet too. If they thought he was sick, they would make him go home and then he wouldn't be able to carry out his plan. They would be afraid of him breathing germs on the little kids. As if that mattered. Soon nothing would matter. Not even Angela.

*   *   *

Murray Steinhart paced the large motel room, a look of fury on his handsome features. "You are incredible, Sylvia, absolutely incredible, do you know that? I've had just about all I'm going to take from you. This time you're going too far. I went along with you before because I was stupid and I wanted to believe what you told me. But this . . . this is too much!"

"If you don't do it, Murray, then I will. What else would you suggest?" Sylvia asked craftily. "Have you a better solution?"

"No, I don't have a better solution, but you aren't having that kid locked up like some criminal. I have something to say about what happens to her. I am her father."

"Some father," Sylvia snorted as she pulled a cigarette out of its package. "Don't think you're going to wriggle out of it all this time by taking off and leaving me to face this alone. That girl has made me a laughing stock for the last time. It's just a matter of time before the newspapers pick up on these visions of hers and then the whole damn town will know that our daughter is a nutcase!" she said, her voice rising hysterically.

"She isn't crazy, dammit!" Murray Steinhart bellowed.

"Oh yeah? Well then what do you call it when a person thinks they can see into the future?" She didn't wait for an answer. "Look, Murray," she said, lowering her voice, "I've finally been accepted by the Mosses and that girl isn't going to spoil this for me, not this time."

"You're a fool, Sylvia," he replied with a look of contempt. "Those people don't care about you. None of the people you associate yourself with care about you.

168

Why can't you understand that? All they care about is money. Jesus, I can't believe you can't see that."

"A lot you know," she said, flicking her ash into the ashtray.

"You've got your priorities all screwed up. Here you are thinking about the Mosses when you should be thinking about our daughter. She needs you. She needs both of us. We're all she's got."

Sylvia took another tack. "No, we're not all she's got." She moved up close to him and brushed an invisible speck of lint from his suit jacket. "Darling, teenagers are committed all the time to various rehabilitation centers for drugs and behavioral problems. I wouldn't even consider such a thing if I didn't believe it was for her own good. Angela is deeply troubled. She needs help. Professional help. God knows I've tried to do what I could for her but I don't understand her. My God, who does?" Sylvia forced a tear from her eye. "This is all my fault," she said, pretending to shoulder the blame. "I should have been a better parent. I should have enrolled her in dance classes and hired someone to teach her to play the piano. Anything to keep her mind busy." She brushed the tear off her cheek. "I don't know what to think any more. It's too late to change her now. She is what she is. I think the best thing for everybody concerned is to have her committed. You must see that," she cajoled.

"Committing her isn't the answer," Murray replied, moving away from his wife. "There's got to be another solution to all of this. I just have to find out what it is."

He paced the length of the room, thinking about the past, his relationship with his daughter. He couldn't lay all the blame for Angela's strange behavior on Sylvia's

169

shoulders. He had to accept some of the responsibility himself. After all, he was her father, though God knows he hadn't been much of a father these last five years. To tell the truth, he hadn't been any kind of a father. Every time Angela had needed something he had accused her of being in trouble, and when she'd assured him she wasn't he'd tried to soothe her ruffled feathers with money.

Angela. Within minutes after her birth, he'd told Sylvia he wanted to name her Angel. Sylvia wouldn't hear of it so he had named her the next best – Angela. In his mind though he always thought of her as Angel. And for the first six years of her life that's what she had been – his little angel. Daddy's little girl. If only he could turn back the clock and do things all over again. He would spend more time with her, talk to her, listen to her. He would do everything differently. Wouldn't he?

Sylvia crushed her cigarette out in the ashtray. "Just let me ask you one simple question, just one, Murray, darling." She drew the word out for emphasis. "What will we do if what Angela says comes true? No, I take that back," she said, shaking her head. "What will we do when what Angela says comes true. Because it will come true, Murray. Her visions always do and we both know it. Before now no one has known about them except you and me, but now a whole lot of people know. And once Timberwoods blows, every newspaper in the country will be carrying the story. I can see the headlines now: 'THOUSANDS DIE IN MALL BOMBING. LOCAL GIRL CLAIMS TO HAVE PREDICTED THE DISASTER'. But you know what, Murray? The public isn't going to believe she sees these things. They're going to believe what's easiest – that she's the one who

170

set the bomb to blow up the center. You know that's what will happen! They'll probably call her a terrorist!" she continued in horror. "How will you explain that to your business partners? When Dr Tyler opened his sanatorium Angela should have been his first resident patient. I thought about it, but when you said to let her try her wings for a while and then decide I went along with you. And this, too, shall pass!" she finished dramatically.

"You're repeating yourself, Sylvia. Let's look at this calmly and discuss it like the adults we are. After all, we are her parents. I've made some mistakes and so have you. Blaming each other isn't going to help her or us now. Fix me a drink and we'll go over it and decide what to do."

"You aren't at home now, Murray. This is a motel, or did you forget that? Your answer to everything is to take a drink, or else it's take a drink and a nap. Alcohol isn't the answer. For once I'll have a discussion with you cold sober. You know what my position is – what's yours?"

Murray looked at his wife helplessly. "I don't know, I honestly don't know. But there has to be an answer."

"Let me ask you another question, Murray. Knowing what you know now, would you go to Timberwoods to shop?"

"My God, no, I wouldn't go there. Why do you ask? Would you?"

"No. Hell no!" Sylvia turned away from him and picked her Chanel purse off the bed.

"Where are you going? What are you going to do?"

"I'm going to find Angela and have her put under a doctor's care. I'm certain that's the thing to do. Everything will work out, I'm sure of it. But if you can come up with something better, Murray, I'm willing to listen."

"There has to be another way. Somebody has to be able to do something. If not, then they have to close the mall," he said stubbornly.

"You're a fool! They aren't going to close the mall and you know it. Not during Christmas week. Don't you understand – no one is going to believe her. Would you if you were in their place?"

"I'm going out," Murray said briskly. "I want to walk and think this over."

"While you're out why don't you stop by the house and see what your little angel did? You'll be lucky if eighty thousand dollars covers it."

"Would you tell me why you have to put a price tag on everything? So what if it costs eighty thousand dollars or even a million? I'm the one who'll pay it, not you," he said, putting on his jacket. "We'll talk later when I get back. This isn't the end of it."

"It's the end as far as I'm concerned," Sylvia glowered. It was the end and there was nothing more to discuss.

The roof of the Timberwoods Mall was an immense sea of drifting snow. The uniformed policemen looked like tiny ink spots staining the surface of a blank sheet of paper.

"Hey, don't go too near the edge!" one of the policemen called to the others. "The abutment isn't very high and it would be easy to go over."

"We'll never find anything up here," his partner said as he slapped at his arms to keep warm. "We don't even know what we're looking for. How will we see anything in all this snow?"

"Yeah, well, just a few more minutes and the captain

172

will be happy. If we go in too soon he'll only send us out here again."

"I thought this bomb business was yesterday's news. Then somebody gives a green light and here we are again."

"Yeah. My wife hates having me work on Sunday but I could use the overtime."

"Christ, did you ever see so much snow? We're in for a hell of a winter, I can tell you right now."

"Yeah," his partner agreed. "I can tell that we won't be up here again. Already the snow is covering everything. I almost broke my neck!"

"I know what you mean. I was going to check that equipment over there when I tripped. Christ, I thought I was gonna go over the edge."

"Did you check out the equipment?"

"Oh, yeah, it's all right. At first I didn't know what it was but then I scooped the snow away. It must be a CO_2 tank or something. Anyway, it says 'Emergency Extinguisher.'"

"C'mon. We've been out here long enough. Call the other guys in – there's nothing up here."

Charlie Roman backed the car out onto the snow-filled road and slipped it into gear. He couldn't explain this compulsion he felt to drive past the center. There was no way he could see if the propane cylinder was still intact. If the police cars were still there then it was safe to assume that it was. If they'd found it, then the parking lot would be empty and the information would have been on the news. His luck was still with him, he was sure of it. After all, the bomb squad would have come in as soon as the mall closed last night. If they hadn't found it by now they weren't going to.

Would the maintenance men be out in the parking lot? It was a good thing he hadn't answered the phone when it rang. He'd guessed it would be the chief wanting him to come in to help clear the snow, make everything nice and easy for all those shoppers who came to the mall with money to spend. Well, how about making life easy for him, Charlie Roman?

He stopped for a red light and decided to drive past rather than go into the lot. You never knew who would be watching, and if one of the men from maintenance spotted him then it would be all over. He craned his neck to peer through the swirling snow and was satisfied to see cars peppered throughout the parking lot. He let out a deep sigh and headed for a U-turn. He could go back home and wait. It wouldn't be long now.

It was eight in the evening when Lex and Heather entered the mall. They had decided it would be best for all concerned if they kept their romantic relationship a secret, at least until after the bomb threat was behind them. Harold and Eric were waiting for them in Richards's office.

Richards was leaning back in his swivel chair, a triumphant look on his face. "The bomb squad has given the center a clean bill of health. I knew they would, but we have to go through these . . . channels. We open the center tomorrow morning on schedule."

"All that is fine, Richards," Eric said coolly, "but what about that other matter we discussed? What are we going to do about that? There've been a few new developments since we last talked to you."

"I told you, we aren't closing this mall. So whatever you have up your sleeve, forget it. The mall stays open. Christ, what is it with you, Summers? Do you have some kind of personal ax to grind with the center? I never saw anyone so hopped up on closing a place down."

"You're deliberately closing your mind to anything I say about the Steinhart kid and you know it. Why can't you listen and make a decision? I called the chief of police to meet us here. If this center blows I want to know I did everything I could to stop it. Lassiter and Baumgarten are on my side. You're sitting alone, Dolph."

"Goddamn it, Summers, you've already made an ass of yourself with this crazy bomb threat. What more do you want? Do you have any idea how many men you tied up today? Men that were needed outside. In case you aren't aware of it, there's a full-scale blizzard going on out there. Those policemen are needed out on the roads. The center is A-1 now. Our own security will patrol the mall all night and tomorrow when the doors open. Now for God's sake, get off this cockamamie kick about that Steinhart kid!"

"There are those that are ignorant beyond insult," Harold said sarcastically.

"All right, all right, tell your story to the police, but when they laugh at you don't say I didn't warn you. They aren't going to close the mall and neither am I," Richards said smoothly, forgetting for once to beam his movie-star smile.

There was a sharp rap at the door. "Come in," Richards called briskly.

The chief of police walked into the room. Eric got up

and held out his hand. "You know Summers and Lassiter," he said. "This is Heather Andrews, my assistant."

Harold sat back in his chair and relaxed. The black man could do the honors. This was a time for action and Summers was damn good at action. He listened intently as Summers told the police chief about the plane crash and Angela Steinhart.

"You can check this out if you want to," he finished. "The question is, what do we do now?"

The police chief nodded to one of his men to make the check and for Summers to continue.

"I know there are people who don't believe in this sort of thing," Eric went on. "I didn't myself. But that doesn't change what I saw with my own eyes. If there's any chance at all that this could be true, then the mall should be closed. Do you have any idea how many people will be here at any given moment this week? Well over one hundred thousand! If this center blows they go with it. Do you want that on your conscience? I don't want it on mine. We have to close the mall! That's it."

"No, that isn't it," Richards interrupted harshly. "If Angela Steinhart was some sort of psychic don't you think the people of this town would know about her? She's just doing this for attention. You can't close the mall just because she thinks something is going to happen. If you think I'm kidding, take a poll of the merchants who have shops here. They'll be down on your backs in an instant. They need this week to carry them through the first half of next year. I wouldn't be surprised if this Steinhart kid wasn't the one who sent the bomb threat in the first place, just to get her kicks out of watching the police bust their

chops. These kids today have it in for the police and you
know it!"

"That's it, Summers? That's all you have?" asked the
police chief. "There are explanations for everything, and
that includes the plane crash. The little girl – did she
die?"

Eric shrugged. "I don't know."

The chief nodded to his captain who left the room to
make a phone call.

"Even if she does die, it still doesn't mean anything.
Angela wasn't sure if she was dead or asleep. The fact
that the plane crashed wasn't just a freak occurrence. This
is crazy," Eric said, pounding his fist in his palm.

"Look, stop and think for a moment," the police chief
soothed. "You say the kid said the center was going to be
leveled. Do you know how much explosive that would
require? If it was here we would have found it. Right now
the center is clean. I can't close Timberwoods on what
you've told me. They'd drum me out of the department."

"I don't believe this," Lex said, jumping up and slam-
ming both hands down in front of Dolph Richards. "Don't
you care? Can't you see that what we've been telling you
could actually happen?"

"There – you said it yourself. It could happen. And it
just as easily could not happen. Think about the merchants.
They're the ones who pay your salary and mine. Don't you
owe them something?"

"I owe them a day's work for a day's pay. Up until
now I've done just that. This is something different.
We're talking about the lives of thousands of innocent
people."

"Thousands of people is right. Our store owners have

families and that also makes thousands of people. What about them?" Richards asked angrily.

"What about them?" Eric demanded. "The worst that could happen is they will lose a little money. We're talking about human lives!"

"I'm warning you, Summers, you too, Baumgarten – if word of this gets out there's going to be big trouble."

"Are you going to go along with Richards?" Harold demanded of the police chief.

"I have no other choice. I wish there was something I could do, but there isn't. I have to have concrete facts. This center was checked out thoroughly – if I were to send you a bill for the manpower you'd choke to death. The police department isn't for your personal use, you know. Richards is right. I'm sorry, Baumgarten."

"We're right back where we started from," Lex said angrily.

Heather drew Lex out in to the hall and whispered to him, "What if we call all the shop owners and ask them to come into the mall early tomorrow, say around eight? We'll ask them what they think. Perhaps they can bring some pressure to bear on the police. It's worth a try." She continued quietly, "After Richards goes home, of course. If you can get Noel over here, that will be five of us calling. It'll take us hours, but it might be worth it. At this point, with the storm and all, I don't think any of us should even attempt to go home."

"I agree. We'll go back to Baumgarten's office and work from there. Richards isn't going to hang around. He thinks he's won so he'll go home and crow a little. Look, here comes the cop and the captain. I want to hear what they have to say."

"The little girl is still alive, just barely," the captain reported. "The hospital said her picture was in the paper about a month ago and the parents were pleading for help. I'm not saying the Steinhart kid saw it and made up the story, but it is possible. The rest of the story checks out too."

The chief of police addressed himself to Dolph Richards, plainly ignoring the others. "That does it then. If there are any changes, if you get something more concrete, give me a call." His tone clearly indicated that there had better not be anything else. "Have a merry Christmas," he called over his shoulder.

Eleven

Harold stood on the dais of the large community room, flanked by Eric Summers and Felex Lassiter. Heather Andrews stood next to Lex.

The chief of the security rapped on the lectern for order. "First of all, let me say that we appreciate the fact that you braved the storm to get here so early. There was no other way this could have been handled. This meeting had to take place before the mall opens. Now, I want your attention and I want all of you to remain quiet while I'm speaking. When I'm finished, you can ask all the questions you want."

Quickly and concisely he ran through the events of the past several days. He ended with, "And the four of us standing here are in favor of closing the mall. But, as I said, the police were here and they, along with Mr. Richards, have refused to close Timberwoods."

"If this is some kind of joke . . ." Harry Walden said angrily, "I don't appreciate it and I'm sure the others agree. What kind of stunt is this?"

"Believe me, Mr Walden, this is not a stunt. We're trying to save your lives. When it comes right down to it, it's money against lives. That's why I called this meeting. If you, as a group, bring pressure to bear, Richards will have to give the order to close the center."

180

Pandemonium broke loose. The shop owners looked at each other, fear, anger and distrust on their faces. Fists were clenched and shaken in the air.

"Money! It always comes down to money!" Harold shouted. "Are your lives worth a few extra dollars? Think about your families! Think about all those innocent people who will be here. Think – I'm begging you!"

"We lost," Eric said angrily. "Just look at them. I told you, Baumgarten, the center stays open."

The chief of security banged on the lectern with his gavel. "All right, the decision was left to you. It's obvious what your answer is."

Harry Walden said harshly, "I'm leaving; the rest of you can do whatever you please. Right now I have to get ready for a sale!"

"If he leaves, the rest will follow," Lex whispered. "How can they be so stupid?"

"Money, that's how," Harold grumbled. "All they want to hear is the ring of their cash registers. Well, we tried," he said in defeat.

"Do you think any of them will carry the story to the outside?" Lex asked.

"No way! You've heard of lips being sealed? Well, this is the perfect example. You won't hear a word of this being mentioned. Not one word."

"We're back to waiting," Heather said softly, tears filling her wide blue eyes.

"It's just like in the story-books," Maria Andretti sighed happily from her narrow bed in the house across the highway in her room which looked down on the Timberwoods Mall. She reached for her little sketch pad and a piece of crayon. She made a few strokes then laid the pad back down. She was too tired to draw. Instead she would watch the busy men shoveling the snow outside the mall. If only she could go over there. Dr Tucker had said that if the outside temperature reached the forties, she could go in her wheelchair.

Maybe if she could manage to stay awake she might see it again – her miracle! What a great secret it was. She had been so excited that she'd thrown up, and then her mother had closed the drapes and told her to take a nap. This time, Maria vowed, she wouldn't get so excited. She would watch and wait. Sooner or later he would be back, she was sure of it. It must be some kind of special miracle that God was giving her because she was so sick. Mommy said that God did make miracles and this had to be one! No one else had seen Santa Claus on the roof of the center. If anyone had seen him her brothers and sisters would have told her about it.

She, little Maria Andretti, was the only one. The only one to see Santa Claus in the daytime. Everything was so wonderful. If the temperature would just get to the forties, then everything would be perfect.

"Hi, honey," Carol Andretti said cheerfully as she came into the frilly pink and white bedroom. "Did you sleep well? Have you been drawing?" she asked, her eyes going to the few crayon lines on the sketch pad.

"I started to and then I got tired. I've been watching the men working at the mall. I never saw so much snow, did you, Mommy?" Not waiting for a reply the six-year-old continued. "Is the temperature high enough, Mommy? Will today be the day?"

"I'm afraid not, sweetie. It's thirty-two degrees outside

and it's still snowing. You know what Dr Tucker said. We can't risk you catching cold."

"But Mommy . . ."

"No buts, little lady. A promise is a promise. I said I'd take you to the mall when the doctor said it was okay. Anyway, today is Sunday and Santa is resting. He'll be back tomorrow. Right now I want to know what you'd like for breakfast. How does a nice glass of eggnog sound? With some French toast?"

"I'm too tired, Mommy. I just want to lie here and watch all the people going into the mall."

A note of panic edged its way into Carol Andretti's voice. "You have to eat, sweetie. Remember what the doctor said? And the doctor's coming over today to see how you're doing." She swallowed hard past the lump in her throat. God, she was so young, so little. Why? "I'll make you some eggnog – at least it will go down easy.""

Lord, why were Maria's eyes so bright? She laid a practiced hand on the small forehead. The ominous statement of the doctor rang in her ears: "If she gets a cold or infection, it's all over. She has no strength, no stamina. Her body resistance is too low. I don't know what's keeping her alive." His tone had been kindly but facts were facts. Please, God, not now, not till she sees Christmas.

Charlie Roman snapped shut the jacket of his Santa Claus suit and threw his colored sack over his shoulders. When was he going to do it? He had to go back up on the roof to be certain that none of the equipment he had set up near the fresh-air duct had been disturbed. He had to be certain it hadn't been discovered. Should he go up now or wait until lunchtime? Should he take a chance and go on the roof in the Santa suit or should he change? Better to go now while it was still snowing. That way his footprints would be covered if someone else from the maintenance department went up there later. 'Now' he kept saying to himself as he worked his way down the mall and up the escalator to the promenade level. Down past the community room and up the ramp to the exit. Once the doors had closed behind him, he moved more quickly.

"Dammit," he muttered as he walked over to the fresh-air duct. How was he going to explain if anyone asked why his suit was wet? And his shoes too. Someone was sure to notice. He would have to go into the bathroom and try to dry off.

Satisfied that his handiwork was untouched and the freshly painted bright red cylinder was just as he had left it, Charlie stood erect and picked up the sack full of coloring books and candy canes. Suddenly he realized that he could be seen from the highway. Timberwoods Mall had been erected in a gully and the old highway looked down upon it. This fact gave Charlie quite a jolt; then it seemed humorous. Dressed in his Santa suit he would just be mistaken for part of a publicity stunt for Timberwoods. He was so relieved he waved his arms and laughed. "Ho! Ho! Ho!" he roared, just as a rooftop Santa should.

Maria Andretti raised a frail arm and waved wildly. It was her own special miracle. He had seen her and waved to her! Her pale little face flushed, her eyes were bright and sparkling. He was her own special miracle.

Angela had left Amy Summers with a brief wave, promising to get back as soon as possible and help her. It was going to be a long cold walk to Timberwoods Mall to pick up her car. But with any luck Charlie would be working and she would be able to apologize for leaving without telling him. She'd decided to tell him that Mrs Summers had needed her. It hadn't been the reason she had left in the first place, of course, but it was the reason she'd stayed away so long, and the reason she was going back. Angela like Amy Summers. Amy made her feel needed and useful.

She would tell Charlie that she'd tried to call him – twice – that she'd let the phone ring and ring. And she would scold him for not having an answering machine to take messages. Everybody had an answering machine these days. Everybody! She hoped he would believe her, and if he was mad at her that he would forgive her. Charlie meant a lot to her in a funny kind of way and she didn't want him mad at her.

Her search for Charlie in Timberwoods led up one alley and down another. The photographer and elves said he was on a break. An over-extended break, they complained. She waited a half-hour and when he still hadn't returned left a hasty message with the photographer. "Tell him I've been trying to call him, that I need to talk to him."

"Yeah, sure, I'll tell him," the photographer said, then waved her away when a customer approached. Something told Angela that her message would never reach Charlie, but what else could she do? She had to leave. Mrs Summers was waiting for her; she couldn't hang around forever waiting for him to get back from wherever he was.

A hour later Angela managed to find her Porsche in the crowded parking lot. An old beat-up Volkswagen stopped within a few feet of her car. The door opened then closed and the car drove off. What was going on, she wondered. Looking down she saw three small round bundles of fur shivering in the snow. She opened her car door and ran over to them. Quickly she scooped up the shivering puppies, cursing long and loud. "Slime dog!" she screamed. "Nothing but slimy slime dog!" she yelled to the retreating VW.

Back in her warm car she turned on the overhead light and stared down at the tiny balls of fur. My God, they were so small. And that awful man left them to die. "You poor little babies," she said to the grunting pups. She cuddled them to her, crooning soft words of comfort. "He just left you to die. How could he? Poor babies. I won't let you die. I'll help you, I'll see that you're taken care of. I'll bet you're hungry."

Cuddling the puppies beneath her coat she went back into the mall and headed straight for the pet shop to ask the owner how to feed them. On her way back out she looked to see if Charlie had come back yet. If he was mad at her the puppies would help soften him up. Maybe he would even let her keep them at his house until they were old enough to be given away. Maybe he would want one.

But Charlie still wasn't there. The photographer was beginning to look anxious.

Disappointed, Angela left the mall for the second time that afternoon. She slipped the Porsche into gear, drove out of the parking lot and headed for the Summers' home.

Her arms full of squirming puppies, Angela managed to find the doorbell and hit it with her elbow.

"Who is it?"

"Angela, Mrs Summers." She heard the chain being removed and the door opened. "Surprise!" Angela laughed as she held open her coat.

"Where . . . how . . . whose are they?" Amy was delighted.

"Some idiot just dumped them out in the Timberwoods Mall parking lot. I couldn't leave them there to die, so I brought them here. I didn't know where else to take them. I bought them some milk replacement. I don't think they're old enough to eat solid food by themselves. Look how tiny they are."

"I'm looking, I'm looking, and I think you're right. How could somebody do such a thing? Poor precious little puppies," Amy said, cuddling one of the tiny bundles to her cheek. "They sound hungry. We'd better fix them some of that milk you brought."

"But what if they're too little to drink it out of a bowl?"

"They probably are, but I have all kinds of baby bottles and things. Let's go into the kitchen and see what we can do. I'll make the bottles and you go into the garage and get an empty box. Then get a towel from the bathroom, a nice fluffy one, and we'll put them in by the fireplace where it's warm."

When Angela came back into the kitchen, Amy said, "I think I'll mix some of this baby pabulum in the milk and make a bigger hole in the nipple. What do you think?"

"Sounds good to me." Angela grinned as she folded the fluffy bath towel. "I wonder if they'll like this color; burnt orange, isn't it?" She giggled.

"All ready," Amy called, her hands full of baby bottles. "You can carry the box and we'll feed them one at a time. Wouldn't you know it, three females," she said as she examined the puppies. "You were right, Angela, they could never eat on their own. Look, their eyes are barely open."

Angela and Amy each took a puppy and put a bottle to its greedy mouth. Angela was suddenly quiet and intent.

"Angela, do you want to talk about it?" Amy asked after a while.

"No."

"Why?"

"Because."

"That's no answer. Because. What kind of answer is that? Didn't they teach you any better than that in school?"

"Sure," Angela said as she put down one puppy and picked up another. "Do you suppose you have to burp them?"

"Burp them? Lord, I don't know. How do you burp a puppy?"

"I guess you rub its tummy. That's what you do with babies. I learned that in health class," Angela said proudly.

"Wrong. So much for health class. You pat their backs."

"Well, I was close," Angela laughed.

At one-thirty in the afternoon the phone on Eric Summers's desk buzzed.

"Summers here."

"Eric, Noel. Listen, I want to try hypnotism on Angela."

"Okay, Noel. She's with Amy now. But I won't have you doing it at my house. It's too much for Amy."

"I need somewhere quiet."

"You'll get it. I have an idea. I can't leave the mall but I'll send Lassiter. Maybe you can use Heather Andrews's apartment.

*   *   *

{off}

Heather opened the door of her apartment to admit Noel, Lex and Angela. She smiled at Angela. "You look frozen. Sit down and I'll get some nice hot coffee. What about you guys? Would you like some coffee or something stronger?"

"Coffee," the two men said simultaneously.

Heather gathered their coats and scarves and hung them in the hall closet. "Be right back."

Angela perched on the edge of a chair as if poised for flight. "Are you sure this is the right thing for me to be doing?" she asked Noel. "I really don't want to see that again. It was so terrible, and what if I see any of you and I say it while I'm under?"

"Then you'll say it, it's as simple as that. We have to do it, Angela. There may be some important details that are hidden in your subconscious. You do understand, don't you?"

"Sure," she answered, taking a cup from Heather's hands. "I really appreciate what you're trying to do, but why can't I convince you that there isn't anything you can do about it? The things I see in my mind's eye – they always happen. There's no stopping them."

"Maybe yes, maybe no. We have to try, Angela. Isn't it better to try than to do nothing at all?"

Angela nodded as she sipped the steaming coffee. "Why don't we just get on with it, get it over with?" she asked fearfully.

"Any time you're ready," Noel said, setting down his coffee cup. "Stretch out on the couch and close your eyes."

Angela did as she was told. Noel watched her and began to speak to her, his voice calm and soothing. "I want you to trust me, Angela. Nothing will hurt you. I'm your friend. Now, just close your eyes and relax. I want you to listen to my voice. You want to listen to my voice. You can hear me. You trust me. You know I'm your friend."

Angela listened to Noel's directions. She visibly relaxed. Soon she felt warm and drowsy . . . so sleepy . . . so safe . . .

"Angela, you know I'm Noel Dayton. Can you hear me?"

"Yes, I hear you."

"You will listen to me very carefully, Angela, and answer me truthfully at all times. You're asleep, Angela, sound asleep, but you can hear me speaking to you. You told me once that you first started having these visions when you were twelve years old. Is that true?"

"Yes. I saw a puppy get killed. I was very frightened. I thought it was a dream."

"After that you saw many things, is that true?"

"Yes."

"How did that make you feel, Angela?"

"Frightened. I told my parents and they took me to doctors."

"That's fine, Angela. Remember now, you're sound asleep but you can hear me. I want to talk to you about one of your latest visions, the one about the Timberwoods shopping mall. You will remember how you had the vision and tell me all about it. Can you do that, Angela?"

"Yes."

"We're going back in time now to the day you had the vision. You're asleep, Angela, but you can hear my voice. It is now the morning of the day you had the vision. It is time to wake up. You have been asleep all night and now it is morning. When you open your eyes you will see the bright light and you will tell me what you see. When I tell you to open your eyes, you will do so."

"Yes," Angela whispered, the fear and strain showing on her pinched narrow features.

"The morning is here, Angela. Open your eyes and see your vision."

"Oh, no, not again!" Angela screamed. "I don't want to look. Don't make me look!" Tears gathered in her eyes as she continued to fight to keep her eyes closed. "Please, please, I don't want to see!"

"You want to tell me what you see, Angela. After you tell me, you can go to sleep and forget it. What do you see?"

"Red. Everything is red. All the Christmas colors. All that red. Blood."

"Are you sure it's blood, Angela?"

"Red. Too much red. I can't see anything but red. Make it go away," she begged.

"Not yet, Angela, you must tell me more."

"There's too much blood. Too much red." Angela sobbed. "I don't know what it is. I can't be in two places at one time. Some man . . . he's bending over. The red . . . I don't know what he's doing! He's afraid . . . his hands are shaking. Too much red, I can't see his face. He's going to kill everyone. He's sick. The blood's in his way!"

"Can you tell me more about him?"

"No . . . everything is in a red haze. He's holding something green, it's big and round. It's soft, there's something in it. He's sick, he keeps wiping his face. He's so afraid."

"What is he afraid of, Angela?"

"I don't know. He has no strength in his hands . . . it won't move."

"What won't move?"

"His hand, he's trying to squeeze something in his hand. He's cold, the wind is blowing all around him. White and red!" Angela's voice was a mere whisper, beads of perspiration broke out on her forehead. "He's cursing. He's angry. Today, he's saying, it has to be today. This has to work! He wipes his forehead, red is going away. No, it's back!"

"Angela, what day is this happening?"

"Today. I have to die today!"

"Angela, what day is it?" Noel asked again, this time more firmly.

"I don't know what day it is . . . the day he has to die. He's very angry . . . cursing . . . oh, he fixed it . . . now he's happy, the red is back."

"Think about the day and time, Angela. Did you go into the mall at all?"

"Yes, I'm in the mall now. Everyone is shopping. Christmas carols are playing. I have to leave now; I have to go outside. Something is going to happen. I have to warn people not to go in there."

"Why do you have to go outside?"

"To warn people. They won't listen but I have to try. He wants everyone to die with him."

"Where is he now, Angela? Do you know?"

"He's walking around the mall. I can't see him but I know that's what he's doing. I can feel him thinking. It's almost time for the explosion."

"Explosion?" Noel queried. "Is it a bomb?"

"It just blows up. It's going to blow up. See all those little boys in their uniforms? They have to leave. The little skinny one who can't see – you have to make him leave! He's going to get lost! It's almost time!"

"The day, Angela, what day is it?" Noel asked, trying to keep his voice calm. Angela was near hysteria now, but he couldn't bring her out of the hypnotic state until she gave them the details they needed. "What day is it, Angela?"

Angela squirmed on the sofa as though hot brands were scorching her. "I have to go outside. It's time. Why are Mr Summers and Mr Lassiter running like that? I'm running too. Fast. Hurry . . . I'm outside in the parking lot . . ." She screamed, pressing her hands against her skull. "Oh, my God! Run! Run! Run as fast as you can . . . another one . . . another one . . . screams . . . make it go away!" Angela screamed again.

Noel, watching her, was deeply troubled. Had he gone too far? The emotions Angela was suffering were so intense that he actually began to be afraid that they were too much for her to handle. He grabbed her wrist and checked her pulse. It was racing far too rapidly for comfort. The girl's lips held a blue tinge, her eyelids fluttered madly, her skin was cold to the touch – all signs of deep shock. Did he dare to continue with this? If he pressed her too far the result could be her death. Noel's voice was unsteady. "Angela, you may wake up now. Come back to the present, Angela."

"No! No!" Angela's voice was a low moan coming from deep within her. She thrust out her hands and shielded herself against a sight that only she could see. "The buildings! They're crumbling! Fire!"

Noel's blood ran cold. Lex was sitting on the edge of

his chair, the color gone from his face, leaving a ghostly pallor. Heather was gripping the door frame, her eyes bright with terror as she watched Angela.

"Angela," Noel called, "Angela, you are asleep now. You are deeply asleep. You cannot see anything but darkness. You are not frightened any longer; you feel peaceful. When I snap my fingers, you will awaken. Sleep, Angela."

Noel's face was bathed in a cold sweat. Putting his hand close to Angela's ear, he snapped his fingers.

Heather ran to the bathroom and was violently sick.

Noel moved the switch on the recorder to off.

Twelve

E ric Summers sat down, coffee cup in hand, his long
legs stretched out. His dark eyes were brooding as he
sipped the bitter leftover brew. "Do you feel it?" he asked,
"The doom, the deathlike air? I know that sounds corny
as hell, but that's what I feel. And those damn Christmas
carols are about to drive me out of my mind! Musak has
got to be the scourge of mankind."

"I know what you mean; this must be how terminally ill
patients feel," Harold commiserated.

"If there was only something we could do. Anything,
anything at all. The kid is standing outside the mall and
telling people not to shop here. I didn't tell her to go
home. If Richards finds out he's going to have the police
pick her up. Christ, at least she's doing something. Say,
Baumgarten, you don't want a dog, do you?"

"No. What's the Steinhart kid saying?"

"Who the hell knows? The truth of the matter is, I don't
want to know. Mike called me when the mall opened. I've
got him stationed at number seven and she's doing her
thing right there. I told him to leave her alone. People
aren't listening to her anyway, they're just calling her
names. She must be frozen stiff by now. She's been out
there for three hours and it's eighteen degrees. She's trying

though – God, she's trying. And what the hell am I doing? Nothing! Not a goddamned thing."

"Well, I know how she feels. I did something this morning and it got me nowhere."

Eric's ears pricked up; Harold had his full attention.

"I called the newspapers, spoke to the editors and in some cases – when I could get through – to the owners, or board executives. I told them what was going on around here and begged them to print it. Each time their answer was an unequivocal no. Finally, in desperation, I said I was going to take out an ad warning people not to shop here. They said they wouldn't print it. They have too much to lose. All the shops here buy advertising space in their papers. No way are they going to take a chance on losing the good will of the shop owners. I'll tell you, Eric, I even thought of having handbills printed and handing them out. But then I reconsidered. I know when someone hands me a handbill I don't pay any attention to it. I always think it's from some subversive group with an ax to grind," Harold said quietly. "Now, how do you think I feel?"

"What are Lex and Heather doing?"

"I saw them down in personnel. Lex wanted to go through the list of employees at the center. Heather was going to talk to some of the shop owners about their personnel. I haven't seen either of them in the past hour. Lex did say that it was an all-day job. He's taken two of the girls from the administration office to help him. If this center is still standing after the new year, it will take us a month to catch up on paperwork."

In a warm two-story colonial home about two miles from the Timberwoods Shopping Mall, the spirit of Christmas was evidenced by the aroma of cookies baking and children decorating a tree. The wall phone in the kitchen jangled and an attractive brunette left her baking to answer it.

"Cheryl, this is Mary," said the voice at the other end of the line. "Listen, I hate to do this but I can't go with you to the mall tonight. I have to take Mack to the airport and it'll be too late when I get back."

"No problem. I want to take Sirena to the vet." Cheryl's glance fell on the tiny Yorkshire terrier that had been a birthday present from her husband Al. "She's having trouble with one of her ears. When do you want to go then?"

"How about Thursday? I can make it for the whole day and into the evening if you want. My mother is taking the kids after school. Why don't you send your kids over there too? Mom is filling stockings and making popcorn balls for the orphanage. The kids can all help. She'll give them dinner and we can pick them up when we finish shopping. What do you think?"

Cheryl smiled. Mary was a live wire. A small compact woman with bright red hair and a perpetual elfin quality. Aside from being quick and sharp, she had a heart of gold. "Great idea," she said. "That'll give me an extra day to see if I can wrangle some money out of the 'Grinch.' Is this lunch and dinner?"

"Let's put it this way – I have twenty dollars cash. I have to buy a gallon of milk and a loaf of bread. What's left over is for lunch and dinner. I was planning on using my charge cards."

"You and me both. Besides, it's the only way to fly. By the way, where are we going?"

"What do you mean, where are we going? We only have one place to shop – Timberwoods."

"That place makes me nervous. They had a bomb scare over there the other day."

"They always have bomb threats," Mary said airily. "Who'd want to bomb that place? Hell, I haven't figured out how to get in and out of there yet. Every time I go over there I get lost and have to walk five miles to my car."

"That's just it," Cheryl complained. "I can never find the exits either. That place gives me the creeps. Too big and too many people."

"You've got two choices – Timberwoods or Wal Mart's out on the highway."

"Okay, but I'm just staying on one level and I'm making sure I know where all the exits are."

"You're nuts," Mary complained. "My charge cards are for all over. How can we stay on one level?"

"Use your Visa then you can shop anywhere," Cheryl answered snidely.

"My Visa is up to its limit," Mary said. "But I haven't used the ones for the individual stores yet. I must have five or six of those. You can never have enough charge cards!" she laughed.

"I wish you'd try telling that to the 'Grinch.' When I tell him somehow it loses something in the translation."

"You worry too much. We have the whole year to pay it off. Think of the fun we're going to have. No kids, lunch and dinner out, and a dozen or more charge cards between us. Do you have any cash?" Mary asked craftily.

"Nope. You'll have to buy me lunch. I'll skip dinner."

"You're lying, Cheryl, I can tell. You think you're going to sidetrack me with all that talk about bombs. How much money do you have?"

"Okay, so I won fifty dollars at bingo."

"And you didn't tell me?" Mary screeched. "You're buying lunch and dinner."

"I knew I'd never be able to keep it to myself," Cheryl grumbled.

"We'll buy the Jordan Almonds for Susie's wedding favors with my money and we'll eat with yours. We'll even buy some of that peanut-butter fudge you like so much. You know how hungry you get when we're traipsing around all day."

"Just what I need," Cheryl mourned, looking down at her more than ample figure. "Seven dollars worth of Jordan Almonds and peanut-butter fudge."

"Shall we get spiffed up or go in our regular clothes?"

"If you mean those worn-out denims and Reeboks you wear, we'd better get dressed up. If I'm taking you to lunch and dinner I don't want you to look tacky," Cheryl said tartly.

"Smartass. Fifty bucks, huh?"

"So, all right, it was seventy-five. I spent twenty-five dollars."

"I knew it, I knew it!" Mary yelled. "Nobody wins just fifty bucks at bingo. I'm glad you told me. You're all heart, Cheryl."

"I hope I still feel that way after I've fed you. See you Thursday."

Angela happened to see Charlie as he was heading for the rest rooms and stopped him. "Charlie! Where have you been? Why haven't you answered your phone? I've been calling you for days. I wanted to –"

"Get out of my way!" Charlie cut her off rudely and pushed past her.

"No, Charlie, wait." Angela grabbed his arm and held onto him. "At least give me a chance to explain what happened. Once you hear you won't be mad at me anymore."

"Nothing you can say will change my mind." Charlie stared at her with cold malevolent eyes. "You ruined everything, Angela. We were going to have such a wonderful Christmas and you blew it. To hell with you. You're just like all the rest of them. I never should have taken you in in the first place. You're a user."

"I'll follow you into the men's room if I have to, Charlie," Angela threatened. "So you'd better listen to me. Besides, there's something even more important that I have to tell you – this mall, it's gonna blow up. I don't know when. I just know it's gonna blow. You have to get out of here, Charlie. Please, I beg you. You've got to get out!"

He wasn't listening to her, she could tell. He was too angry to hear a word she was saying. When she met his gaze she was taken aback. She had never seen such hatred in a person's eyes in her life. Short of getting down on her knees and begging him, there was nothing else she could do. His face beneath the beard was grayish white as he stared at her. His beady eyes hadn't blinked once and that frightened her more than his stony silence.

Like a wounded dog Angela whimpered then walked away. What was the use? He was too angry to listen to anything she had to say, even when what she was saying was meant to save his life. She pushed through the double-door exit and went back outside.

She stamped her feet and rubbed her numb hands together as she tried to keep warm. What was she doing here anyway? People were avoiding her as if she had the plague. The few people she had managed to talk to had laughed at her. One of them had called her a coke-head. Well, what had she expected? You couldn't just go up to people and tell them not to go into the mall without giving them a reason why. She could just hear herself saying: "Don't go in there, it's going to blow up." Then they would really think she was crazy. All she could do was tell them that something was going to happen. Secretly she was surprised that the police hadn't come for her. She knew the security guard had reported her after one of the customers had pointed her out to him.

There was a lull in pedestrian traffic and Angela huddled up against the cold. She didn't know which was worse – the freezing temperatures or the cold she had felt inside ever since that afternoon when Dr Dayton had hypnotized her. When Dr Dayton had played the tape of her own voice back to her, she had realized that if she was ever going to do anything she had to do it now! Believing wasn't enough. Somebody had to do something! Starting with herself. She shivered violently. And if that wasn't bad enough, now she had Charlie to worry about.

"Angela, honey, what are you doing out here in the cold? Do you know it's only eighteen degrees?" Murray Steinhart put his arm around his daughter's shoulders.

Angela stiffened at the physical contact and tried to draw away from him. Run, her mind screamed, run!

"Daddy, what are you doing here? Look, I have to go now," she said, jerking her arm away from him.

"Angela, please, I'm not here to make you come with me. I just want to talk to you. Let's get some coffee. My word on it, no one is going to make you do anything you don't want to do. All I want is to talk to you. I know it's a little late . . . it's a lot late . . . but I'm here now to help you any way I can."

"Oh, Daddy, I'm so glad," Angela cried, wrapping her arms around her father, tears streaming down her thin cheeks. "I'm so glad!"

"Me too, Angel," Murray said huskily. "Let's go get that coffee before we both freeze to death."

Angela, the coffee mug cupped in her cold hands, stared at her father. "I don't know what to do. I did everything I could think of. I even let Dr Dayton hypnotize me. He said it helped, but I don't know how. They won't close the mall, Daddy. I keep coming back here, hoping I'll think of some way to stop it but . . ."

"I know," Murray said wearily, rubbing his eyes, "I understand. I'll stay here with you. Your mother went . . ."

"Don't, Daddy, I understand, I really do. I don't want to talk about Mother. I'm so glad you're here. Boy, you don't know how glad." She smiled.

"You know something, Angel, I'm glad too." Murray sounded surprised, even to himself. "Real glad," he repeated softly.

"Whatever happens you can't blame yourself. You know that don't you?"

"I know."

"What you said a moment ago, about coming back here. Is it the mall itself that draws you or someone in the mall?"

Angela replaced the coffee mug on the table. "What did you just say, Daddy?" Her pinched narrow face looked stunned.

"I said," he repeated quietly, "is it the mall or someone in the mall that keeps bringing you back here?"

She stared at him, thinking. "That's it," she said suddenly. "It isn't the mall." She slapped her forehead. "God, how could I have been so stupid? Of course. It's someone I know here that's responsible. That's why it can't be stopped and why the vision is going to come true. It's a person."

Murray felt real fear for the first time in his life, gut fear. Somehow he had always believed in his daughter's visions even though he had never let the belief surface until now. "Okay," he said more calmly than he felt. "We've established that it's a person. Let's run down your list. Who do you know that you feel is capable of blowing up a mall and killing thousands of innocent people?"

"Daddy, that's heavy stuff. I know a lot of kids from school who work here. There are a lot of freaks and a lot of straights. I know a few of the mall personnel, some of the security people, the Santa Claus and a few of his elves. There's no way I could pick out anyone and say that he or she is the one."

"I'll tell you what," Murray said. "You come back to my motel with me and we'll spend the evening running down your list, one by one, together. Maybe we'll come up with something. How's that sound?"

"Good," Angela said.

*   *   *

Maria Andretti woke from her nap, her face more flushed than usual. Feebly she tried to kick off the covers. She wanted a drink, she felt too hot, like in the summertime when you lie on the beach and there's no shade. "Mommy," she cried weakly.

"I'm right here, honey. I'll get you some juice and then you rest."

"Will you open the drapes? I want to look out. Is it nice today?"

"Very nice, but very cold."

"Mommy, you promised to . . ."

"I know, honey, and we're watching the temperature very closely. As soon as it's warmer, we're going to take you over to the mall. But first we have to make this pesky fever of yours go away. I'm going to rub you down with some alcohol as soon as you've drunk this juice. That'll make you feel better."

Maria gazed out of the window across the highway to the mall. She couldn't see very well. Yesterday she had been able to see right to the roof of the center. She blinked and rubbed her eyes. She still couldn't see across the highway. Maybe it was the fever. After Mommy rubbed her down with alcohol, she might be able to see better. When was she going to get well? When would the doctor let her get out of bed so she could play with her brothers and sisters? When was she going to be able to go back to school? She missed all her friends and the teacher.

"I just have to get better, I have to!" Maria cried, burying her face in her pillow.

Charlie Roman walked nervously up and down the mall.

From time to time he handed out a candy cane and a coloring book. Every so often he uttered a hoarse "Ho! Ho! Ho!"

He couldn't remember ever being so furious in his whole life. Did she have to come to the mall? Why did she have to pour salt into his open wound? Wasn't her blatant rejection of him enough? Was this the way she got her kicks? And to think he'd ever thought she was a special person. She wasn't like the rest of them, she was worse. She had used him and then betrayed him. It struck him as almost funny that she'd warned him about the mall blowing up. What would she think if she knew he was the one who was going to make it blow? He'd show her. He'd show them all.

He had to get back up on the roof. He had to! The maintenance men had been up there since early this morning, clearing away the snow. Tomorrow the weatherman predicted that the temperature would be going up and Miguel, one of the maintenance crew, had told Charlie they were going to continue with the patching work. If he could find the missing propane tank, that was.

Perspiration beaded Charlie's forehead when he thought of what could happen if Miguel put two and two together. Miguel had complained to Dolph Richards about the missing propane tank, but the manager had ignored him. Now, with the predicted rise in temperature, the roof would start leaking again and it would be all systems go. Someone was sure to mention the missing tank then. Charlie had heard Miguel say that the crew was waiting for the delivery man to come around to check how many tanks he had delivered. Because of the cold the demand for bottled gas had increased and the supplier was two

205

days behind schedule. Many houses in the outlying areas needed propane for their stoves and the delivery man had stated that his residential customers came first. Besides, he was insisting that he had delivered four tanks, not the three that remained. According to Miguel, he refused to consider there might have been a mistake.

Charlie had heard that there wasn't that much snow on the roof; the snow blowers had made quick work of it. So what was taking so long? Surely they couldn't be working up there on anything else. Maybe he had missed them somehow. If only he could think of a way to get one of the crew down here, or manufacture a reason for him to go up.

Charlie's body was bathed in sweat beneath the heavy red velvet suit, and the Santa beard was almost more than he could bear. He pressed the tiny button on his digital watch and noted the time. Conceivably he could take a break, but where and what would he do?

"Charlie, have you seen Ramon?" Harry Walden asked, tapping him on the shoulder. "It's time to change the day on the billboard outside my store and he isn't here. Do you think that on your way downstairs you could tell him to come up? I've called up there but they're not answering."

"Sure thing, Mr Walden," Charlie said hoarsely.

"That's some cold you have there, Charlie. I didn't think Santa ever got sick," the shop owner joked.

"Sounds worse than it is," Charlie said agreeably. "I'll get Ramon for you."

How could he be so lucky? Quickly the big man walked to the escalator and rounded the corner. His breathing was ragged as he bolted through the exit door leading to the roof. He could pretend that he didn't know where

Ramon was and that would explain why he was up on the roof.

Halfway up the long flight of stairs he had to stop and rest. Instead of feeling better from all the medicine he was taking, he was feeling worse. His chest felt as though it were on fire, and he could barely swallow.

He opened the door leading to the roof, stuck his head out and decided to go all the way. He was already sick – what did the cold matter?

"Miguel, is Ramon up here?"

"Yeah, he's over there on the snow blower."

"Mr Walden wants him to change the sign."

"Why don't you do it, Charlie? I need Ramon up here. And it's almost quitting time. On second thoughts, forget it," Miguel said, eyeing Charlie. "You look awful. You'd never make it up the ladder."

Miguel waved to the short slender man riding the chugging snow blower. Ramon shut off the machine and walked gingerly over the rooftop to his boss.

"Old man Walden wants the sign changed."

"All right, I do it now. I work the day shift tomorrow, remember?'

"Si. Mañana. Hey, Charlie," Miguel called, "did you steal one of my propane tanks?"

Charlie shook his head, his stomach churning.

"Hey, don't look so scared. I'm only kidding. Some son of a bitch stole my tank. I report and nothing. Nobody do anything. Who pay for the tank when the time comes to take it back? Not Miguel. They think because I'm Puerto Rican I'm stupid. But Miguel no pay."

"They can't blame you, Miguel," Charlie croaked. "It's probably just some mix-up. Nobody in this place knows what anyone else is doing. It doesn't pay to complain. When you complain you lose your job." That should give him something to think about.

"Si. You right, Charlie. Let the bosses do what they want. I come, I do my work, and I go home. No more I tell them anything. They pay for the propane tank."

"Forget it," Charlie muttered. "Nobody will even remember. See you later."

"Si, Charlie. Later. You take whiskey for that cold."

"Sure, sure," Charlie agreed, going down the stairs. Good, everything was still okay.

Maria Andretti sat propped up in her bed, fluffy pillows behind her thin wasted body. She still couldn't see across the highway. She didn't feel so hot any more but she still didn't feel good. It was such an effort to move.

"Mommy, will you look across at the roof. Do you see anything?"

"There are some men working, that's all. Why?"

"Are you sure there isn't someone else?"

"No, honey, just some men."

"They're getting the roof ready," Maria said weakly.

"Getting it ready for what?"

"For Santa. It's my miracle."

"Maria, what are you talking about?" Carol Andretti asked nervously.

"I was going to surprise you when we went to the mall and Santa recognized me. He waved to me from the roof. He's getting ready. Don't you see? That's why I have to go to the shopping center. It's my miracle. He's waiting for me. I saw him three times! Mommy, are you sure he isn't on the roof? When I wish very hard, he comes. Look, Mommy, see if he's there."

Carol Andretti swallowed hard and looked across the highway at the Timberwoods roof. Oh, God! There he was! Her eyes widened. "He's there, honey, I see him! Look," she said, lifting the frail child. "Can you see him?"

"No, I can't see that far. Yesterday, I could see the roof, but my eyes are too tired today."

"Shhh. He knows you can't see him. But he knows that I'm here and that I'll tell you he waved."

"Isn't it a wonderful miracle? Mommy, when will I be better?"

She found it difficult to swallow and her eyes burned, but Carol forced herself to answer. "Soon, baby, soon."

"Mommy, can we go tomorrow? You promised. I want to go tomorrow."

Carol held the frail figure close. "Yes, darling, tomorrow. I promise. But now I have something to tell you. Do you think you can be very brave?"

"Uh huh."

"After . . . after we take you to the center we have to take you back to the hospital. You may have to stay there over Christmas."

"Okay, Mommy." Little Maria's voice was tremulous. "As long as you take me to the center first. You won't break your promise, will you?"

"No, baby, I won't break my promise. We'll go late in the afternoon and then go to the hospital. I'm going to get you some more juice and I want you to drink it all and then have a nice nap. You have to be strong to go to the center."

"Okay, Mommy. Oh, thank you, thank you. Mommy, you really did see him, didn't you?"

209

"Oh, honey, I wouldn't lie to you. Yes, I saw him."

By the time Carol got back with the juice Maria was asleep, her dark lashes casting shadows on her pale cheeks. How many days – one, two, three? Could she make it? She had to make it! There wasn't any other way. You had to go on. Somehow you managed to survive, to endure. Please, God, help us, Carol cried silently.

Amy Summers laid the puppy back in its box and was about to scoop out the other when the phone rang.

"Mrs Summers?"

"Speaking."

"This is Bill Simmons from Simmons Leather Shop at Timberwoods Mall. The briefcase you ordered came in this morning. I sent it over to be engraved and you can pick it up tomorrow any time after five o'clock."

"That's fine. You couldn't have it ready sooner, could you?"

"I tried, Mrs Summers, but they have so much work I'm lucky I got it squeezed in at all."

"There's no problem, I can manage. But I might not be there until after six. Thanks for calling."

Eric would be so surprised. It was a beautiful attaché case. If she could just get out of the doctor's office in time to pick it up.

When the phone rang, Dolph Richards picked it up and spoke quietly. "Richards here. Yes, put her through." He gave an audible sigh as he listened, pencil in hand. "Yes, Mrs Andretti, how can I help you?"

"Mr Richards, I don't know how to say this, but . . . What I mean is, I want to thank someone at your center for something. I live across the highway from Timberwoods and I have a little girl dying of leukemia. She can see the center from her room and she was absolutely thrilled to d— . . . overjoyed when she saw the Santa Claus on your roof waving to her. It seems he has done it for the past three days. I know it isn't important to you but it was to Maria. I want to thank you. I also want to ask you when would be a good time to bring Maria to the center tomorrow. What time do you think it will be least crowded? I have to bring her in a wheelchair. She's being admitted to hospital immediately after the visit. If it isn't too much trouble, do you think you could have the Santa seek her out? I can't tell you how much I'd appreciate it."

Dolph Richards frowned. What was she talking about? What Santa on the roof? She must be saying it for her daughter's benefit, he decided. "Between six and seven would be best, Mrs Andretti. I'll see to it that the Santa is available to you. Come in the employees' entrance and go straight to the Toyland display. I'll take care of the rest. You did say your little girl's name is Maria?"

"Yes. Thank you, Mr Richards, thank you," Carol Andretti said humbly.

"No need to thank me, Mrs Andretti, this is why I'm here," Richards said magnanimously.

Thirteen

Charlie Roman, his body one massive ache, parted the curtains and looked outside – the last time he would look out of this window at the world. Today was the end of everything, for him and for everyone at the center. His life would cease, all the hurt, the anger, the loneliness.

It was going to snow again. The sky was swollen and gray, the air cold and damp. He could feel it seeping in between the window frame and the sill. Shivering, he put on his robe and slippers and staggered down-stairs.

His brain was fuzzy, he couldn't get it together this morning. "Damn it," he muttered, "I have to be sharp today or I could ruin everything." Coffee laced with brandy might help.

It took several applications of nasal spray before he could breathe through his nose. His chest felt as though a great weight was leaning on it and his back ached too. His vision seemed to be blurred. He felt his forehead with the inside of his wrist the way his mother used to do when he was little. He was shocked at how hot and dry it felt. It really didn't matter whether he was sick or not, he persuaded himself. The only thing that mattered was getting up to the roof during his lunch hour and squeezing the clay around the piano wire. That was the only thing that mattered. And then . . .

Charlie prayed for snow while he measured instant coffee into his cup. If it snowed then Miguel and his men wouldn't be out working on the roof.

He thought of Angela and her percolator coffee. In spite of hating her for running out on him, for making a fool out of him, he missed her. The few days they'd had together had been the happiest days of his life. His hands trembled so violently he had to grasp the heavy mug with both hands. He gulped the fiery liquid and swallowed, oblivious to the pain as it scorched his swollen throat.

Even after he'd finished his coffee he didn't feel much better. Should he have another cup? No, it wouldn't make any difference. "Ho! Ho! Ho!" he croaked. His eyes began to tear and he sneezed four times in rapid succession. He would have to keep quiet when he got to the center, stop himself from sneezing. If anyone heard him they might send him home. And he couldn't afford for that to happen. It had to be today! Everything was set for today.

Felex Lassiter held the door open for Charlie Roman. "How goes it, Roman?" he asked, not really caring about the answer.

Charlie shrugged, not wanting to open his mouth.

"I think there are more kids in this mall than ever before. What do you think, Charlie?"

Charlie shrugged again. Christ, wasn't the man ever going to shut up? If Lassiter kept it up, he'd have to say something sooner or later.

Lex looked at Charlie suspiciously. "You got a bug up your ass about something, Roman? No one in this mall likes the extra work during the holidays. But we have to do it and we do it courteously. Courteously, do you have that? When someone speaks to you, you answer him. I'd better not get any reports from the mothers of these children about your sullenness. You got that, Roman?"

Oh, Jesus, Charlie thought. "I'm sorry, I didn't mean to be rude. It's just that I have this cold," he said hoarsely, "and I've been saving my voice."

Lex turned and looked into the man's face. "Christ, you do look sick as hell. What are you doing here? Report to the clinic before you go on duty. If you have a fever, then go home. Max can fill in for you."

Oh, Jesus, Charlie groaned inwardly. "I'm all right. I sound a lot worse than I feel."

"Maybe so, but all I need is one complaint from a mother that our Santa Claus is spreading germs and that's it. I don't have to tell you what some of these women are like. You go to the clinic right now and I'll check in later to see how you are."

Oh, Jesus, Jesus, now what was he going to do? He couldn't go home, he just couldn't. He had to get up on the roof – how could he do that if he was sent home? He would report to the nurse, get some aspirin and give her some cock and bull story that would get him off the hook. Old Jessie was a sucker for a good sob story. She'd cover for him, Charlie was sure of it. He'd stay out of Lassiter's way at least until after lunch. And if worse came to worse and he was sent home, he could always come back as a shopper. They couldn't throw him out for shopping.

Just hang in there till after lunch, he told himself, and it will be okay. Just two and a half hours.

He paused when he saw a familiar figure walking by.

Holy Christ, what was he doing here? "Hey, Malinowski," Charlie croaked hoarsely, "where are you going?"

Dan Malinowski turned around at the sound of his name. "Oh, it's you, Roman. I'm here to see the big man. I don't want to hear any of that crap about not delivering four propane tanks. I delivered them and I got a signed receipt. What's Miguel think he's pulling? I'm going to see Richards – he'll fix Miguel's ass."

"Wait a minute," Charlie said hoarsely. "If you do that Richards will fire Miguel on the spot. You know Richards, Dan, he's a bastard. Miguel has a large family to support. Can't you wait till after Christmas? He's an old guy." Charlie pressed home his point. "You don't look like a mean guy, Dan, give Miguel a break. The damn tank is probably on the other side of the roof covered with snow. I'll check it out for you myself and call you this afternoon. Don't get the old guy into trouble."

"Ah, that Santa suit must've gone to your head," Dan Malinowski said with a grin. "Okay, but if you don't find that tank you let me know. And if I were you I'd go home and go to bed. You sound like you've got pneumonia."

Charlie forced a smile. "I sound a whole lot worse than I feel, believe me. Actually I'm much better today. Can't disappoint the kids – you know how it is."

"Yeah," Dan laughed. "You better call me by three o'clock or I'm gonna get mighty upset. In the end it's me that's got to account for that tank. Okay, Charlie?"

"You've got my word," Charlie muttered. "Look, I've got to check in at the clinic and get some aspirin. Give Miguel a break, okay?"

"I said I would. I'm no Scrooge."

As soon as Dan had walked away Charlie leaned against

the cold terrazzo wall . He felt faint, his head was reeling and it was all he could do to get his breath. That had been so close. Now, go to the clinic he told himself. He should put his suit on first; Jessie would be more receptive to the Santa suit.

A light snow was falling as Heather drove her car into her reserved parking space. In spite of the cold she felt all warm and fuzzy inside. She and Lex had spent a second night together – a wonderful night. Funny, she thought, that it had taken a bomb scare to bring them together.

She wondered what Dolph Richards would say if he knew that two of his employees were sleeping together. Actually she knew what he would say and it wouldn't be congratulations.

She and Lex had talked long into the night about Timberwoods and their jobs there. Neither one of them was overly happy with their positions. If Richards decided to make them an example of what would happen to employees who became involved in an office romance, they would simply quit. In fact, they might quit anyway once this bomb business was out of the way.

Once she'd cut the engine, Heather sat in her car for a few minutes, staring at the massive complex. Her mind went back to the day she and Lex had gone to Angela's home and questioned her. She could still hear the girl's voice in her head: "Fire . . . buildings collapsing, first one and then another . . . thick, black smoke . . . flying glass . . . people screaming . . . rivers of blood . . ."

Heather shut her eyes and leaned her forehead against the steering wheel. God, what she would give to just be able to start up the car and pull out of the parking lot.

But she couldn't. That would be cowardly and she wasn't a coward.

Reaching Harold's office, she removed her coat, threw it down on a spare chair and poured herself a cup of coffee. The warm fuzzies had given way to feelings of fear and wariness. She looked at her boss and sipped the scalding brew. "Sorry I'm late, but there was so much traffic I could only inch my way here. It's snowing again."

"Not again!" Harold exclaimed.

She approached his desk. "Chief," she said in a low voice, "do you feel it?"

Harold nodded, his expression grave. "As soon as I got into this damn building I felt it. I actually stood there like a statue for a few minutes and just looked around. Everything is the same and yet . . ."

"I know. I have the same feeling," Heather said, going back to the wet bar to add more coffee to her cup. When she turned around she saw Angela Steinhart and her father standing in the doorway. Her heart fluttered at the look on the girl's face. "What is it, Angela?"

Angela licked dry lips and took a deep breath. "I don't know how I know . . . but today is the day." There was a long pause.

Heather and Harold exchanged I-told-you-so-glances.

Tears blurring her eyes, Angela continued, "Don't ask me to try to explain it, I can't. When I got up this morning I saw all that red, all that blood. It stayed with me till I screamed for my father. I felt all tingly and there's something wrong with my hair. It feels like it's full of electricity." She looked at Heather. "It's going to happen today. You have to believe me."

With shaking hands Heather poured Murray Steinhart

and his daughter a cup of coffee. "Drink this. Sit down and we'll talk."

Angela took the closest chair. "There isn't anything to say. I just said all I know." She started fidgeting. "You see, I can't sit still. Something is forcing me to move and . . . I don't know. It's like I'm supposed to do something but I don't know what it is!"

"Drink the coffee, Angela," Heather said firmly. "Try to be calm." Over her shoulder she said to Harold, "Call for Eric. Now!"

Harold needed no second urging. He pressed the button on the intercom. "Margaret, page Eric Summers. Tell him to come here to my office. Immediately!"

Eric was at the office door in minutes. He only needed one look at Angela's face to confirm his worst thoughts. She nodded and jumped up from the chair, pacing the room while Heather repeated her story.

Eric turned to Angela and studied her for a moment. The poor kid – she was showing the effects of the past week yet, somehow, she looked more alive than he had ever seen her. Her eyes were bright and her color was good. He was actually finding himself liking Angela.

"You're sure today is the day?" he asked as Heather handed him a cup of coffee.

"I'm as sure as I can be. I have to do something, I just can't sit here." She screamed suddenly, "Close this mall!"

"Angel, take it easy," Murray comforted, laying a hand on his daughter's shoulder. "Remember, slow and easy. Just take it one step at a time."

"When?" Eric interrogated, forcing himself to remain calm. If only Angela could tell him when it would happen, he could get on the loudspeaker and clear the mall.

Angela ignored him. "Daddy, I have to get out of here. I have to move!"

It was one-oh-five before Charlie was back out in the mall again. His chest was hurting him so badly he could barely breathe. He had really managed to fool old Jessie, the clinic nurse, though – it had been a real coup. There were three people ahead of him so he'd just marched up and asked for three aspirin, complaining all the while about the noisy kids. Jessie had nodded absent-mindedly and waved him away. She would remember he had been there though, and hopefully that would be enough if Summers checked up on him.

All he needed was another ten minutes after that he didn't care what happened. He thought of the long flight of stairs to the roof and winced as a sharp pain stabbed his chest. He would have doubled over if a little boy hadn't taken that particular moment to grasp his leg and point to his sack. Charlie drew out a candy cane and a coloring book and handed them to the child. Then, moving as fast as the pain in his chest would allow, he hurried toward the exit and the stairway to the roof.

Could he make it? One step at a time, both feet on one step. That was the way to do it. It would take longer but there was no way he could force his legs to do anything else. When he got to the top of the stairs, he collapsed, his breathing ragged. What if I die here, alone? he thought. That spurred him on. Move, Charlie, he ordered himself, just a little farther. A few more steps, that's it. You did what you said you would do. Just a little farther . . .

Doctor Francis Tucker held the little girl's frail wrist in his hand, his eyes on the antique pocket watch he carried. It was one-thirty-five.

He shook his head at Carol Andretti. "I should have had her admitted to the hospital yesterday but I'd hoped against hope that she would improve so she could be home for Christmas."

"Doctor Tucker, will you look out the window and see if you can see anything special across the highway?" Maria said in a strained whisper.

Francis Tucker looked across the highway and smiled. "I sure can, young lady." He turned toward the window. "Well, I'll be darned – there's a Santa Claus on the roof of the Timberwoods Mall. Looks like he's stuffing his bag with something. Now, that's clever," he added to Carol Andretti.

Maria tried to raise herself up but her strength gave out and she fell back down. "Do you really see him?" She sounded out of breath. "He's my special miracle. Isn't he, Mommy?"

Carol Andretti squeezed her daughter's small hand. "Yes, darling, he's your own special miracle."

"Is he waving, Doctor Tucker?"

"Why, I . . . Yes, he is. Do you want to me to wave back?" He turned to Maria, his eyes twinkling.

"Oh, yes, wave back. I can't see that far any more and I want him to know that I know he's there. Wave, please, wave for me."

Francis Tucker felt slightly foolish but he did as the child asked, then turned around and smoothed her fevered brow. "You look tired. Why don't you go to sleep now. I want to talk to your mother for a minute and then she'll be right back."

"Okay, Doctor Tucker. But first . . . you didn't say when I'd be better. Will you tell me now?"

Francis Tucker closed his eyes for a brief moment. Somehow you were never prepared for things like this. "I think, Maria, that soon you will . . ."

Luckily for him she fell asleep, saving him from having to give her a reply.

"I couldn't have answered her," he said to Carol. "Let's talk outside. Surely you aren't going to take her to the shopping center, Mrs Andretti? Maria has a fever and you heard her breathing. She's bordering on pneumonia."

Carol Andretti squared her thin shoulders. She drew in her breath. "Will you be able to get the fever down?"

"We can only hope . . ."

"Can you ward off the pneumonia?"

"As I said, there's always hope and . . ."

"Will she live through Christmas?"

"There's always . . ."

"Hope, Doctor? I'm asking you for your medical opinion. Will Maria live to see Christmas?"

"No."

"How long? Tomorrow, the next day, Christmas Eve? When?"

"Not days, Mrs Andretti, hours." His shoulders slumped. No, you were never prepared.

"Thank you, Doctor. And the answer to your question is, yes. I am taking her to Timberwoods. I have to let her see her special miracle. Don't you see? It's all she has left. It's all I have left."

Francis Tucker left the small clapboard house convinced that he was going to change his field of medicine. Dermatology – that was fairly safe. In the new year he would look

221

into it. Acne and psoriasis weren't all that bad. At least patients with those complaints stayed alive. You smeared a little ointment on them and hoped for the best. Just acne and psoriasis, he promised himself for the thousandth time since entering medical school.

"You want to know something, old buddy? That was the worst lunch I ever ate," Mary complained as she lit a cigarette. "Our only hope is to buy those Jordan Almonds for Susie's wedding favors and stuff ourselves."

"If it was so terrible why did you eat it?" Cheryl asked testily.

"Because you paid for it, that's why. I didn't want to hurt your feelings."

"Since when did you ever worry about my feelings? I thought the lunch was good."

"That's because your taste buds are deformed."

"I would have thought that anyone who can eat pickled herring with ketchup has deformed taste buds," Cheryl's voice dripped honey.

"Are you going to start a fight?" Mary demanded, her elfin face full of mischief.

"I'm too tired to fight. We've been here since ten o'clock. It's now two-thirty and we haven't bought anything. That's four and a half hours. What the hell did we come here for?" Cheryl protested indignantly.

"It's not my fault you want to buy all the wrong things. I bought you a foot massage and I expect something of equal value."

"Ah, the true meaning of Christmas," Cheryl snorted. "How can I buy you something when all you keep saying is 'tacky, very tacky – I don't want that under my Christmas tree!' If you aren't careful, I'm going to stuff you into one of those sequined stockings with a tag that says 'Don't Open Till' . . . and I'm going to leave the year blank!"

"What's bugging you, old buddy? We came out for the day to have fun. All you've done is complain. And you haven't even bought my present."

Cheryl sighed. She knew when to quit. "Why don't I ever win?" she asked her friend, a winsome smile on her face.

"You always win! You won seventy-five dollars at bingo. Pay the bill and let's go."

"Pay the bill and let's go," Cheryl grumbled as she struggled out of the narrow booth. "I suppose that means I have to leave the tip too."

"Suit yourself. The food was lousy, I wouldn't leave a tip. Do you want me to write a complaint on the napkin?"

"No, I'll take care of it," Cheryl answered through clenched teeth. She pulled two coins out of her wallet and left them on the table in plain sight so that anyone seeing them before the waitress picked them up would know what kind of service they'd received. Leaving two cents said it all.

"Where do you want to go now?" Mary asked brightly. "Oh, listen – don't you just love 'Jingle Bells?' "

Cheryl looked around. "First of all I want to get my bearings. Where are all the exits? I can't see one. Which store are we going to next?"

"Let's see, I have a credit card for Stedmans, and they're on this level and so is Simmons Leather Shop. I want to get a wallet for my hairdresser and a camera for Patty. You know, one of those instant things."

"I'm not moving till I find out where the nearest exit

is," Cheryl said, grabbing hold of the railing leading to the lower level.

"Oh, for God's sake! What do you think is going to happen? Tell you what, if you buy me two presents I'll get you a pair of worry beads."

"Mary!"

"It's over there, next to the community room. All you do is go down the hall by the snack bar. That's an exit."

"Okay, we'll go to Simmons first then Stedmans. Maybe I'll look for a key holder for the mailman while you're looking for a wallet. What do you think a leather key holder will cost?"

"Who cares? We aren't using money, remember?"

"I forgot," Cheryl said agreeably.

Simmons Leather Shop was crowded with shoppers. Mary looked through the selection of leather wallets and finally found one that looked right. "What do you think?" she asked, holding the wallet up for Cheryl's inspection.

"It looks okay to me, but what do I know? I don't use a wallet, you know that."

Mary rolled her eyes and walked over to a very pregnant black woman who was waiting at the checkout counter. "Excuse me, but could you give me your opinion about this wallet? I'm considering buying it for my hairdresser. Do you think it's too plain?"

The woman smiled and took the wallet from Mary's hand. "Plain? No, not at all. I think it's elegant. I'm sure your hairdresser will be delighted with it."

Mary let out a sigh of relief. "Oh, good. I couldn't decide and my friend here is no help at all. She doesn't use a wallet. She just throws her money into her purse."

"Ah, Mrs Summers," the sales clerk broke in, "I have your briefcase right here, all wrapped up and ready to go. Will that be cash or charge?"

After paying for the wallet Mary and Cheryl headed for Stedmans. At the front of the store there was a Polaroid Camera display.

"Oh, look, Cheryl," Mary cried, "the sign says you can take a picture to try the camera. Say, that's clever. Back off into the mall a little and I'll take your picture."

Cheryl obliged. Out of the corner of her eye Mary saw Santa Claus. Who wanted a picture of Cheryl anyway? She turned the viewfinder toward Santa Claus and pressed the button. Cheryl was going to have a fit. Maybe if the salesman wasn't watching she could snap two pictures. Cheryl was hell on wheels when she got mad.

Snap, zippp and the picture was out. Snap, zippp and out came another.

"Hey, lady, what do you think you're doing?" the sales clerk asked.

Mary set the camera down and gave him her innocent look. "Taking pictures, what does it look like?" she snapped. "We'll take two of these. Cheryl, you don't want to try this, do you? I already took two and he's having a fit."

She turned back to the clerk. "Put them on my credit card, please."

"Some day I'm going to learn," Cheryl complained. "Who did you take the other picture of?"

"Santa Claus, who else?"

"Oh," Cheryl said, slightly mollified as she put her credit card into her purse. "Did we get a good buy?"

"Absolutely. Would I steer you wrong? Oh look, they're

225

coming into focus. Oh, nuts! There's something wrong with my Santa Claus picture. Look, it's all blurred and red. Nothing but red." She held up the other one. "Yours came out good, though. Look how nice your teeth look. What do you suppose happened to the first one?"

"Don't worry about it, it probably wasn't focused right."

"Guess so," Mary said, putting the pictures into her purse. "Shall we get the nuts now or later?"

"Later, Mary, much later."

Dan Malinowski looked at the clock on the opposite wall and grimaced. Damn that Charlie Roman. He should have known better than to believe him. "I'll fix his ass," Dan snorted. He dialed the number of Timberwoods Mall.

"Summers here."

"Dan Malinowski. Can I speak to Charlie Roman?"

"Charlie Roman? Our personnel manager sent him home this morning. Can I help you?"

"Nah, guess not. It can wait. He looked sick when I saw him but that was about eleven this morning. Guess he couldn't take it, all those kids and that bad cold. I'll call him next week."

"Are you sure there isn't anything I can do?" Eric asked.

"Nah. He was just going to check on that missing propane cylinder for me. But like I said, it can wait," Dan said, remembering what Charlie had told him about Miguel. "No sweat. Sorry to bother you."

"No bother," Eric said, sounding puzzled.

Dan hung up the phone. Poor old Charlie. He must've been really sick to go home. That was why he hadn't called about the cylinder. Dan congratulated himself on

226

keeping his word and not getting Miguel into trouble before Christmas. Even he had a heart at Christmas.

"Damn that Charlie," Eric mumbled as he pressed a button on the phone. "Summers here. Is Charlie Roman here or did he go home? Get back to me . . . Well, how long? . . . For Christ's sake, I could run around the mall faster than that . . . Yeah, I know there's been some accidents . . . No, I don't want to shovel snow . . . Okay, get back to me."

Dolph Richards stomped into Eric's office, a furious look on his face. "Now what the hell do you want?" Eric asked, not bothering to hide his agitation.

"I've had it up to here with you, Summers. Do you know how much work I have piled on my desk? Do you know that over the past three days there have been eleven accidents in this damn parking lot? Accidents, complaints, dying children, missing propane – who the hell do they think I am? And you sit there playing games! Well, you can just start moving your ass and do something! For starters, you can handle these complaints. The people in question are waiting in my outside office. Right now, I have to go find that asinine Santa Claus and arrange for a private sitting for some little girl who is dying. Don't open your mouth, Summers, because if you do I'm going to stick my fist in it!"

"There is no Santa Claus – at least I don't think there is. Lex told Charlie Roman to go home. He was sick as a dog."

"Are you telling me there's no damn Santa Claus? Is that what you're telling me?" Richards snarled.

"That's what I'm telling you and, no, I can't do the job. I don't think I'm the right color."

"You could have told me!" Richards shouted. "God-damn it, you could have told me! What the hell am I going to tell the kid's mother?"

"He might be here, I'm not sure. Someone called for him a little while ago. He said that Charlie was still here around eleven o'clock."

"One of these days, Summers, one of these days . . ."

It was five-forty.

Angela stood up from her seat on the bench, her face haunted. "Daddy, this feeling is getting worse by the minute. I feel as though I'm going to erupt."

She paced around nervously, her movements uncoordinated and jerky. "You have to get out of here, Daddy."

"I'm not leaving you. Look, why don't you call your friend, the one who has the puppies? Talk to her for a few minutes and maybe you'll calm down," Murray suggested helplessly as he looked into his daughter's tortured eyes.

Angela walked around the corner to the phone booth, her mind whirling. Would Mrs Summers's calm voice soothe her? It was worth a try. Anything was worth a try if this feeling would just go away.

"Could I speak to Mrs Summers?" Angela asked a voice she did not recognize.

"Mrs Summers isn't here right now," the woman answered. "She had a doctor's appointment and then she was stopping by Timberwoods to pick up a gift. She should be back in a little while, around seven, I guess. Do you want to leave a message? I'm her sister, I'm babysitting the puppies."

"She went where?" Angela screamed.

228

"To the doctor's office and then . . . to Timberwoods. Say, what's the matter?"

"Are you sure?" Angela pressed. "What time was she coming to the center?"

"I'm not sure. She said something about it depended on how long it took at the doctor's. The roads aren't too good so she'll be driving slow. What's wrong? What's the matter?"

"What's the name of her doctor? Do you have his number? I have to reach her as soon as possible." Angela chewed on her fingernail while she waited. "Okay, I've got it, thanks," she said, breaking the connection. She dialed the doctor's number and counted the rings.

"Hello, I'm trying to reach Amy Summers, is she still there? . . . How long ago did she leave?' Angela let the phone fall and raced to find her father. Quickly she told him of the phone conversations. "We have to find her, Daddy, and stop her from coming into the mall. We'll go outside and check the entrances. Hurry, Daddy, we can't let anything happen to her."

"That's doing it the hard way. All we have to do is call Eric Summers and he can station a man at each one of the doors to catch her."

"I don't know why I didn't think of that, Daddy. She can't come in here, she just can't. Mr Summers will take care of it." Her eyes brightened momentarily in thanks to her father and his quick thinking.

Once they had called Eric Summers, Angela and her father prowled the mall, each intent on their own thoughts. No matter which way they walked Angela invariably circled back and headed toward the North Pole display.

It was someone in the mall. She was certain of it. But

who? Would she recognize him or her if they came into her line of vision? She wasn't sure. The only thing she was sure of was that the center was going to blow up within minutes. She stopped and looked at her father imploringly, tears swimming in her eyes. A flash of red appeared and then disappeared. Angela blinked the tears away and stared transfixed at the sight to her left. It was Charlie Roman trudging down the mall with his sack over his shoulder.

"Oh, my God. Daddy! It's him. It's Charlie. The Santa!" She grabbed her father's arm in a vise-like grip. "I don't know how he's done it, but he has. We have to tell Mr Summers right away."

"Okay, Angel, whatever you say."

Charlie's first reaction when he saw Angela pointing him out to the man she was with was to run. She knew. He wasn't sure how she knew but she did. He could see it in her horrified expression, in her tear-filled eyes.

He ran into the closest store – a health food shop – and ducked behind a vitamin display. Who was that man with her? he wondered. Probably one of the plain-clothes police officers Eric Summers had brought in to investigate the bomb threat. Only it wasn't a threat. Not any more. He pulled back his red velvet coat sleeve and looked at his watch. In just a few minutes it would be a reality.

"He shouldn't be too hard to find, Angel," Charlie heard a man say outside the store.

"I have to find him, Daddy, I have to. If I can find him I may be able to stop him."

Recognizing Angela's voice, Charlie peeked out from behind the display.

"He's not a bad man, Daddy. He's just misunderstood and lonely, like me. If you knew him you'd like him. I know you would."

"I'm sure I would, Angel. Come on. Maybe he went that way."

Charlie turned around and leaned his back against the display. "Angela," he whispered, then let out a long sigh. She still liked him, even after the way he'd treated her, even knowing that he was the one who was going to blow up the mall. Had he jumped to the wrong conclusion about why she'd left him? Maybe he should have given her a chance to explain. She might have had a good reason. Christ, he'd never thought about that. There could have been any number of reasons why she'd left. She'd told him that she'd tried to call several times. Damn, if only he'd put on the answering machine . . .

He checked his watch again. It was too late to stop the mall from blowing but, if he hurried, maybe he could get Angela and her father out in time.

"Angela" he cried as he ran out of the store. "Angela!"

Carol Andretti, her husband at her side, pushed the wheel-chair down the hall toward the center's lower level. Maria was propped up with pillows and a safety belt was fastened about her waist. Her eyes were feverishly bright as she tried to look in all directions at once. She wanted to tell someone how beautiful it was, but she felt too weak to talk.

"Mr Richards said he would meet us over here by the Toyland display," Carol whispered to Joe Andretti. "Look, there's Santa sitting by that old lady. I guess we're never too old," she said, trying to smile.

"Come on, honey," she said brightly to Maria, "one special miracle coming up."

Mary and Cheryl sat in the manager's outer office complaining to each other.

"There really isn't any point in complaining, you know. What's he going to do?" Cheryl demanded. "It's almost six-thirty and we haven't eaten dinner yet."

"How the hell can you be hungry? You just ate half those stale nuts."

"That's because I'm starving," Cheryl gritted. "We could be eating, but oh no, you have to come here and complain about the stale candy and nuts. He's not going to do anything; these guys are just fixtures. All they do is play games with the public."

"It's the principle of the thing. Seven dollars is seven dollars. And that clerk was rude. I don't have to put up with that. And as long as we're here, I'm going to bitch about that searching business at the door."

"Speaking of doors, I didn't see . . ."

"I'm sorry I even mentioned it. Look, here comes somebody who looks like he's ripe for complaints."

"How can you tell?" Cheryl muttered.

"Because he has a clipboard and he looks efficient. He also looks like he's in a hurry so he'll make short work of these two ahead of us."

"Yeah, yeah," Cheryl said as she stuffed more Jordan Almonds into her mouth. "And did you notice she gave us all white almonds? I like the pink ones, and the blue ones too. I hate white!"

"Do me a favor and save a few so this guy can see that they're stale."

Cheryl rolled her eyes and continued to chew. The guy was speedy, she would give him that. Their turn came almost immediately.

"Two things," Mary said firmly. "Don't hurry me like you did that other lady. I have something to say and I'm going to say it. We bought two Polaroid cameras. As a matter of fact, we spent almost six hundred dollars in the mall this afternoon. Actually, six hundred and seven, if you count the Jordan Almonds and the peanut-butter fudge, which is why I'm here. The almonds are stale. We bought these cameras after we took a couple of pictures. See these pictures? This is Cheryl," she said, holding out the first picture, "and this is Santa Claus. We bought two cameras, so we were entitled to two free pictures. This one of Cheryl is okay but look at this one. Isn't it a mess? All red. Makes me think of blood. I do hope there's nothing wrong with the cameras and they work right when we get them home. Anyway, after we put our things in the locker, we bought these almonds and candy and they're stale. We thought you should know. Here, taste them. We want our money back. We complained to Nanette herself and she just said, 'I'm fresh!'"

"Nanette's Nut House," Mary babbled as the man stared at the blurred picture. "Well, aren't you going to do something? Did you hear me? I spent seven dollars on stale candy and nuts and I want my money back!"

Fourteen

E ric Summers stared at the picture, his thoughts whirling. The tape Noel Dayton had made of Angela came to mind. He could hear Angela's voice in his head: "He's sick, he keeps wiping his face . . . he's cold, the wind is blowing all around . . . everything is red . . . he's holding something green, it's big and round . . . soft . . . there's something in it . . . he's sick . . . he's sick . . . he keeps wiping his face . . ."

Eric almost staggered under the impact of his thoughts. He looked at the picture the woman had handed him, all blurred and out of focus . . . it did look like blood. Charlie hadn't wanted to go home. Angela had said under hypnosis: "He wants to die . . . he wants everyone to die with him . . ."

Then another thought hit him. That guy on the phone – what was his name? Dan Malinowski. What was it he'd said – that Charlie was supposed to check on a missing propane tank? Propane! Angela had predicted an explosion not a bomb! And what about that note Richards had left on his desk – something about a Santa on the roof?

"Jesus!" Eric yelled. He dropped the picture and ran past the two women.

234

"Hey! What about our money?" Mary yelled after him.

"Forget it!" Eric called. "Just get out of here! This place is going to blow! Get out now!" he shouted as he ran down the hall.

Eric passed Lex and grabbed his arm. "Come with me, Lassiter. I know how the bastard did it. I hope to hell it isn't too late, but we have to try. Heather!" he called back over his shoulder. "Get on the loudspeaker and tell everyone to leave the mall. I don't care how you do it. Just do it!"

Cheryl looked at Mary. "What did I tell you? This whole damn place is crazy. Where's the exit? There's no exit up here."

"Yes, there is, it's right over there." Both women ran, leaving a trail of Jordan Almonds behind them.

"I hope that Nanette's Nut House is wiped out!" Mary grumbled as she thrust open the door.

"It's snowing," Cheryl yelled as she raced for the parking lot only to collide with a young girl. "Don't go in there," she babbled, "the place is going to blow up!"

"I know," the girl said quietly. "Any minute now."

"Attention all mall shoppers and storekeepers. We have an emergency situation. We have reason to believe there is a bomb in the mall. For your safety, we ask that you leave the mall immediately. I repeat, we have an emergency situation. There is a bomb in the mall. Please proceed to the closest exit in an orderly fashion."

"That mealy-mouthed bastard locked the door," Eric cursed. "He didn't leave a damn thing to chance."

Eric fumbled in his pants' pocket. "I've got the key somewhere."

He pulled out a key ring. "Jesus, which one is it?" He tried first one, than another. "I should have labeled them. Oh Jesus, what time is it, Lassiter?"

"Two minutes after seven."

"Got it!" A split second after he'd spoken an explosion ripped through the night. Then another and another.

"Oh, my God!" Lex shouted when he'd recovered from the shock wave. "We have to get out of here, Eric!"

Screams, shouts and explosion after explosion sounded throughout the mall. "Eric, come on!"

"Not yet. I've got to see for myself!" Eric ran across the roof, a black shadow against the eerie whiteness of snow. "Over here," he called to Lex who had followed him. "The fresh-air intake duct. Look what the bastard did! He hooked the propane up to the duct and the blowers have been sucking the gas in. The tiniest spark could have set it off!"

Eric turned the ball valve to off although he knew that the tank was empty of its volatile liquid. Another explosion hit and the roof quaked beneath them. "Jump, Lex, jump!"

Eric followed Lex as he plummeted through the night air into an eight-foot snowbank which had been plowed close to the building. He dug himself out and looked around for Lex.

"I'm okay, over here. I think I wrenched my shoulder."

Eric lifted his eyes to the roof where he had been standing a moment before. The flames were shooting up into the sky.

"We've got to get back in there – maybe we can help! Do you think you can make it, Lex?"

"Yeah, but I need something to tie up this shoulder or I won't be worth a tinker's damn," Lex replied. He removed his belt to use as a support.

As the two men ran around the building to a side entrance several more explosions rocked the mall. "Christ! It's still blowing," Lex gasped, the wind knocked out of him.

"It's the propane. It builds up into pockets and then it blows," Eric explained.

Screams rose and fell. The sky was a crimson glow and the shrill sirens of fire trucks and ambulances could be heard in the distance.

"Head for the first ambulance you see and get that shoulder taken care of," Eric instructed.

"Nuts. The shoulder can wait! I'm coming with you."

Angela watched the horror, the death and destruction. She had to do something! People were running, screaming, pushing and shoving to get through what remained of the plate-glass doors. The fire was everywhere! A woman, her clothing on fire, ran outside and threw herself into the snow. Angela blinked as something sailed by her and landed near her feet. An arm, wearing a gold bracelet.

All Angela could hear was screaming.

Firemen and ambulance men ran past her, carrying stretchers between them. Where was her father? She ran toward the entrance, over broken glass and rubble. Her pants' leg caught fire and she beat it out with her hand. There was nothing left. She stopped her scramble over the rubble and looked around. Feeling something wet on her face, she looked up and saw a great black void. The roof had caved in and a light snow was falling into the mall, the snowflakes bursting into droplets of water as they hit the smoking heat.

She shook her head and started walking again. She had to help, she had to!

A small child in a wheelchair caught her attention. Tears were streaming down her pale little cheeks as she struggled with the safety belt. Angela worked her way over to her, undid the belt and took the little girl in her arms.

"Where's your mommy and daddy?" she asked. The little girl pointed to a couple who were pinned beneath the rubble. The side of the man's head was crushed in; he had his arm around a woman who lay lifeless beneath him.

"Put me over there," the little girl whimpered.

Angela gulped. "Oh honey, I can't do that. I'll take you to one of the first-aid men – they'll help you."

Maria Andretti opened her eyes and looked at Angela. "Please, put me over there by my mommy." The child's breathing was ragged and torn and her eyes were bright as stars. Angela started off with the child in her arms. She looked down again and saw that the ragged breathing had stopped. There wasn't anything a first-aid man could do now. She staggered with her burden past a flaming overturned bench and gently lowered the child down next to her parents. The tinny sound of 'Oh, Come All Ye Faithful' floated through the choking smoky air.

On her feet again Angela felt a hand on her shoulder. A minister, his collar askew, his eyes blank and staring, was repeating over and over again, "The Lord giveth and the Lord taketh away . . ."

"Shut up! Shut up!" Angela shouted, shaking away from him.

"Help me," came a feeble cry. Angela turned in the direction of the sound and bent down to help a woman with a small child. She picked up the child and grasped the woman by an arm, literally pulling her away from the fire erupting nearby.

"I'll take the baby to one of the ambulances and come back for you."

"Take care of her!" the woman sobbed.

"I think she's more scared than hurt," Angela smiled reassuringly.

Another woman, her eyes wild with terror, her arms hanging limply at her sides, screamed, "I can't find my children! Please, help me find my children! I can't move my arms. Please, help me find my children!"

Angela heard Eric Summers's voice behind her. "Watch where you're going, the floor's gone! Stand still, I'll come for you!"

"I can't find my children," the woman whimpered. "Please help me!"

"We'll find them, just don't move," Eric shouted as he climbed over a smoking mass of twisted girders.

The woman turned and looked dazedly at him. "Will you help me?" she pleaded, taking a step toward him. She turned and lost her balance, toppling into the dark cavernous emptiness.

"Mommy, Mommy," came a weak wail.

"Where are you?" Eric shouted to be heard over the fire.

"Mommy!" came the cry. "Mommy, help me."

"I'm coming," Eric said huskily. Jesus, where was the

kid? His eyes smarting from the smoke, he crawled on his hands and knees in the direction of the child's voice. "Oh, my God!' he yelled. "Doctor, over here! Somebody! Over here!"

A small child with his legs pinned beneath a beam had a ten-inch shard of glass sticking out of his ribcage. A man in white rushed to Eric, took one look at the little boy and shook his head.

"He's only a kid," Eric whispered. "He's only a kid!"

A voice broke through the shock. "Summers, have you seen Angela?" Murray Steinhart asked.

Eric shook his head. "She's alive. I saw her pull some kid out from under all the rubble. I don't know where she is now though."

"I've dragged so many bodies out of here, I've lost count," Murray said, his eyes reflecting the tragedy he'd witnessed. "I think every ambulance and doctor within a fifty-mile radius is here, and we aren't even making a dent in this . . . holocaust. What are we going to do?"

"Do? We're going to keep dragging them out of here till we drop."

"The western section has collapsed entirely and the middle is hanging by a thread. This section has some flooring at least. The fire is under control in this wing, but it keeps flaring up in Walden's end of the mall. If you see Angela, tell her I'm all right."

Eric nodded and made his way toward a young girl who was moaning and crawling around on her hands and knees looking for something. It was dark in the mall and the emergency spotlights from the fire company cast a dark gray shadow where the young woman was searching.

"Easy there," Eric warned as he came close to her.

"I'm looking for my husband, he was here before . . . before . . . I know he was here!" Her voice rose to a wail.

"It's all right," Eric soothed, helping her to her feet. "We'll find him. Where did you see him last?"

The young woman turned her face toward Eric, her expression shocked and dumbfounded. "I don't know . . . I don't know . . ." she whispered over and over.

Eric took her to the rescue team working nearby. He wondered if she would ever know.

"Heather . . . Heather!" Lex called as he picked his way over the debris on the Promenade level. He shone the flashlight he had borrowed from someone on the rescue team into the all-encompassing blackness. She had to be here – she had been making the announcement to clear the center when the explosions stared.

"Heather . . . Heather!" Please God, don't let me lose her, he thought. I've only just found her.

In the acrid smoking darkness, Angela stood and watched the busy doctors, nurses and firemen. She hadn't seen her father since they had both gone outside to find Eric Summers. Where could he be?

"Watch it, the floor is gone," she warned someone as she walked around a great gaping hole. There was Mr Lassiter with Heather. He was on his knees holding her, kissing her. Angela crawled past the debris and rushed over to Lex. The fear in her eyes was evident, the question didn't need to be asked.

"She's all right, Angela. I think her leg is broken and she's fainted. Have you seen Eric Summers?'

"The last time I saw him he was helping carry a man to one of the ambulances."

"I haven't seen him in a while either," Lex added, the strain of carrying Heather with his injured shoulder showing on his face. "Dolph Richards is dead." He looked over to the rescue team carrying stretchers. "I found him when I went up to look for Heather. I'll talk to you later. I want to get her to an ambulance."

Angela worked her way around the gaping crevice to a small boy who was sniffling and afraid to move. How the hell had he been overlooked, she wondered angrily.

"Listen to me. Just stand there and don't move. One wrong step and you'll go over. I'll come and get you. Don't move now."

"I won't," his small voice quivered. "I'm blind and I don't know which way to go."

Angela's lips tightened and she forced her mind to concentrate on the matter at hand. She got to her knees and crawled along the edge of the floor. A piece of cement fell away and she held her breath as she continued her slow progress to the child.

"Just bend your knees, don't move your feet. When you bend your knees, reach out your hand. Remember now, not your feet, just bend your knees. Can you do it?"

"I can do it."

"Good boy. Okay now, bend your knees and hold out your hand. There we go. I knew you could do it. Now stoop and walk toward me, like a fat duck. Pretend you're a fat duck and make your feet go. You can do it, I know you can. See, what did I tell you?" she said, clasping the thin boy to her. "Come with me, I'll take you to one of the ambulances and they'll take care of you."

"Will you look for my friends, Mickey and Jackie? They were with our den mother."

"I'll look for them, I promise. Just hold my hand and walk where I tell you. I'm proud of you. Not many little kids would have been as brave as you."

Harold and Eric had found each other amidst the confusion and teamed together in the rescue. Now that most of the wounded had been carried to safety, Eric was concerned about his wife.

"Hey, Harold, I've got to go and see if I can find someone to get word to Amy that I'm all right. This mess must be all over the radio and TV by now and she must be worried sick."

"Yeah, go ahead. I'll see what I can do here," Harold answered, wishing he had someone in this world who cared if he lived or died.

Eric was heading outside when he heard Harold calling his name. Whirling around he saw that Harold was waving his arms frantically. "Over here," he shouted. Eric inched his way back over the jagged remains of the floor.

Harold pointed to a man huddled over three people, his arms trying to cover them. "Do you see that beam?" he shouted. "It's going to come down on them any minute, and this man won't move. Help me get him out of here. He's so dazed he doesn't know what he's doing. It's his wife and kids, I guess. He won't accept the fact that they're dead. He won't leave them."

A snapping sound jarred Eric and he looked upward and saw the beam loosen further. "Okay, you grab one arm and I'll take the other. When I say pull, yank him backward and don't lose your balance, for God's sake, or we'll all go over! The floor's gone over there. Okay, you got him?"

"Yup," Harold wheezed.

"Pull!" Eric yelled and the man toppled backward. Just as they dragged him clear, the beam fell over the three inert bodies.

"You can't do anything here," Harold insisted. "Come with us. It's too late for them, but there are others who need you."

"Ann . . . Ann, darling!" came the man's anguished cry. Turning to Harold, he said, "I loved them so much, they were my life! They were the reason for everything. Now they're gone!" He wiped a hand across his eyes and stared at Eric and Harold.

"Take him outside, Harold. I'll see what else I can do."

"What about your message to your wife?"

Eric looked back at the three bodies and shrugged. "It can wait. Somehow I have the feeling that Amy knows I'm all right. I don't know how, I just know."

Harold left with the grief-stricken man. Eric picked his way around the smoldering fire and heard a soft whimpering cry. "I'm sick . . . help me . . ."

Eric looked down and gasped. A man clad in red velvet reached out for him. "I don't want to die . . ." the fallen man gurgled, blood pouring out of his mouth.

Eric turned and walked away, fighting a sudden wave of nausea.

Charlie Roman watched him leave.

Murray Steinhart caught sight of his daughter leading a little boy toward what remained of the exit. "Angela! Angela, wait for me."

"Daddy! Where have you been? I've been looking all over for you. I was afraid . . ."

"Hush, Angel, I'm here now."

The adrenaline which had kept Angela working so fast and furiously seemed to seep out of her body. She deflated. Here was someone she could turn to. "Daddy!" she cried, dissolving into Murray's arms.

Out of the corner of her eye she saw a flash of red – the Santa suit. Charlie.

"It's Charlie, Daddy. It's Charlie." She broke from her father's arms and ran over to him.

"Angela," Charlie croaked.

Angela bent down beside him, her eyes swimming with tears. She could tell by his breathing that he wasn't going to make it. "Oh, Charlie? Why? Why did you do this?"

She was torn between hating him for what he'd done and caring for him as the friend he had been to her.

". . . so glad you're okay . . . didn't want you hurt . . ." Charlie whispered, not answering her question.

Angela felt her father's hand on her shoulder. "Leave him be, Angela. He's the cause of all this. He doesn't deserve your sympathy."

"No, Daddy. Wait." She shrugged him off and returned her attention to Charlie. "You have to tell me, Charlie. You have to make me understand why you would do such a terrible thing. Is it because . . . ?" She hesitated, afraid to ask what she was thinking. "Is it because you were mad at me?"

A trickle of blood ran out of the corner of Charlie's mouth.

"Is that it, Charlie? Because if it is, that means . . . I tried to call to tell you what happened. I let the phone ring

245

and ring and ring. I was coming back to spend Christmas with you."

The anguish on her face must have told him what she was thinking because he reached out and took her hand. "No, Angela," he managed, his voice weakening by the moment. "Nothing to do with you . . . you were the only one who ever cared . . . the only . . . one . . ."

Angela squeezed his hand. "Oh, Charlie. I'll always care. Always."

He fell backward, his eyes glazed and unseeing.

"Come on," Murray said, wrapping his arms around his daughter and lifting her from the ground. "I'm taking you home. Home, Angela, just you and me."

Angela's eyes burned. Charlie was dead and her hope for their friendship along with him. "No, Daddy, please. Anywhere but that mausoleum we live in."

Murray grinned. "I was thinking of the Holiday Inn down the road. We can stay there till we get our heads together and decide what we're going to do."

Hope lit Angela's face. "Just you and me? Not Mother?"

"Just you and me, Angel. We'll deal with your mother later."

They made their way through the smoking rubble, searching for the exit that would lead them to the parking lot. Everywhere there was chaos and people running with stretchers. Sirens wailed as more police and help arrived.

Eric Summers saw them first and walked over. "Congratulate me," he said, forcing a grin. "I'm a father. A baby boy. Amy and the baby are in the ambulance over there," he said, pointing. "Both are fine." He stared intently at Angela but said nothing.

"I tried, I really tried," Angela muttered.

"I know you did. I'm sorry it took us so long to believe you. We're only human. It's hard for people to understand . . . What I mean is . . ."

"I understand. If only they could have closed down the mall none of this would have happened."

"Don't think about it. It's not your fault, Angela." Eric took her by the shoulders and stared deep into her watery eyes. "It's not your fault. Do you understand what I'm saying?"

"Of course she understands and you're wrong. It is her fault," a shrill voice cut into the small group.

"Sylvia!" Murray cried in surprise. Angela drew closer into the circle of her father's arms.

Sylvia Steinhart ignored her husband and centered her attention on her cowering daughter. "I always knew you were crazy, I just didn't want to believe it. You'll do anything to gain attention. How could you? How dare you blow up this shopping center? You're insane and I'm going to see that you're locked up for the rest of your life. It's your side of the family, Murray," she said, finally acknowledging her husband.

Angela seemed to shrink before Eric's eyes.

"Shut up, Sylvia," Murray said through clenched teeth.

"Don't tell me to shut up, you . . . you ghoul. Look at you! How can you bear to touch her? She's some kind of devil. Did you listen to me when I tried to warn you years ago? Oh no, you said it was growing pains. Well, Murray Steinhart, look what your growing pains grew into. You're a bigger fool than I thought. You should be locked up with her."

"One more word and those perfect teeth in your perfect

face aren't going to be perfect any more. Neither will that perfect nose that cost me a fortune. In short, Sylvia, shut up!"

"If you won't call the police, I will. I'll tell them this . . . this monster blew up this whole place, that she's the one responsible for killing all those people. My God, Murray, open your eyes!"

"I have opened them and it's something I should have done a long time ago. I don't know if you can understand what I'm going to tell you, Sylvia, but force yourself to try."

"What are you babbling about, Murray?" Sylvia raged. "I'm not stupid. I can understand English. What I don't understand is this crazy person we call a daughter blowing up this shopping complex to get attention. Now, what is it you want me to understand? Make it quick before I call the police to take her away."

Murray gently moved Angela from the protective circle of his arms. Instinctively Eric gathered the young girl close to him. Tears glistened in Murray's eyes. His face was a mask of reproach. "We did this to Angela. She's in no way to blame. Now get out of my way. I'm taking my daughter home."